Illicit Illustration

E.L. KOSLO

Copyright

Table of Contents

This one is for all the neurospicy girlies who were told their entire lives to keep the "inappropriate" intrusive thoughts on the inside.

F that shit. Life's more fun when you grab it with both hands... Like Hazel is about to do to her brother's *pierced* best friend before she rides him off into the sunset.

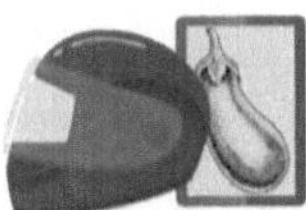

You are perfect exactly as you are.
Your neurodivergence does not define you.
You are a beautiful soul who just happens to experience life in a way unlike any other.

Chapter
One

"**N**O. JUST NO. I'M not doing it." While I was not exactly social lately, I also had zero desire to take part in this ridiculous experiment with modern dating. I had a hard enough time finding guys I clicked with face to face, much less having to flirt with strangers through an opaque screen.

"Come on, Haz," Charley implored—staring at me from where she was seated on the floor sorting things she'd pulled out of her closet to pack—with what I knew was an intentionally pathetic expression. She knew I couldn't resist the pouty face and was clearly not above using it to get what she wanted. "I need one more woman to balance things out. I promise none of the guys are creeps, I vetted them all myself. They even went through Hudson's rapid fire asshole finder questions. All of them passed with flying colors."

"Does Hudson know you're asking me? I can't see him being okay with this. He doesn't like it when I try to date guys who come into the bar. Even though I rarely leave this place lately. Where else am I supposed to meet guys in this town? The grocery store?"

"That's not a bad idea, but please try this first. Worst case, you don't click with anyone, and you don't have to give your number out. Best case, you meet a few nice guys, you flirt via text, and then at the party in two weeks you get to meet them in person. Won't getting to know them be easier if it's through the written word? It'll weed out the disinterested ones."

"Or I'll get fricking catfished. You know I've been a creep magnet latcly, Char. I'm going to be a forty-year-old virgin at this rate."

"Haz. Seriously? I doubt you'll even be a twenty-five-year-old virgin. I think it's admirable how you've managed to get two degrees and have yet to fall victim to the hook up culture."

"Yes," I scoffed, rolling my eyes at my formerly *One-Night Stand Queen* roommate. She may have been blissfully committed and moving in with my brother in a few days, but I remembered all the nights she brought home her various companions.

Spending the money from my first large commission had been worth it for the noise canceling headphones that kept me from listening to my best friend mid-climax with her headboard ramming into the wall.

"Because you had such a terrible time being fucked by all the random college guys who used to spend the night. Thank God you don't bring Hudson back here. It's bad enough watching the two of you flirt, I don't need to hear that. At all. Like I'd need to bleach my brain if I knew what Hudson sounded like when he…"

"Hazel! Breathe, you're spiraling again. Back to the blind speed dating. Please try. If you hate it, then you can make me sit in weird poses for hours so you can draw them, and I won't complain."

It wasn't the female form that I needed a figure model for. And I was definitely not telling Charley about the kinds of commissions that now filled my ever-expanding waitlist. She would tell Hudson, and my brother would steal my tablet to keep me from being corrupted from the smutty side of Bookstagram.

"Only if you promise this is a one-time agreement. If it goes how I assume it will, then I'm never subjecting myself to one of your events again."

"Yay!" Charley cheered. "I would say I'd help you get ready, but you could wear pajamas to the first night if you wanted to because you won't be seeing any of the very eligible bachelors. But you will not be disappointed. There are a few I think are perfect for you."

But I didn't want perfect for me. I didn't have mildly pornographic dreams about who should be perfect for me.

No, my stupid subconscious kept having shadowy sex dreams about the man who lived above the tattoo shop on the other side of the parking lot. The man whose surprised post orgasmic face had haunted me for almost two years.

The same man who I tried not to picture every time I needed to relieve myself after listening to all the smutty audiobooks I had over the past few months.

It was all a part of my job as an illustrator who worked with romance novelists. I'd been binge listening to each of the books to better understand what the authors I was working with wanted in their character art commissions. They'd all given me specifics of which chapters and scenes I was drawing, but with some of them I'd been so curious about the rest of the story that I'd listened to the whole thing while I worked.

Which was an epically bad idea when I had been working more nights. Going to the bar to watch Reid pick up women when I was horny from listening to word porn all day was literal torture.

"Are you even listening to me?" Charley laughed, taping one of the boxes that she was using for her move closed. Surprisingly, she was almost finished, even though she still had a few days left until Hudson was planning to transport the rest of her belongings to his house a few miles away. My brother did not know that his incoming girlfriend was just as much of a hot mess as I was growing up. "You've got a weird look on your face right now. If this really makes you that uncomfortable, I had a few alternates chosen in case we had anyone back out."

Shaking my head and trying to banish the lingering image of a mostly naked Reid from my mind—again—my chest heaved with an exaggerated sigh as I sat down on the edge of her bare mattress. She hadn't slept here in weeks, and I was going to miss her even if she was only going to be a few miles away.

"It's fine. You're right. I'm just being whiny. Maybe I will meet someone. Doesn't hurt to try. It doesn't count when I punch my own v-card, might as well find someone with a real penis."

Charley laughed, shaking her head as she sat down beside me and pulled me into a side hug. "Don't throw it away because you think you need to. If you've waited this long, you might as well have it be with someone you like. Someone you trust."

"I'm gonna die a virgin," I groaned dramatically, falling back on the mattress and covering my eyes with my forearm.

"You could always ask Reid to help you out."

What...the...fuck...

A blush stole across my cheeks as she gave me a pointed look.

"That was mean, even for you."

"Not saying it to be mean, Haz. I'm saying it because the two of you have been dancing around each other since Halloween and maybe banging it out would help relieve some of the tension now that you don't flee the room every time he enters."

"He's my friend, Char. And Hudson would murder him. Like legitimately torture him in a slow and painful manner with his own tattoo needles."

She rolled her eyes. "We both know your brother is all talk. He might threaten Reid's dick if he hurts you, but if you two actually wanted to take things past your awkwardly tense friendship, then go for it."

"He's got a type, and I am not it." Reid liked women who had much bigger assets than my smallish A-cups and slim frame. And I didn't have any tattoos or piercings, despite always having been curious about them. Every time I was near Reid on Halloween, I had to fight off the thought of playing with his nipple piercings, since the attractive jerk had spent the entire night without a shirt on.

And every time I thought about what was hidden underneath his tight shirts, questions I would never get the answers to ran through my head. Like... If I tugged on one, would it make him hard?

"I think now that Hudson and I are moving in together, Reid is realizing that they're not lost boys who don't have to grow up. He hasn't been picking up women here for a while. Coincidentally, he's been a good boy since...you took a bat to someone's twat and then flirted with a cute baseball player all night on Halloween." Charley grinned, clearly laughing at the memory of finding out that I'd assaulted my brother's toxic monster of an ex. "Which he extensively told your brother about on multiple occasions, because *Haz deserves better than some minor leaguer wannabe who won't stick around, anyway.*"

"Christian was just being nice to me. We texted for a few days, but then I never heard from him once their conditioning started. He's busy with school and practice. And Reid's right, even if he doesn't play after he graduates, he won't want to stay in a small college town in rural Colorado. All the students end up leaving eventually." I shrugged, and she rolled her eyes at me.

The transient nature of living in an area heavily reliant on tourism was why a lot of locals never dated the college students or the tourists who flocked to Sage Springs and the surrounding small communities during the ski season. My cousin Colette was a ski instructor, and she'd warned me years ago not to fall for any of the smooth-talking tourists.

"Not all of them do."

Yet another reason I wasn't sure about this whole blind dating thing. Since I had no way of identifying the man on the other side of the screen, what if I ended up with someone who didn't have plans to stay here?

Although that might be a good solution for my virginity problem. If I was terrible at it, he could just leave town, so I didn't have to hide above my brother's bar. I could just be the weird word porn illustrator who lived a life of seclusion with her dildoes and a collection of penis art because she was allergic to pussies.

The animal kind, not my vagina.

"You're doing it again, Haz."

Yet another reason I wasn't sure I was cut out for blind dating. I had five minutes to pitch myself to someone as a date. With my ADHD, I'd probably end up getting distracted, go off on a tangent with weirdly specific knowledge about what was supposed to be a conversation starter topic and then get flustered and clam up from mortification that I couldn't have a conversation like a normal person.

My friends and family may tolerate my social quirks, but I knew my tendencies to interrupt and have rapid-fire topic changes during a conversation annoyed most people. I irritated myself regularly, but no matter what medications I took, how much I tried to mask it, or how often I attended cognitive-behavioral therapy, it happened anyway.

Sometimes my ADHD could be a blessing. I had hyper-focus when I was working on commissions as long as I stuck to my usual routine, but it also meant I forgot to do things like feed myself, drink water or check the clock so I wasn't late for my shifts at the bar.

"Just... Fine. I'll do it. But I swear to God, if I get any dick pics during the texting part of this whole experience, then I'm printing it out and plastering copies all over Hudson's garage door with my craft glue like a phallic collage art master*batory*piece."

"Sounds reasonable, but I think we managed to weed out the unsolicited peen pic posters during the vetting stage. Pretty sure Hudson made some of them hand over their phones so he could scroll through their camera rolls."

He'd better not ask to look through mine. Because it was currently full of source photographs from my various 'research' sources. Some illustrators used 3D models, posing diagrams, and illustration textbooks to help them capture realism in their work.

I also used Pinterest, Instagram, and porn.

The last one hadn't been helping with my dirty fantasies about Reid. No matter what they looked like, every man in a video I watched—for purely research purposes, only...*obviously*—turned into him.

And every time I got myself off thinking of him, it made it harder to resist the urge to run away from him when we were forced to be in the same room.

"I promise you'll have fun. Or you'll at least have funny stories to tell me afterward. Since you're debriefing me about the entire process so I can improve things for next time. If Hudson is convinced the experience was a success, he's more likely to let me make it an annual thing."

She grinned at me, and I felt terrible that I really did not want to support my friend. But I also knew she'd thrive off my embarrassment when I inevitably did something cringeworthy.

"If no one texts me the next morning, I'm going to never speak to you about this again."

"Fair enough," she laughed. "But I don't think you'll have anything to worry about. You'll probably have a few guys fighting for your attention, if not all of them. You're funnier than you give yourself credit for, and some guys find humor sexy. Everything will turn out fine."

Spoiler Alert: Everything indeed did not go fine.

Chapter

Two

"WHAT IS HE DOING here?" I hissed, but my attention was quickly averted to watching the way the muscles rippled beneath the short sleeves of Reid's shirt in a way that should not have had me salivating and wanting to take a picture so I could sketch it later.

I never expected to be the kind of girl who got off from observing some arm porn. But I realized how wrong I was as I watched, hypnotized, as the tendons in his forearms flexed and shifted. Reid was currently across the room holding up one end of the divider screen, so Hudson could attach the support feet, his back flexing while he tried to hold it steady.

"He's helping with set up. Hudson asked him to come get everything ready for tonight. Then I think they're going to drink beer with the cooks and guard the doors."

"Reid's not doing the event, is he?" I asked, shifting uncomfortably as my hands began to sweat. There was no way I could go through with this if she asked him too.

"I hope not," Charley joked, her expression sobering when she realized I wasn't. "No. He's not. I mean, I asked him, but Hudson vetoed it. He's not sure Reid would take it seriously."

"Because if he's doing it, I'm out. There's no way I can do it if I'm worried every guy I'm talking to is him." And because I'd recognize his voice and then over-analyze every word that came out of my mouth, which would make me too flustered to talk to anyone else.

Which was another reason I had to go through with the plan. I needed to stop crushing on Reid and find someone who could help with my problem. I was tired of scratching my own itches. I wanted a big, hard, thick...

"Calm down. You're going to do fine. Just be your charming self and you won't have any issues."

"Why do people always say that? I'm not charming, Char. I'm not you. You give off sex vibes with your witty banter and I just give off desperate feral cat lady vibes."

"You're allergic to cats, Haz."

"Great, just add sneezing to my lack of vibe and none of these guys are going to be interested."

"Did you take your meds today? You're a little extra right now."

"Yes," I hissed, wanting her to keep her voice down. No one was here yet, but I didn't need her broadcasting it. "I even made sure my alarm was set, so I took it on time."

"Then you'll be fine. Just relax. I have a good feeling about this. The whole anonymity element will help you stay calm, and you'll be texting your little heart out for the next two weeks before you meet your Prince Charming."

"I'd just be happy if he's not a frog."

"I think you're mixing your fairy tales, but no frogs in the bunch, I swear."

I wasn't so sure I believed her. There was always a catch. And if someone could embarrass themselves during a blind date, I could. Even through a barrier.

"Just go change into something that makes you feel sexy and confident. Then come back down and wait in Hudson's office. Once the other women start to show up, I'll come get you."

Nodding, I took a deep breath and escaped into the kitchen. If I was going to survive tonight, I needed some emotional support potatoes.

Tater tots made everything better.

"**Y**OU IN HERE HIDING?"

I visibly startled at the unexpected voice coming through the open door, instinctively flipping my sketch pad over so he couldn't see what I'd been drawing. At least I'd thought ahead and left my penis study sketchbook upstairs. Not that I knew what his penis looked like up close…even if I desperately wanted to.

"No," I replied, busying myself by lining Hudson's pens up by color on his desk. Maybe if I avoided looking at him, I could keep my blush at bay. "Just doing some line work while I'm waiting for Charley to come get me."

He sat down in the chair across from the desk, extending one long arm in my direction with his palm up. "Lemme see."

"Absolutely not," I stuttered, grabbing the pad, and holding it to my chest.

"Oh, come on, Haz. It can't be that bad. I want to see what you've been working on. It seems like you're permanently attached to your iPad when you're not working the pass."

"I was just practicing some shading." On the forearms I drew as soon as I sat down in this chair. Forearms I was trying not to stare at in person, although it wasn't working as my eyes zeroed in on the way Reid's currently flexed.

"Then let me see."

"It's not as good as what you do, but I've been taking some workshops on creating depth with shading. I still feel like I have a long way to go as far as skill level—and it's hard to get the right brush set calibrated with my stylus—but my sketches haven't looked as flat lately. It's really helped with my rendering."

"I've had a bit more practice than you," he laughed, leaning forward so he could snag the edge of my notebook with his fingers.

They brushed the bare skin of my collarbone, and I shuddered, my traitorous cheeks beginning to heat at his accidental touch.

He pulled the notebook into his lap, his eyes scanning the page. Without looking up, he extended a hand toward me. "Pencil."

"What? No. You're just going to show off and make me feel inferior."

"Haz, all I'm going to do is show you how to vary the crosshatch and how hard you press with the pencil to create a more realistic shade along the edge. Drawing skin is hard, but you've done a great job so far."

My blush deepened at his praise, and I reluctantly handed over my pencil. He studied the barrel, the teeth marks in the middle drawing his attention. His eyes flashed to mine with a knowing look, and I glanced away.

"Don't judge me. Sometimes I need something in my mouth. The wood... The pencil *wood*. I put it in my mouth, so I don't lose it. Every time I set one down, it suddenly disappears."

Or I don't remember where I put it down and spend more time trying to find it than I should, and then I get distracted and forget what I was looking for in the first place.

Reid's lips quirked at the side in amusement, and I opened my mouth to clarify, but he nodded, interrupting me. "I do the same thing sometimes. All my pen caps have marks in the middle from my teeth."

I'd like to have marks on my middle from your teeth.

But what I really said was, "Nice to know it's a common trait in artists to identify as a beaver."

He cracked up laughing and my eyes widened as I realized what I said.

"Love beavers, but I identify more with the wood they gnaw on."

"Sounds painful," I giggled. Again, I pushed down the impulse to think about Reid's wood. It was hard. Cue random giggles that had him smiling in a way that made my stomach twist and my wayward vagin...

Nevermind.

I stopped the thoughts of Reid and being hard in the same context from taking over.

"You gonna share what's making you giggle with the class?" he asked, turning his attention to my sketchbook. His nimble fingers cradled my pencil as it danced across the page. "Why are you drawing arms, anyway? Is this for one of your figure drawing commissions?"

"No...not exactly." There was no way in hell I was telling him that the arm he had been refining was his own. "Just a self-development exercise. Never hurts to practice drawing something that catches your attention."

"And forearms catch your attention?" he asked before the tip of his tongue traced along his top lip.

"Sometimes." I glanced toward the door, hoping Charley would show up and rescue me from this conversation.

"Any reason?"

The words escaped my mouth before I could let my faulty brain to mouth filter take a crack at them. "Because they're sexy."

"I can think of sexier things," he murmured, his gaze briefly flitting to mine before it returned to the paper.

"Like what?" I'd always wondered what someone like Reid found sexy.

"Eyelashes. The way they flutter when a woman is aroused. How they make their eyes look when they glance up at me through them."

"Mm hmm," I hummed, swallowing hard; my gaze suddenly focused on my hands. I felt his eyes on me, but I couldn't look at him. One flutter of my eyelashes and he'd know I was aroused around him.

"That little dip above a woman's collarbone, and the way she squirms when I ghost my lips across it."

My mouth went dry, all the moisture pooling in other places as he cleared his throat. I looked up, noticing the way he shifted in the chair, widening his legs.

"The curve of a woman's hip. It's one of my favorite places to ink. So feminine and soft, but also strong."

Goosebumps prickled my skin as his sensuous voice dropped, and I drew in a shaky breath as his gaze lifted to meet mine.

"Have you ever wanted any ink, Haz?"

Clearing my throat, I decided to tease him, or I would have confessed all the places I wanted his big hands to trace my skin. The places I wanted him to mark me. "What makes you think I don't have any?"

"You better be fucking joking, Haz. If you've let someone else touch that pristine skin, I'm going to…"

"Going to what, Reid?" Charley asked, leaning against the door-frame. My cheeks flamed as I looked toward my best friend, her eyes flitting between the man who sat on the other side of the desk and me.

"Tell them to back the fuck off," he growled, and my eyes widened, my nipples a lost cause against the material attempting to conceal them. "If anyone is touching Hazel's skin with a needle, it's me."

"What if Hazel wants someone else to touch her?" Leave it to Charley to draw even more attention to the fact I was thirsty for my brother's best friend. *So…damn…thirsty…*

"Then they're going to have to go through me first. There's no way in fucking hell I'm letting someone else be her first."

My face was fully red, and my breaths came in shallow pants as I tried not to melt into a puddle and slide right off Hudson's desk chair and onto the floor. I knew he was talking about tattooing me, but I would have literally given my right tit to have Reid be my first.

"Hmm," Charley hummed, trying not to laugh as she glanced over at my reddened cheeks. That bitch knew exactly what she was doing. "Then let's hope none of the bachelors tonight know their way around marking up virginal skin."

I was going to fucking kill her. She was dead.

"Hazel's a smart girl," he murmured, turning toward me with a smile. "She knows who to come to when she's ready for her first."

Fuck *me*.

"Alright, fuck boy, get out of here. Hudson is waiting for you in the breakroom. Just try not to clear him out this time...and no more poker with real money. I'm tired of listening to him whine after you guys convince him to go all in and he loses it."

"Not my fault your boy is quick on the trigger," Reid laughed as he stood from the chair and tucked my pencil above his ear.

"You going to give it to me, Reid?" I asked, reaching for my sketchbook. Charley's snicker from the door confirmed she'd taken that innocent comment somewhere dirty, and I tried to tamp down the urge to blush again as Reid turned to face me.

"I'll give you whatever you want, Haz," he responded, his voice low and his gaze lingering on the low neckline of my dress. I reached for the pad again and fought off a shiver when my fingers grazed his. My eyes followed his hand as it fell to his side, his thumb hooking into his pocket. The pocket right next to his...

"You can keep the penis," I whispered, my eyes widening when I realized what I'd said to him. "THE PENCIL! Keep the pencil. Okay, bye."

Charley laughed hysterically as I sprinted toward the door, passing her and yanking open the door to the ladies' bathroom. I needed to just drown myself in a shallow bar bathroom sink before I said anything else embarrassing.

It was going to be a long night.

Chapter Three

"**D**ID SHE REALLY JUST tell me to keep the penis?" I asked, trying not to be utterly charmed by the woman who'd just sprinted across the hallway to the bathroom.

The Hazel I knew—or thought I knew—was likely in there muttering to herself in mortification.

"Shut up, Reid. You know you make her nervous."

"Is she ever going to get over that?"

"Probably not," Charley laughed, checking the hallway to make sure no one was listening before she stepped toward me. "She's anxious about tonight. And you know she overthinks everything and freaks herself out. She was supposed to be in here relaxing so she could flirt with some eligible bachelors, but you've clearly undone what I was trying to achieve."

My neck prickled with irritation as I thought about what would happen shortly. Charley's little dating experiment seemed kind of cool from the outside, but I still didn't understand why she'd roped Hazel into it.

"Speaking of..." Charley led, lowering her voice again. "You're not really going to play poker with the guys. It's canceled because Hudson had to go deal with something at home. So, it's going to be our little secret that you will now be bachelor number seven."

"What? No." Charley had already tried to rope me into this thing and Hudson had been very vocal about me *not* taking part. I wasn't sure if it was because he didn't want me flirting with his sister or if he thought I was too much of a slut—his words—to take it seriously. But I'd quickly been eliminated from his selection process.

"Yes."

"No, not with..." I gestured across the hallway toward where Haz was still hiding in the bathroom. "She'll freak out. You know she will. Even if I manage not to flirt with her, she won't be happy when you tell her."

"That's why we're not telling her. I can tell you her number, so you act aloof and distant if you really don't like her like I think you do, and then I won't have to figure out which woman to cut because the numbers are uneven."

I wasn't even touching the bait of her trying to figure out if I liked Hazel. Watching from afar was about as close to her best friend as I was going to get. Hazel didn't go for guys like me. She went for nice fuckers like that pretty boy baseball player who'd followed her around way too closely at the Halloween party.

"Does it even matter that the numbers are even?" I whispered, trying not to draw attention to our conversation for fear Hazel might overhear it. "The women don't have a limit on who they give their numbers to. And there isn't any guarantee that people will follow through on texting. The outcome won't be any different if I do it or not."

"But then the numbers won't match up for the rotations."

"You'll figure it out. You're a smart girl."

"Reid," she growled, hands on her hips. "If you don't do this, I'm going to take Hazel to Butterfly Ridge and have my cousin's friend consult on the tattoo she's been talking about."

Charley was fighting dirty. I knew it was ridiculous, but I was very possessive of my friends' skin. Not in a creepy, serial killer way. In a concerned tattooist way.

If they were making the commitment to permanently mark their skin, I wanted to make sure it was done correctly. With over a decade of experience, I knew my way around a tattoo gun and always ensured my clients were satisfied after it was done. Some were *very, very* satisfied.

"Her friend is looking for people to practice on for free."

Which was how I'd started, too. But no one that inexperienced was touching Hazel's flawless skin.

I might not have a fancy art degree in illustration, but I'd been winning regional art contests since I was ten years old. If my family had been able to afford tuition, I would've gone to somewhere like Rocky Mountain College of Art and Design, like Hazel.

Unfortunately, most of the prestigious art schools were on either coast, and I'd barely been able to scrape enough money together to get my associates in business management at the community college.

Then I'd busted my ass while I apprenticed at a shop near Boulder before I came back home to open my studio in Sage Springs the year Hudson took over the bar for his old man.

"Come on, she's coming back out soon, and she'll freak if she knows I asked you."

"Which is why this is a terrible idea."

She eyed me, lifting a brow. "Or it's an opportunity you shouldn't squander. I've watched you two dancing around each other for months. You clearly need help seeing what's right in front of you. So maybe not being able to see each other will help."

"Hudson would kill me." Especially since my thoughts about his little sister had not been innocent lately. Not since the night she'd nailed Hudson's ex in the crotch with a bat like a fierce little angelic warrior—wearing a halo to boot.

"He'd only kill you if you took advantage of her. You're not going to do that, are you?" Judging by the tone of her voice, I felt like I was being set up. "And if you take advantage of her, it will be because she asked for it."

"What does that..."

She held up her hand, whispering the sentence that sealed my fate.

"Because he'd want someone he loves to treat his sister with respect. And who better to do that than his best friend? His best friend who hasn't been able to keep his eyes off her for months.

Who would make sure she enjoys her first time? You, or some inexperienced college boy who might not know what he's doing?"

"Charley…" I growled, clenching my jaw and balling my fists at my sides.

"I'll see you in a bit, then. Go wait outside until I text you."

"Seriously?"

"Do you want to know her number, or are you going to guess?"

It wouldn't take me much effort to guess. If Hazel wore a paper bag over her head, I'd still be able to pick her voice out of a crowd.

"She's going to kill both of us."

"Not if you're as charming as you think you are. Then she will definitely *not* be killing you. Jumping you, maybe. But not killing."

Before I could curse her for trying to drag me into this, she was turning on her heel and disappearing into the bathroom to retrieve her best friend.

Her best friend I had been imagining in a very inappropriate way for months.

Who was the little sister of my oldest friend.

And the last person I should have been touching.

But the thought of anyone else laying their hands on her had me escaping out the back door of the bar and waiting for a text I should have ignored.

Charley: It's showtime.

Reid: I want it noted that I'm doing this under duress.

Charley: Noted. Now get in here and convince my best friend to give you her number.

Reid: No guarantees. I might not be her type.

Charley: Trust me, you're her type.

And that was exactly what I was afraid of. Because I had started to think she was my type, too.

Mikey, THE BOUNCER WHO'D worked here for years, smirked as he held the door open, gesturing toward the side of the temporary wall where a group of men loitered next to the bar. "Have fun. Try to leave some numbers for the rest of them, charmer."

"Just here as a favor," I whispered, patting him on the chest as I passed.

"Charley might be persuasive, but we both know why you're here. Or should I say *who* you're here for?" The laughter that followed was obnoxious.

"Not you too," I groaned, hoping I hadn't been that blatant with my observations of a certain redhead.

"I get paid to watch people all night, and you haven't exactly been subtle the last few weeks. I'm going to make an educated guess it's because you haven't been laid in a while. At least not by anyone drinking here. Because I've seen you turning away tail left and right."

"Does everyone think I'm a slut?" I growled, hating that everyone in my life seemed to know way too much about my sex life.

"Nah, you're young and you're not tied down yet, but you kind of have a reputation around here. At least you did."

"Maybe tonight will change that."

"Maybe," he laughed, slapping me on the shoulder. "I hope you get what you came here for. She needs someone fun who won't take advantage of her. Which you're not going to do, right?"

"Fuck, why in the fuck does everyone think I'm going to take advantage of her? You think I enjoy feeling like this?"

"Dude, you gotta get a hold of yourself before you sit down in that chair." He nodded toward tables lining the temporary walls with fourteen chairs waiting for the fourteen victims—or *bachelors,* as Charley kept calling them. Lowering his voice, he continued. "Because those college boys came to play, so if you want a chance, you've gotta take it."

Before I could respond, Charley noticed me lingering by the door and dragged me away, pressing a glass into my hand before pushing me toward the chair at the table with a sign taped to the back with a number seven printed on it.

"Lucky number seven, Reid. Come with me."

Sniffing, I realized she'd given me water instead of vodka, but I probably needed to keep a clear head for the next few hours, anyway.

"I would give you a shot for luck, but this is a dry event." She aimed me toward the table, picking up a notebook and pressing it into my hand. "This is to take notes. Please take this seriously. I know you're saving my ass here, but I think this could be good for you too."

Nodding, I flipped through the book, noting that it was unlined, which was good for me because I had a tendency to doodle when my attention waned during situations with limited visual stimulation.

That was part of why I'd gravitated to tattooing. Drawing had always had a calming effect and my attention to visual projects was much better than any other activity. And since it was something I could listen to music while doing, it was a perfect fit.

"I'm gonna get this show on the road. Just breathe and focus on your objective for the night."

Sighing, I looked down at her. "Char, if she doesn't want me like I am, then why is she going to want me two weeks from now after she's been lied to?"

She gripped the front of my shirt, pulling me down until our noses were practically touching. "Listen here, shit for brains. She likes you, but she's scared of you. So, you're going to convince her to give you her number and then you're going to show her who you are with your pants on, and at the end of two weeks, she's going to have enough confidence to think she can handle someone like you. And then you're going to rock her world and treat her like a princess. Because deep down, underneath all that testosterone, we both know you want to settle down, and who better to do it with than a woman who is loyal and funny and has the potential to be the love of your life if you'd get out of your own damn way."

Charley released her grip on my shirt, smoothing down the wrinkles she caused with her palm. "Are we clear?"

"Crystal," I murmured, smiling when I realized that my best friend really ended up with his perfect match, and that she was right...maybe it was time for me to find mine.

Chapter Four

Reid

"**S**O, HE WAS LIKE, tall and handsome and built, like covered in tattoos with a motorcycle..."

Bachelorette number five was not Haz. And while she was describing me to a T, her voice really grated on my nerves.

"And like he just couldn't understand that I'd spent too much money on my extensions to cover it with a helmet and risk the wind pulling one loose. So, I like insisted he drive his car, and it totally didn't match his personality. He drove a freaking used Mazda 3, and it didn't even have like tinted windows or anything. It was like totally boring."

And she was clearly superficial as hell. I'd asked her about her ideal type of man, and she went on some rant about her ex-boyfriend. She hadn't stopped talking since and every other word out of her mouth was *like*.

When the bell rang indicating this round was over, I scrubbed my hand over my face, scratching the hair covering my jaw. I'd been debating getting rid of the beard for months, but at this point in my life, it was my emotional support facial hair. Weren't beards supposed to make every man exponentially more attractive?

And Colorado winters were cold as fuck, so it was like having a built-in face warmer.

"It was like nice to meet you," she chirped, and I braced myself for the next woman. Charley hadn't warned me I'd be bored out of my fucking mind during this.

Adding one last crosshatch to the bottom of the letter E on my paper, I drew a line through the #5 written at the top of the page and chuckled at the incredibly detailed block letters spelling out the word LIKE that covered the *like* page.

It was clear I did not *like* number five.

Number four wasn't much better. She didn't talk unless I asked a question, and even then, she gave one sentence answers. After asking most of the questions on my prompt sheet, we lapsed into awkward silence for the last minute. She didn't even say goodbye when the bell rang, and I wondered why some of these women had taken part if they weren't taking it seriously.

I was trying to, but after three more soul-sucking rotations, my patience was waning. Number three whispered everything, and after I asked her to repeat herself multiple times, I just ended up sketching a very detailed set of lips across the page with tiny words floating around it.

By the time I got to bachelorette fourteen, I was ready to just lay my head down on the table and take a nap. If I wasn't afraid of Charley grabbing the pink bat she now kept stored underneath the counter at the bar and whacking me with it, I would have.

"Hi," she greeted, and a grin pulled across my face. Finally. Even from one word, I'd know that soft dulcet anywhere. It had been haunting my dreams for months.

"Hey," I responded, pitching my voice slightly lower so she hopefully wouldn't recognize it. While actually talking to each other over the last few months was a recent development, we'd spent enough time shooting the shit at the bar while she cleaned glasses after a shift for her to know what I sounded like.

"Okay, I'm just going to ask..." she trailed off, and I sat up straighter, ready for her to call me out. If she flat out asked me who I was, I wouldn't lie to her.

"Hmm," I hummed, hoping that was enough of a prompt for her to continue.

"Are you super bored right now?"

Laughing, I looked down at the once blank sheet with the #14 written on the top. The soft jawline of a woman had curved around the page, my fingers moving on autopilot as I shaded a slight dimple in her right cheek, the shape of her lips long committed to memory.

"Like you would not believe."

Her soft laughter did something to my chest that I was not going to acknowledge right now. But this was the first rotation where I dreaded the clock counting down and our turn being over.

"So, we should probably get to it. Do you want to ask the first question, or should I?"

"Go for it, H…" I trailed off, clearing my throat before course correcting after I almost said her name. "Hun."

"Ah, a nickname guy. Do you call everyone *hun*?"

"No, not really. At least not in everyday conversation. I'm more of a nickname in the heat of the moment kind of guy."

"Oh, really?" she laughed. "And what's your go to?"

"This is our first date, and you already want to know what I call women in bed? Aren't you getting a little ahead of yourself? We're supposed to be asking *getting to know you* questions."

Her laughter warmed my heart, and I was almost embarrassed for myself at how much I lit up when I talked to her lately. I was a thirty-one-year-old grown ass man, not a sixteen-year-old.

"You can tell me," she coaxed, her voice taking on a throaty quality that had other parts of me taking notice.

"Are you going to be a *good girl* and use the questions on the sheet if I do? Hmm?"

She let out a little squeak of surprise and I turned my attention to the page I had absentmindedly been sketching on. The image of Hazel's lips on the paper prompted me to lick mine, and I shifted in my chair because that unassuming noise should not have been turning me on.

"I think you just gave yourself away, handsome."

"How do you know I'm handsome?" I asked, deciding to tease her a bit.

"Just a hunch. Any man with a voice like yours and delivery of a *good girl* that smoothly has to be attractive. You've clearly got practice with those words coming off your lips."

"Is that so?" I hummed, wanting to keep her talking. Even though we were completely off the rails and only had a few minutes left, I was enjoying this flirtatious side of her.

"Oh yeah, and the deep flirty tones coming out of you without hesitation means you've got practice at seduction. Which I find incredibly attractive. What do you find attractive, bachelor number seven?"

"Women with a sense of humor."

"Then you're in luck, I'm freaking hilarious. People laugh *at me* all the time."

Deciding not to rise to the bait of her putting herself down, I continued with my list to see how she'd respond.

"A woman who loves her family."

"Considering I can't seem to escape mine; I must love them a lot."

"That didn't sound too convincing. Do they meddle in your life too much?"

"Not really," she sighed, clearing her throat. "I just have a very protective older brother, who is also my boss. So, it's hard to step out of my comfort zone when I feel like he's watching my every move."

"It's probably because he cares about you and doesn't want to see you make mistakes."

"Or because he's the world's biggest cock block."

I choked, trying not to laugh at her assessment of Hudson.

"I just want to break out of this mold he's shoved me into. But maybe now that he doesn't have a psycho bitch for a girlfriend, his new one can keep him distracted enough that I can finally breathe. Even if he stole my best friend."

If I didn't already know the story, I would have asked more questions about that. But now that I was fairly certain this bachelorette was Hazel, I suddenly wanted to march over to Charley and break her damn timer.

"And now that you can breathe, what do you plan to do with your freedom from cock blocking older brothers?"

"Well," she hummed, and the sound sent a shockwave through me. Now that her nerves were calmed by the anonymity of the opaque screen between us, I felt like she was letting her personality really shine through. I'd been trying to get her comfortable around me for months, but our history had clearly made her more skittish than I'd realized. "I want to finally be brave enough to do the things I've always wanted."

"Which are?"

"Dance all night. Find a guy who understands me and doesn't try to change me. Steal my brother's motorcycle just to feel the wind on my face... Get a tattoo."

"You know you should wear a helmet if you steal his bike."

She laughed, and I glanced at Charley, who was standing at the end of the barrier screens, imploring her to not call out the time like I knew she would in less than a minute. She winked, and I sighed in relief as she flashed her phone. The screen was paused on the two-minute mark, and I knew she was waiting for Hazel to lose interest before she called out time.

Part of me felt sorry for the guys stuck with *like* girl and the whisperer, but maybe they were into that.

I was into the woman on the opposite side of the screen from me.

"You sound just like him."

"Or maybe I just want to protect the pretty face of the woman on the other side of this screen."

"Yeah," she scoffed, her voice taking on a tone that had me wanting to knock this screen over and take her by the chin. "That would involve me being pretty. I'm average at best."

Hazel had a natural beauty about her, nothing superficial like so many of the women that came into the bar. Her high cheekbones, dark brown eyes, freckles that dusted her cheeks, and silky auburn hair...

Damn, she was a stunner. Even if she didn't see it.

"Well, I find your laugh very attractive."

"Oh, don't worry. My personality is quite sparkling. Well... when I'm not rambling about random things because I'm nervous. Or turning bright red when I'm embarrassed, which is often because I have a word vomit problem. And I know lots of random facts I add to conversations to make them more awkward. Then there's the whole interrupting people and over-sharing. Yup. So hot. It's a wonder I'm here with all the men beating down my door."

"I'd happily beat down your door. I enjoy listening to you."

She laughed, "Well, buckle up. Cause if we ever meet in person, I'm sure I'll word vomit all over you. Or just freeze and run away. I'm good at that too."

Yeah, I was well aware of her propensity to run away from uncomfortable situations. She'd been running away from me for years.

"Then I'll have my running shoes on so I can catch you."

"Oh, you're smooth," she chuckled, and I could just picture her blushing while she chewed on her lower lip.

"Seeing as we don't have too much time left, why don't we ask a few questions from the sheet?"

"Oh...yeah...the sheet. I completely forgot about that. Sometimes my brain gets started on a tangent and I can't seem to get my train of thought back on the tracks."

"You first, what question do you want me to answer?" I offered, curious which one she'd pick.

"What is one mistake you never want to repeat in life?"

Fuck. There were a lot of mistakes I wouldn't want to repeat. Starting with not realizing how attracted I was to my best friend's little sister. But it also would have been torture, because she needed to settle into who she was as an adult before some older guy tried to rope her into a relationship.

But there was one I was determined not to make now. And that was letting this opportunity go. Getting to know her better was worth the deception. At least on my part. Hopefully, in a few weeks, it would be on hers as well. If she freaked out, then I could just bow out after the reveal. It wasn't like she hadn't perfected avoiding me over the last few years. We'd get past it, even if she hated me.

"Not chasing opportunities. There are too many times in my life where I played it safe and regretted not taking the risk. The greater risk, the greater reward, right? I used to think that was bullshit, but there have been times I waited too long and missed the opportunity altogether."

"So, are those regrets with women, or...?"

"No, not really. I just played life a little too safe when I was unsure of my direction, and now I'm playing catch up to get where I should have been in the first place." I could've started my own shop earlier, but the fear of failure had kept me away from home years longer than I'd intended. I'd spent years in a city I hated, working for someone else when I could have taken the chance on myself, since I eventually ended up doing that anyway.

"I can relate to that."

"How so?" It had always seemed that she knew exactly where she wanted her career to go. I knew she was doing freelance—and that wasn't without its own set of risks—but she seemed so confident in her work.

"I let my fear of rejection keep me from putting myself out there. Now I feel like I'm way behind on life in general." She paused, my heart rate increasing while I waited for her to finish her answer. "And I'm tired of watching other people get what I want. I want to be adventurous and do things that scare me for once in my life. I've been scared of things and some people for too long."

"What people are you afraid of?"

Charley had said Haz was scared of me, but I wanted to know why. Other than the obvious incident that happened a few years ago. One I wish I could take back because of how it'd driven a wedge between us.

"There's a...*friend* I used to have who I distanced myself from when something embarrassing happened a few years ago that I miss. We used to talk a lot when I was younger, but then he moved away. He's been back for a while now, but I saw something I shouldn't have, and I let it get in the way of our friendship."

"Sounds like you might want to be more than friends."

She laughed, and it wasn't her typical carefree one. "There's no chance of that happening. And I'm tired of obsessing about it, so maybe something like tonight is a good opportunity for me to let go of childish fantasies."

Fuck.

I didn't want to take the conceited route and think she was talking about me. But I knew she was. And the last thing I wanted her to do was let me go.

Chapter Five

M Y CHEEKS FELT HOT from how hard I was blushing, knowing that my flirtatious banter with bachelor number seven was not how I typically reacted to men. There was something about his voice that helped ease my nerves, and he seemed genuinely interested in getting to talk to me instead of turning this whole thing into something about himself.

Not that it was all about me either, but the conversation seemed to flow, unlike some of my previous unsuccessful blind dates. I'd already gone through two dude bros, one humble bragger, two obnoxious laughers and a one-word answerer so far.

By the time I got to number seven, my hopes weren't very high that I'd be giving my number to anyone tonight, no matter how much I knew Charley wanted me to.

"You know, sometimes fantasies can be made a reality." I tried not to read things into his statement, but my nipples didn't get the memo, tightening as I thought about what fantasies I'd like bachelor number seven to bring to life. Ones that'd increased in frequency over the last several weeks, brought on by Reid's insistence not to let me hide from him any longer.

While he'd always been Hudson's friend, we'd once been close, too. But he'd never seen me. The real me. He'd seen the shy, reserved, completely inexperienced little sister of his friend I'd been in my teens. And I wasn't sure I wanted to be that person to him any longer.

"Well, play your cards right and in a few weeks, you might be able to put your money where your mouth is..."

"Trust me, my mouth is not where it wants to be right now," he practically growled, and I knew without a shadow of a doubt that this man would get my phone number at the end of the night.

Charley would be beyond smug, but I wouldn't let my nerves get the best of me and miss out on the possibility of pursuing something with him. Even if things went bust after we started texting or he wasn't who I wanted him to be in a few weeks when I'd get to meet him for real, I would not be shy or talk myself out of things any longer.

"And where would that be?" I knew I was pushing the boundaries again since this was supposed to be a friendly date to see if our personalities were compatible, but I knew I'd kick myself if I didn't follow my instincts. Even if my instincts were telling me that this man on the other side of the wall was vastly more experienced than I was.

"You're trying to be *naughty* again, ha..." his voice trailed off abruptly, and I wondered what he was going to say. After he cleared his throat, he continued, his voice a bit deeper. "Have you always been this much of a rule breaker?"

Surprised laughter flowed out of me, and goosebumps raced across the backs of my arms—not helping at all with the nipple situation—when he joined in, his deep timbre evoking feelings only one other man in my life could ever create.

"No, I'm about the exact opposite of a rule breaker. You're currently conversing with a bona-fide *goody two shoes*. If rule following was a sport, I'd be a world champion."

"Hmm, I..." he hummed, and I thought he'd ask for more details, since he seemed to be more curious about me than revealing much about himself, but he didn't, the sound of my best friend's voice cutting him off.

"Thirty seconds, boys and girls, then we're onto your next match."

"Fuck," he cursed, and the smile that pulled across my cheeks was obnoxious. "Okay, one last question."

"Hmm?"

"What's your hidden talent?"

If only he knew what talents I'd been pursuing lately. Charley was the only one who knew about all the commissions I'd been working on. But as the seconds ticked by, I decided that playing it safe wasn't what I wanted anymore. And at the end of the night, this guy—this man—on the other side of the screen was worth disclosing all my naughty secrets to. Because I had a feeling he wouldn't judge me.

With a nervous laugh, I glanced at Charley out of the corner of my eye, and she flashed me a thumbs up while holding up her phone that was counting down the end to the weirdest, but most satisfying date I'd ever been on.

"Drawing naked people."

He was quiet for a moment, and I thought maybe he was put off by my answer, but then his response moments after the timer went off on Charley's phone had my heart beating faster.

"Don't think for one second that timer is saving you from answering more of my questions. We're continuing this discussion later."

"Um," I laughed, a bit startled by the gruff tone in his voice. "Pretty sure our date is over."

"You better turn over that phone number at the end of the night, because I'm telling you now, this discussion isn't finished."

Glancing to the side, I noticed the next woman who'd be going on a date with bachelor number seven giving me an impatient look. Well, she could wait a fucking minute.

"Maybe that's for me to decide," I teased, knowing full well he was the only man to have earned my number so far. And I had a feeling he might be the only one.

"We both know you wouldn't have told me that if you didn't want a response."

"Hmm, I guess we'll find out." I knew I was throwing off Charley's schedule, but I also wanted to say fuck it and knock down this stupid divider to beg bachelor number seven to get me out of here.

"I look forward to your text."

"So cocky." The arrogance suddenly coming off this man should have been a turnoff, but it had the opposite effect.

"You have no fucking idea," he chuckled, and I really, really wanted the next two weeks to fly by so I could meet him for real.

"Bye, number seven."

"This isn't a goodbye, fourteen. Not if I have anything to say about it."

No amount of pissed off blondes scoffing as I refused to move on to my next bachelor quickly could have wiped the smile off my face.

"So..." Charley had been waiting for me at the end of the event, grinning obnoxiously as I deposited the card with my phone number on it into two of the numbered boxes lying on the table by the entrance to the bar. "Looks like you didn't totally hate it."

"Shut up."

"Oh, come on, you give your number to a guy—actually two guys—after an event you were very much against doing and you think I'm not going to ask you how things went? This is huge, Haz!"

"It's not that big of a deal." It kind of was, but I didn't want to get ahead of myself. Just because I'd given them my phone number didn't mean they'd follow through with texting me. The ball was in their court, and I was suddenly nervous that neither one of them would respond and I'd feel even more like a loser than I already did.

"Yeah, I see what you're doing." She gave me the side eye as she started gathering up the question sheets and table numbers from the ladies' side of the room. I could hear a few people milling around on the other side of the screens, but all the other women had already left out the front and Charley had escorted the men out the back door before she'd come back in to interrogate me. "You're trying to convince yourself that you didn't have fun. That this idea wasn't awesome. And now you don't want to acknowledge that maybe this was exactly what you needed."

"Wow, humble much?" There was absolutely no way I was confirming anything, because she was already feeling smug about how the event had gone. And if best friends were good for anything, it was keeping you grounded when your ego was at stake of getting obnoxiously large. "I wouldn't go bragging about your success until the end of this thing."

"It's okay. I'll wait to say I told you so until after you meet the love of your life at the party. I might even wait until after your wedding to say it. Just to be extra humble. But I'm expecting Charlotte as the middle name of your first-born child."

"Just looking for someone to punch my v-card, Char, not looking for a soulmate. Not everyone has to be in love since you are."

She frowned, and I felt a little bad about raining on her parade, but I wasn't holding out for a soulmate anymore. I just wanted to feel wanted by a man for once. To be the center of someone's attention—even if it was fleeting.

I wasn't gorgeous and curvy like her. I wasn't confident like her. I wasn't the object of a man's obsession like she was. And that was okay. I would be okay if that never happened for me. But for the next few weeks, I wanted to pretend it could.

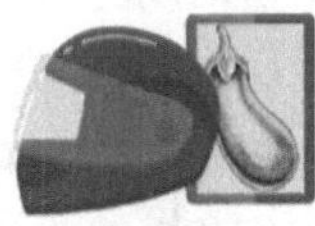

"Y OU'RE UP LATE." MY hand jerked at the low voice coming from behind me, but thankfully digital illustration had made it so mistakes, like the dark line now marring the face of the woman I was drawing, could easily be erased. Luckily, I had the image zoomed in close, so Reid couldn't see the rest of it, but I still slammed the magnetic cover over the screen of my iPad and laid my hand on the top before I turned to face him.

"What are you still doing here?" I asked, my pulse skyrocketing as I turned on my barstool to face him. His hair was a chaotic mess, like he'd been running his hands through it. Under different circumstances, I would have automatically assumed it'd been someone else's hands who'd made the mess, but I knew he'd been with my brother all night playing poker with the cooks.

"Was just helping break down the extra tables for Char. She and Hudson just took off. Wanted to make sure everything was locked up before I left." Glancing up, I noticed the kitchen was dark, the bar surrounding us quiet, but the air around us felt charged. "I thought you'd be upstairs asleep by now."

"Hmm." My fingers absently tapped at the cover beneath my palm, my usual nerves around Reid surfacing. But I was trying to fight the urge to flee, like I normally did. Maybe Seven had been right, despite my unwanted feelings for him, maybe I could be his friend again. "Knew I'd never be able to sleep, so I was working."

"Didn't want to use that fancy new workspace upstairs?"

Reid and Hudson had been the ones to set up my new desk while I hid downstairs in the bar sketching, so I wasn't tempted to drool over Reid using power tools. Once they were done, I'd been surprised to walk in and see they had set up the desk pad I'd been waiting to cover the surface with. And there was a fresh box of pencils I liked to use sitting on a brand-new leather-bound sketchbook. The only issue was, the sketchbook had metallic embossing on the front cover, clearly a joke from my best friend because it was in the outline of a cartoonish looking kitten. I'd wanted to call them out for getting me such a childish gift, but it was cute, and I'd kept it next to my bed to doodle in when I woke up in the morning.

But it also cemented in my mind that they still saw me as the awkward little girl who spent more time with her face buried in a sketchbook than anything else. Which was the last thing I wanted Reid to think of when he looked at me.

"What are you working on? Not forearms this time, I see."

"No," I scoffed, hoping he didn't press me for details, because while the face of the woman with her eyes closed on the screen was unassuming, if I zoomed out, he'd get an eyeful of where she was supposed to be straddling a man's face. Explaining that it was my latest romance book commission was the last thing I wanted to have to do right now. Never mind that it was unfinished while I was still trying to get the positioning right.

"Care to share?"

"No." My palm flattened on the case covering the screen, hoping he'd take my answer and move on.

"What are you so secretive about suddenly? The last few weeks, anytime anyone asks you what you're drawing, you slam the cover closed on your tablet."

"Maybe I'm just protecting the privacy of my clients."

"I wasn't aware that illustration commissions were such heavily guarded secrets."

"Well. They are. I like to maintain the integrity of my work, and some things I've been drawing aren't ready to be shared publicly yet."

"Hmm. And what are these things you've been drawing?"

Maybe I'd been listening to too many of my client's books lately, but I could have sworn that Reid's eyes darkened as they slowly tracked from where my hand held the cover of my iPad in place to my eyes. If I didn't know any better, I'd guess he knew what I'd been drawing, which seemed impossible, because even Charley didn't know all the details.

And after being caught by her, I'd started keeping my sketchpad full of dicks locked in the bottom drawer of my new desk along with all the source material I'd printed out. Just because I lived alone didn't mean I could risk leaving cocks lying about if I had any surprise visitors. Because my mother would give me a talk about being safe—which seemed laughable with all the sex I was so clearly not having—Charley would tease the shit out of me, and

Hudson would go all protective older brother on me, and he did that enough.

"It's private," I muttered.

"What?" He grinned, leaning in closer. "I didn't hear you. Did you say *it's privates*?"

Since I couldn't refute his question because that'd be lying to him, and I was trying not to do that, I just did the only other thing available in my virginal arsenal. I blushed. Hard.

Reid cocked one eyebrow, and my face flamed hotter, but I maintained eye contact, determined not to back down. He could tease me all he wanted, but I was proud of my commissions, and my growing list of clients, and nothing anyone else said about it would make me stop.

If drawing fictional naked people was my happy place, then everyone else could fuck themselves, Reid included. Although that thought just had me picturing him doing exactly that. Fucking himself with... *Stop it.*

Stupid intrusive thoughts were trying to get me in trouble again.

"Haz," he murmured, his fingertips brushing against the back of my hand. Biting my lower lip, I fought off a shudder, my stomach fluttering at the contact from his calloused fingers. Fucking attractive asshole. I knew what he was trying to do. But I knew I was going to fall for his bullshit, regardless.

"Yes, Reid?"

"Give it to me." I knew the command wasn't inherently sexual, and I should not have been thinking of throwing my panties at the man like a brazen hussy, but I was. I most definitely was thinking about giving him things. All the things. The things being the clothing I wore that suddenly felt too tight.

"No," I whispered, despite my intrusive thoughts. Those horny little fuckers needed to stop getting me in trouble.

"You know you want to show me. You thrive on positive feedback, just like I do. So why won't you let me give it to you?"

Nope. No. I could not allow my mind to wander down that trail of thought.

"Because it's not perfect, so your feedback might not be so positive."

He gently pried my hand free, setting it down on the smooth surface of the bar. Holding it down with his palm, he picked up the tablet with his other hand, pressing the button to wake the screen. "Passcode."

Shaking my head, I tried not to swoon at the feeling of him holding me down, even if it was just my hand.

Using his thumb, he quickly typed in a code, grinning when the screen opened. I knew I should have been more original than using my birthdate, but this tablet also never left my sight.

His ability to zoom out from the image on the screen was limited since he only had one hand available, but that didn't stop him from scrolling down the page, his eyes widening as he likely took in the female form that I'd mostly finished the line work on. The very, *very* nude female character.

"You've been a naughty girl, Haz. But this is fucking hot. Why were you so afraid of me seeing this?"

"I think you know why," I whispered, watching his gaze flicker back and forth between me and the risqué image on the screen.

"The female body is nothing to be ashamed about. And this is... This is not what I was expecting. But it seems incomplete."

"Because it is." My voice was quiet, but the look in his eyes had me transfixed. I couldn't look away even if I tried. And I wanted the source of the desire in his eyes to come from me, not some illustration on my tablet. He was looking at her in the way I'd always fantasized about being looked at by him.

Somehow it seemed fitting that I was jealous of a figment of my imagination holding more appeal to him than me.

"What do you need help with?"

Nibbling on my lower lip, I averted my eyes to the screen, so I didn't have to look at him. "I can't get the posing right."

"What's she kneeling on? Maybe I can help."

"Um…" While I refused to look up, I still knew he was smirking, I could feel it burning into the side of my head. "I don't want to tell you."

"Haz…"

"His face," I blurted, after a few charged moments of silence. "She's sitting on a guy's face. And since I can't find a reference picture at this angle, I've been having a hard time getting it right. And I don't have any firsthand experience with…*that*…so I'm just making it up as I go and it sucks, okay? Happy now? Ready to tease me some more?"

Reid didn't say a word as I internally freaked out, mortified that I'd basically just told him I'd never sat on a man's face before. Or even had my lady parts anywhere near a man's face, for that matter.

"Actually," he said, clearing his throat. "Maybe I could help you out with that."

Um, excuse me. What?

Chapter
Six

Reid

"**I**'M SORRY, WHAT?" SHE asked, panic in her eyes.

Shit, I'd basically just inferred that she could sit on my face. Not that I'd be all that opposed to the idea, but that wasn't what I had in mind.

"I was going to ask if you wanted someone to help you with reference photos."

"Oh," she said, sounding relieved. "Oh...uh. Maybe?"

"I don't have any clients until noon tomorrow. Want to do it in the morning?"

She started chewing that pouty lower lip again, and my fingers twitched with the urge to pull it free and soothe her abused lip...with my tongue.

Fuck, I needed to keep it together. After flirting with her during our blind date, I had to get my head in the right place, so I didn't give myself away. I still needed to text her from the VPN phone number I'd set up moments after walking out the back of the bar earlier. I'd already input her number into the texting app, but I wasn't sure what to say.

I also felt guilty about the deception, but it wasn't like I could contact her from my personal number or the shop mobile number, since she knew both. And while volunteering to help with her commissions might put me at risk for exposure, I could also see if this attraction between us was really happening or if it was something I was imagining.

She'd probably think I was a piece of shit later for not coming clean, but she'd been hiding from me for years, and it was time she stopped. Because the more time I spent with her, the more time I wanted to *keep* spending with her, and I wasn't going to let her fear of the man I used to be stop me.

Maybe it was turning thirty or the fact that I'd never been in a serious relationship before. Hell, maybe it was because I was finally seeing—and was really fucking attracted to—the woman she'd become over the last few years that'd infused me with this craving to be around her.

"You know I'll just show up if you don't give me an answer. And while figure drawing is not where I concentrate most of my energy, I know how to do it. Unless you have some art school friends who'd be happy to help you…"

Hazel's cheeks remained pink even as she shook her head, trying to dissuade me from continuing to pry into this situation.

"None of them know what I've been working on."

Stepping closer, I pulled her closer, cupping her cheek. "You know this isn't something you should be ashamed of, right?"

Her eyes were soft as she stared up at me, the pad of my thumb absently stroking the apple of her cheek. She truly didn't know how beautiful she was. How brave she was. But I was determined to be the one to clue her in on just how amazing she truly was.

"Haz, I think it's impressive you're building a business on your own terms. It isn't easy, but if you love what you're doing, it's worth it. Your dreams are worth it."

"Okay," she murmured. I wasn't sure if it was her accepting my offer to help her or if she was confirming what I'd said, but she wasn't fighting me. And I'd give just about anything to keep her attention right now.

"So, you'll let me help you?"

The soft skin beneath my thumb pinkened, and I knew I had my answer. She may have been apprehensive about letting me in, but she wasn't hiding from me anymore.

Leaning in, my lips brushed her cheek as I whispered in her ear. "Don't worry, you're in good hands. I'm an excellent photographer. And I'm very good at giving direction."

"Wait." Her eyes widened as I stepped back. "You're not meaning that you're going to take pictures of *me*, right?"

Shrugging, I stepped backward, knowing if I didn't leave soon, I'd never want to. And I had a text yet to send.

"Reid, this isn't self-insert artwork here. I don't need pictures of me."

"How else do you intend to get reference photos to work from? Are you planning to ask Charley?"

She cursed under her breath as she followed me toward the back door, and I tried not to laugh. She really was a fierce little kitten sometimes.

"You CANNOT tell her."

Holding up my hands, I adopted an unassuming expression. "You need reference photos of couples, so unless you're willing to get in the shot with me, it'll be hard to set up what you need without a second person."

"What?"

"Let me put it to you another way. *You* want my help? *You* pose with me."

She sputtered, her panicked expression only making me feel a little remorse for talking her into this.

"You can't be serious about this, Reid. You saw what I was drawing."

Nodding, I tried to hold back how much her drawing had truly affected me. "Very serious, Haz."

"But…"

"See you in the morning. I'll bring my tripod."

"Your what?" she squeaked, her eyes briefly darting toward my pants, and it took all my fucking willpower to hold back a laugh. This girl had a much naughtier mind than I'd ever expected.

"Get your mind out of the gutter," I teased. "That one won't do much good for holding up a camera, but thanks for the ego boost."

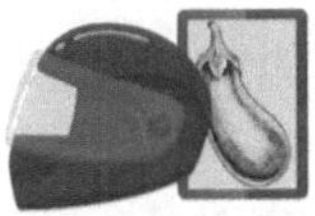

MY PALMS WERE FUCKING sweating as I pushed the back door of the shop closed, making sure the security system was armed before I escaped up the back staircase.

I didn't remember ever being this nervous about texting a woman, not even when I was in high school.

This was ridiculous. I was over thirty, not thirteen, but here I was, staring down at my phone like a fucking pussy, trying to figure out what to say.

I hadn't been kidding the last time Hudson had given me shit about my dating habits. Women pursued me, I didn't pursue them. And to be completely honest, I didn't even exchange phone numbers with half the ones I messed around with.

My reputation preceded me most times, and they knew what the score was. Sage Springs wasn't that big. If you wanted no strings attached, one night of fantastically dirty sex, you either came in and got a tat with me or tracked me down next door.

Most of the locals steered clear, but with an influx of tourists and college girls—let's just say my dance card was full. And nearly everywhere around my shop had been defiled, but never my bed.

I didn't take women upstairs. It seemed too...intimate.

The time Hazel walked in on me at the bar had been an anomaly. While I may have engaged in some borderline inappropriate displays of affection on the dance floor, I hadn't fucked anyone at the bar before—or after—that. We'd just been interrupted by Haz coming to look for something in the back room at the same time.

Unfortunate timing.

Definitely for me, because I felt like it'd been a mistake I couldn't escape, even after two years. Hudson had held a grudge for my lapse in judgment, and Hazel had retreated inside herself, taking away a valuable friendship. I hadn't realized until it was gone that I would miss her so terribly. While Hudson knew all my dirty secrets, Hazel had been someone who understood my need to create.

It was rare for me to click with someone on a purely artistic level. Even when she was in high school, Hazel was a very skilled illustrator, and we'd spent a lot of time drawing with each other. Watching her skills grow and flourish from afar since things fell apart had been bittersweet, but I *was* proud of the business she was creating. She may have been embarrassed to tell me what she was really doing, but I'd admired her ability to dive into something so sex positive at this step in her career.

Women shouldn't have to hide their sensuality, and artwork like the one on her tablet was just one avenue to explore that side of their sexuality.

I just hadn't expected it from her. She had a shy, demure vibe about her that had kept me away, but now that I knew what she'd been hiding from me, I was going for it.

Charley and Hudson had never outright told me that Hazel was inexperienced sexually, but I could read between the lines, especially after Charley's little pep talk earlier in the night.

The responsible best friend of her older brother should have stayed far, far away from her, but everyone knew I was a bit reckless. I wouldn't be reckless with her though, and I sure as hell didn't want to risk some dipshit college guy breaking her heart.

Blowing out a breath, I sat down on the edge of my bed, laying my phone down on the blankets beside me. Staring at it while I tried to plan a response in my head, I flexed my fingers, cracking them nervously before I picked it back up and typed out my first message...which would definitely not be my last.

> *Seven: Told you we weren't done with our discussion, fourteen.*

Chapter Seven

I WASN'T SURE HOW that smug fucker—number Seven—expected me to get any sleep after that kind of text. It was bad enough I had escaped back to my apartment all wound up after Reid discovered my dirty little secret. Now I had to figure out how to respond to the only bachelor who'd texted me last night. Part of me figured I wouldn't receive any texts from the bachelors, but I knew if I got one, it'd most likely be from him.

Bachelor Ten had been sweet and funny, making me laugh at several points during our brief conversation, but I hadn't felt that spark I did with Seven. He'd had my whole body on alert, my pulse racing every time his voice dropped lower, and he'd say something vaguely suggestive.

I knew that wasn't what the experiment was about. It was supposed to see how we'd react to each other without being able to see each other, but I'd never experienced that kind of instant sexual chemistry with someone. And the rush was a little addictive. Was this why my apartment had been a revolving door of dick for Charley before she settled down with my brother? Was this how other people normally felt around the opposite sex?

It was certainly unlike anything I'd ever experienced before, because the way I felt around Reid was just me being a neurotic mess, not mutual attraction, no matter how much I wished it were. But that interaction with him volunteering to help with my commissions had thrown me too much to respond to Seven last night. It wouldn't have been fair of me to reply to him when I was thinking about another man.

Another man who would be at my apartment any moment and I was still under the covers wrapped in blankets staring at a sentence that I knew had the possibility to change my life. If only I had the balls to respond to it. Which right now, I did not.

The screen of my phone lit up with a text message and I immediately dropped it, my pulse racing at the idea that either man had texted me while I was having a sleep deprived existential crisis. Nervously glancing at it, I frowned because Christian hadn't texted me in months.

> *Christian: What are you up to today? I've got classes all day, but I'm looking forward to catching up with you.*

It seemed innocuous enough, but I didn't have space in my brain to decipher the intentions of another man, so I just laid it back down and ignored it.

Right now, I had to get my shit together because I looked as if a hibernating squirrel had taken up residence in the messy bun on the top of my head. And if I didn't fix it soon, Reid would get an up-close viewing of how much of a hot mess I was.

Three sharp raps against the apartment door had me scrambling out of the bed and racing to the bathroom. I tried fruitlessly to unfurl my crazy hair, but the ponytail holder got stuck and was now trapped in the center of my wild, tangled mane.

"Fuck me," I hissed, throwing it back up into a messy bun. Hopefully, he wouldn't notice I was an epic disaster this morning or at least would be nice enough not to point it out in the time it took me to tell him this was a terrible idea, and he needed to go back home.

"Haz?" Reid's deep, masculine voice echoed through the wooden door, and I knew he'd stand there all day if I tried pretending I wasn't home. He knew I was. Hell, I practically never left the building now that all my classes were online.

"Just... Hold on! I'm..." *a fucking mess.* Swiping at the crumbs on my baggy hooded sweatshirt, a litany of curse words rolled through my brain, but they didn't budge. The curse words or the crumbs. Wow, I was just the epitome of a sex goddess this morning.

"If it makes you feel any better, I have donuts and coffee," he chuckled, and I tried not to picture how attractive he looked when he laughed. It really wasn't fair how good I was sure he looked on the other side of the door and how *not* attractive I looked in contrast right now.

"Depends on what kind," I replied as I gripped the latch on the deadbolt and turned it, the door swinging inward before I could even touch the handle below.

"Well," Reid mused, stepping forward and pressing a cup into my hand before he skirted around me. My skin burned where he touched my arm through my sweatshirt and my eyes widened as he leaned in to dust a chaste kiss on my jawline. "I know what you like."

That was *new.*

Had I woken up in some alternate universe where my brother's best friend now kissed me on the cheek? And brought me warm beverages and donuts without prompting? Was there a full moon I didn't know about?

Pulling the cup to my lips, I sniffed, the scent of cinnamon and chai immediately calming my frazzled nerves. He *did* know what I liked. And he'd clearly been paying enough attention that he knew real coffee made me a hyped-up, jittery mess. But I would never turn down a Chai tea latte.

"I'm not sure this is such a good idea," I mumbled, still huffing my mildly caffeinated drink. "While I appreciate the offer, I think I can manage to do this on my own."

Reid laid the paper bag from my favorite bakery, *Ice My Cake,* down on the kitchen counter, turning and bracing his hands against the edge of the countertop. "I think it's already too late for that, Haz."

"I'm really not in the mood this morning." Taking a sip of my hot drink, I tried not to squirm under his gaze, but he looked like a man on a mission. He wouldn't leave, and part of me was glad he was here. That part also would have liked to not look like woodland creatures were taking up residence in her hair.

"Then go take a shower and I'll eat my fritter while I wait."

Shaking my head, I almost groaned as I took another greedy gulp of my tea. His methods for gaining entry to my apartment were really on point this morning. "I think I'm just going to keep things low key before I have to work tonight."

"Is there a reason you're so resistant to help this morning?"

You mean other than that he looked like a fucking male model—which I guess was technically what he was here to do—this morning and I looked like a person who should shop in Walmart at 2 am?

"I'm just not in the right headspace for explaining to you why this is a bad idea."

He pushed off the counter, stepping forward until my head tilted back to maintain eye contact. Then his much larger hands closed around where mine had a death grip on my cup to get my attention.

"Haz, go put on something comfortable, brush your hair—and maybe your teeth—and I will wait for you. We both know you'll let this derail your whole day and I don't want to see something that could easily be fixed keeping you from making progress on your commissions. I've seen how much you've been glued to that tablet, and I know how fast you work, so don't even try to convince me you don't have authors lining up with requests."

Well, fuck. Maybe Reid paid much more attention to me than I thought he did. Because he was right, after a few authors told their writing groups about me, my DMs had been nuts with requests. I'd not only had to create a calendar and spreadsheet to track them all, but I also had several authors tell me I wasn't charging them enough and was now making twice what I thought I would be doing this.

What had been an idea to generate a bit of extra income while I was taking more advanced digital illustration courses online had turned into a legitimate business overnight. One that had taken a turn I never expected. Which was why I was now stuck in said existential crisis.

How workable was it for a virgin to run a successful illustration business that specialized in artwork that was firmly in the *not suitable for work* category?

And how long was I going to keep that virginity status from the man I'd had a crush on for over a decade?

"You know I'm right." He was. But I wouldn't tell him that. His ego was big enough.

Why couldn't I be the confident friend? Charley would know what to do in this situation, while I was still standing here huffing chai tea and looking like I'd not only rolled out of bed, but into the woods behind the building to become one with the woodland creatures.

"I am not at liberty to confirm or deny that statement."

"Seriously, Haz. What harm will it cause to let me help you?"

It would murder my panties for one.

If he wanted to go full on reenactment for the scene I was supposed to be focusing on, I'd have to straddle his face and then take a picture. Surely my unexciting plain white cotton full coverage underwear would expire if that were to happen.

"Why are you so fixated on this?" Because he wasn't showing any signs of backing down and going away. In fact, he had the audacity to take a seat on my couch and make himself at home while I remained there gaping at him. "I'm not seeing how this benefits you."

My pulse skittered to a stop as I waited for his answer and then took off into a gallop when he licked his lips, his gaze turning predatory. If I didn't know better, he was looking at me like he'd looked at the sketch on my tablet last night.

"Because I think what you're doing is…admirable. And if I can help you, I want to. Isn't that what friends do? Help each other?"

"So, drawing people doing…*things* is admirable now? There are plenty of people who I'm sure would disagree with you." My brother being one of them. I knew he supported my art, but he still didn't seem to understand that I was a grown adult. And that I thought about sex. So much so that I was now embracing those thoughts and the ones of others and bringing them to life as pieces of artwork.

"Then they're fucking stupid." His arms stretched along the back of my couch, and the fleeting thought that he belonged there quickly ran through my overwhelmed thoughts. That was not something I should have been considering, much less acknowledging.

Reid and I didn't make sense. Not on paper and certainly not in real life. It wasn't even that I thought he was too good for me, because I knew my worth, it was that we were in such different parts of our lives that I couldn't imagine him being interested in someone younger and much less experienced than he was.

For most of my life, I'd stayed inside the little box people put me in. I was the shy bookworm who loved to draw. I was the good girl who followed all the rules and didn't cause problems. And now, I was discovering a part of myself I'd denied for so long.

Maybe I wasn't so shy, and maybe I wasn't such a good girl. Maybe I wanted to be more adventurous and try new things. I wanted a lot of things I never thought I did before, but most of all...I wanted to be wanted.

That was why the idea of Seven was so appealing. He didn't care what I looked like or who I was to everyone else. He genuinely seemed to want to get to know *me*. And that was something I'd never experienced before.

"You still in there?" Reid teased, his gaze never wavering from mine. I'd been off in La La Land, and he was staring at me like he was waiting for something. Technically, he was waiting for my approval to go along with his half-cocked scheme to help my posing, but it felt like I was still missing something.

"Fine. We try it once. But if it still doesn't help, you let it go. And you cannot use any of this as fodder to tease me. And you sure as *fuck* aren't telling Hudson a damn thing about my art."

His answering grin was almost obnoxious. "The word fuck sounds good coming from your lips."

I faltered as my brain caught up to him using the words *fuck, coming,* and *your lips* all in one sentence, and I couldn't help the blush that crept up my neck and cheeks.

"And the fact me saying that made you blush is really fucking adorable."

And he had to ruin it by calling me adorable.

Raccoon videos on the internet were adorable, grown women with sex appeal were not. Which meant Reid still clearly only saw me in one way.

"Shut up." My clever response was met with a deep chuckle, and I took that as my cue to escape into my bathroom to make myself look less like a feral cat lady.

I thought I'd escaped further embarrassment, but as I crossed the threshold into my bedroom, he couldn't help making one more comment. "Don't worry, I'll have to shut up while you're sitting on my face."

And there was the mic drop...

Chapter Eight

Reid

I'D NEVER ACTUALLY SEEN someone scurry before, but as Hazel's expressive eyes widened and she turned abruptly toward her bedroom and escaped into the bathroom, I was pretty sure that was exactly what she'd done. I knew that being here like this was kind of a dick move on my part, but when I woke up this morning with no response to my text, I was even more determined to see where her head was at.

Hazel was the type of person who wore her heart on her sleeve and couldn't keep a secret to save her life. If I spent enough time with her, eventually she'd crack and give me a hint on whether I should continue to message her as bachelor number seven. If she wasn't into him, I wouldn't force myself on her.

Her non-response wasn't exactly encouraging, but I also knew she over-thought everything. I was sure that at least once in the past twelve hours she'd spent a significant amount of time staring at the open text thread—much like I had waiting for her answer.

But that was fine, I'd give her time to process how she wanted to move forward, and in the meantime, I'd come up with any excuse to see her in person. Starting with this project to help her get pictures to use as posing references. While I could tell she was intimidated at the thought of reenacting some arguably hot positions, her eyes had lit up several times in a way that I'd never seen before.

Not so little anymore Hazel Rivera was aroused, and that was exactly how I wanted her to be when I was around. Because I was hard as fuck this morning when I woke up and thought about her straddling my shoulders like she'd need to for this picture. So much so that I'd already taken care of things twice—once in my bed, and once in the shower. But the thought of her being wet and naked on the other side of the wall had things perking up again.

Which was why I'd worn a pair of compression shorts underneath my athletic shorts, because I didn't want to scare her. She'd had a hard enough time on Halloween keeping her eyes on my face and not my piercings. It probably didn't help that they were at her eye level while I spent the entire night shirtless, but I'd seen her staring more than once when she'd noticed me watching her.

As a result, my nipples had ached the entire night from being the object of her attention. At the time, I'd tried to rationalize it as a reaction to the blizzard that'd taken us all by surprise. The same blizzard that had stranded her brother with her best friend for an entire weekend and seemed to be the spark that had led to her deciding to stop fleeing every time I was in the same room.

Even now, I'd seen lingering glances when I wore tight T-shirts because she knew what lay underneath. It wasn't a secret that I was pierced because she'd seen me in a swimsuit dozens of times over the ten years since I'd had them, but the way she looked at me seemed to have changed over the last decade.

If only she knew that those weren't my only piercings.

But I wouldn't be that guy. The one who talked about his dick piercing to entice women. It was just a bonus for those who had the chance to find out. And having Hazel find out about that particular piece of body jewelry was the source of all my fantasies lately. The thought of watching her on her knees before me, her pink tongue darting out to play with the ring, tugging on it with her teeth, feeling it against the roof of her mouth while she sucked on my cock...

"Are you okay?" she asked, and I blinked hard, trying to refocus and not let all the blood in my entire body rush straight to my aforementioned cock.

Hazel had been adorable when she answered the door all disheveled, but now I was forced to clench my fists as I took in what she was wearing—or not wearing—after her shower.

Her hair was down and damp, her face freshly washed showing off the freckles that covered her cheeks, but it was the tight sports bra and tiny athletic shorts that had me wanting to bite my fist.

Fucking hell. She was hot as fuck, and she genuinely didn't know it.

"Yeah, uh…" I cleared my throat, shifting, so it wasn't obvious that thinking about her with her lips around my dick while she was in the shower had gotten me worked up.

"How exactly do you want to do this?" she asked, avoiding eye contact as she crossed the room and sat down across from me on the coffee table. My eyes wanted to zero in on the way her shorts rode up even higher on her thighs, but I forced myself to make eye contact and keep it. Because if I kept succumbing to my baser urges, I'd have her splayed out on that table with my face between her thighs. Tongue lapping at her clit, her cries music to my fucking ears…

Shaking my head, I realized she was waiting for my response. "I think maybe someplace like a bed would be the best place to do this. The perspective would be better, and we can adjust the tripod to get the angle you need."

Her teeth tugged on her lower lip as she contemplated that, her eyes darting toward her room and then at the door across the hallway where her studio was set up. Hudson and I had dismantled Charley's old bed before we'd assembled Hazel's desk, but I knew it might invade her personal space to suggest we do this on *her* bed.

"I've got a futon at the shop we can use if you don't want to do it here."

Her nose wrinkled. "Yeah, not sure I want to be thinking about your conquests the whole time."

She had a point, and there were quite a few places over there that had been defiled over the last few years, but this was in one of the few places I hadn't brought women to hook up.

"I was thinking about the one in the break room. There's enough floor space to lay it flat and the lighting in there is even, so you wouldn't have to worry about any weird shadows. No one will be in until late afternoon, so we wouldn't run the risk of being interrupted."

"You mean you don't want your employees to catch you in the break room with your best friend's little sister straddling your face?"

I honestly didn't give a fuck. And most of my employees wouldn't either. But I didn't want anyone else seeing her like that, no matter however innocent our arrangement was.

Call me possessive.

Call me obsessed.

All I really wanted to be called was *hers*.

"You think that would embarrass me?" I asked, brow lifted.

She met my stare, that rosy blush from earlier spreading across her cheeks again, but my girl had fire. "I think it'd take a lot to shake you, Reid, and I hope I'm around to see it when it happens."

You already are my fierce little kitten. You don't even know.

TEN MINUTES LATER, AFTER she'd thrown on some sweats for protection from the crisp late January air and bundled up in her bright pink floral coat, I was unlocking the back door of the shop and holding it open for her.

She'd been to my shop a few times, but since I spent a lot of my time when I wasn't working in the bar, it'd just been brief encounters at the reception desk in the front of the building. As she stepped further inside, her eyes darting around the wide-open area, I just followed while she studied my space. The building had once been a glassmaker's shop, with tall ceilings and an entire wall of windows overlooking the snowcapped mountains in the distance.

It was part of what had drawn me to the property. That and the price, since it'd sat abandoned for years after the original owners left Sage Springs.

Purchasing the building had been an enormous risk, but since I'd done a lot of the renovations with help from friends and my uncle, I'd been able to keep the costs low. My mentor in Boulder had also come on as a silent partner, providing equipment that I'd finally paid off recently.

Since the closest tattoo shop was over 30 miles away on the far side of Butterfly Ridge, it'd filled a gap in the local economy, and I had a sizeable roster of clients.

Speaking of things to fill...

When I refocused my eyes, Hazel was bent over at the waist, studying the stencil book on the coffee table in the lounge next to the reception desk. A lot of the designs we used regularly—as I found college students didn't always have discerning tastes in their body art—were in that book. I hadn't drawn all of them, but most of them were designs I'd been perfecting for years.

I had a similar book in my office with all my custom work, along with client photos, and I suddenly had the urge to drag Hazel in to show her that one as well. To sit her down on the couch in there and start a custom sketch for her. As my eyes traced her bulky outfit, I imagined the curves underneath.

Although Charley's threats of someone else tattooing Hazel's pristine skin bothered me, I still wasn't sure what she wanted... Did she want something delicate and flowy? A quote that spoke to her in a tiny script wrapping around her side? A sternum tattoo to drive me insane with temptation as my hands spent a lot of time right next to the breasts I ached to cup in my hands?

I didn't have time to contemplate it further when Hazel stood abruptly and locked those expressive brown eyes on mine.

"Should we get started? The faster we get this done, the quicker I can leave." Her tone may have sounded confident, but I could tell by the way she was clutching her coat, knuckles turning white as she held the unzipped sides, she was nervous.

That made two of us. This girl had me all twisted up inside. And not just because of the illustration help. She still hadn't responded to the text. I'd thought maybe she would when she escaped into her bedroom earlier, but I was still on read. And I didn't like it one bit.

"Typically, I like to take my time with these things, especially when I'm really invested in a project." Her eyes flashed with surprise, and she stepped back, bumping into the table behind her, but thankfully she didn't fall. I wanted to keep her on her toes with the subtle flirting, not knock her off them.

Without waiting for an answer, I turned toward the hallway leading to the back, glancing over my shoulder briefly to make sure she was following me.

"Well, must not have been invested in that girl," she muttered, and I bit my lip to hold in the chuckle that wanted to escape. She was right in a sense, I wasn't invested in anything other than fucking the girl she'd caught me with, but clearly Hazel had no idea how enjoyable it was to have frantic sex against a wall.

Something I should not have been picturing with her. I had a long way to go to make sure she was comfortable around me. And I was still withholding information from her. But I hoped that in a few weeks she'd see me as more than just who I fucked.

Because the only person I wanted like that for the foreseeable future was her.

"This is it?" she asked as I unlocked the door to the break room and let her inside.

The fluorescent lights overhead flickered on, and I stepped aside, setting my camera bag on the small table before I shed my jacket. Hazel was still standing in the doorway, yet again dissecting one of my spaces. It wasn't much, just a place for my staff to come and rest between clients. It had a fridge and coffee bar along one wall, a large wardrobe cabinet for coats on the other, a small round table in the middle of the room, and up against the window that faced the woods was a black leather futon.

"Is that where you want to…?" she trailed off, nodding at the futon.

She was so fucking adorable, so full of fire, but so uncertain of herself. I hoped the next few weeks would change that.

"Get comfortable, I'll nab the heater from my workspace and bring it in here, so you aren't cold." If she would ever release the death grip she had on her coat, I didn't want her getting chilled when she'd stripped back down to the outfit she'd come out of the bathroom wearing earlier.

"And by comfortable, you mean?" she asked as I stepped forward, her eyes widening as she backed herself against the doorframe.

"I mean, you need to get rid of this," I responded, uncurling her fingers from her coat. Then I traced the back of my fingers down her sweatshirt, enjoying the way she shifted her weight from my touch, even if it was through several layers of fabric. They lingered at her waist as she stared up at me and I fought the sudden urge to pull her into my arms and kiss the fuck out of her. Instead, I tugged on the drawstring peeking above her waistband. "Then you need to take these off."

"And what will you be taking off?" she asked, her voice low. But she immediately covered her mouth with her fingers like she hadn't intended to say it like that.

"Whatever you want me to, Haz. You're in charge here. If you want me to take something off, all you have to do is ask."

At her quick inhale of breath, I stepped around her and escaped into the hallway, needing to cool myself off for a few minutes so when I started shedding clothes, she wouldn't see the massive hard on she'd caused.

This project, and my dick, were going to be so fucking hard. But I hadn't been lying to her. She *was* in charge, and I would do whatever she asked me to do. The only thing I wished could change about this situation was that I wanted to be doing the things in her commissions *to* her, not just pretending.

Chapter Nine

Hazel

MY HEART WAS POUNDING as Reid stepped around me and into the hallway, leaving me a shaking mess. The way he looked at me lately left me wanting to melt into a puddle at his feet, but I knew I was just imagining it as desire. He didn't really want me like that.

Knowing he'd give me shit about it if I was still standing here all bundled up when he came back, I shed my coat and laid it next to his, trying to fight the urge to pull his to my face. It was bad enough I secretly tried to huff him anytime he was near me. He didn't need to catch me in the act.

Sitting down on the edge of the futon, I pulled off my shoes, tucking my socks inside.

"You're being an idiot," I muttered as I braced my feet on the cold tiles and lifted my hips. Slowly lowering my sweats, I tried to remain calm and focused. Instead, all I could focus on was the fact that he would probably smell how turned on he'd made me this morning when I was straddling his...

My phone buzzed in the pocket as I pulled the waistband over my knees. I froze, leaving my pants half pulled down as I reached for it, my fingers shaking as I unlocked the screen.

A text alert was blinking up at me from the number I'd saved in my phone as *Seven*.

Fuck, I'd completely forgotten to text him in my Reid induced haze this morning. I needed to stop thinking about Reid's dick and start thinking about number Seven's. Wait. No. I needed to stop thinking about anyone's dick and get my shit together because Seven was a real possibility to explore, and Reid was not.

> Seven: Leaving me on read all night isn't very nice, Fourteen. Are you feeling a bit naughty today?

My eyes widened as I tried not to read something dirty into the context of his message. My mind was just stuck in the gutter lately.

> Fourteen: Would you like it if I was naughty?

His response was almost immediate.

> Seven: I didn't like being ignored.

> Fourteen: Aw, did I make it hard for you?

> Seven: Yes. You've definitely made things hard.

Well, damn. So much for not being flirty.

> Fourteen: I'm sorry. How would you like me to make it up to you?

> Seven: I want you to finish telling me about this secret talent of yours. How exactly does one get into drawing naked people?

> Fourteen: By accident.

> Seven: Don't play coy. You're much too clever to do anything accidentally. I want to know more about you, so when I meet you in a few weeks, we'll have gotten all the awkwardness of getting to know each other out of the way. Talk to me.

> Fourteen: We're not supposed to actually talk to each other right now.

> Seven: Then type to me. Tell me all your dirty secrets.

> Fourteen: Not many dirty ones. Despite my flirting, I'm not that experienced with dating. Or dirty things.

Seven: But you seem like you're curious and ready to learn. Now, back to the subject at hand. How did you learn to draw these naked people?

Fourteen: Can you stop saying naked people? You're making me blush.

Seven: I wish I was there to see it.

Me too, was what I wanted to say, but I wasn't brave enough to type it. So, I did what he asked.

Fourteen: Figure drawing courses at art school. I'm an illustrator.

Seven: Wasn't aware drawing nude studies was a lucrative endeavor.

Fourteen: You just have to know the right places to look. You'd be surprised at how large the market is for what I draw. I make more illustrating than I do in my other job.

Seven: Which is?

Fourteen: Are you always going to focus the conversations on me? You're supposed to be telling me about you, too.

Seven: But you're much more interesting.

Fourteen: Not sure about that.

Seven: I am. But I'm also in an artistic trade. People pay me to mark things for them.

Fourteen: That wasn't vague at all.

His responses stopped, and I straightened up as I heard a door down the hallway close. The last thing I needed Reid to do was catch me texting Seven. He'd tease me relentlessly.

> Seven: I need to go for now. But don't ignore me that long again, I'm not sure I can stand it. Might make me beg the event coordinator for your address so I can see the answers to my questions come from your lips in person.

While I wanted that, I knew I wasn't ready yet.

> Fourteen: You have to earn seeing me again. Start making a list of answers to all these questions you've been asking me. I'm not taking no for an answer next time.

> Seven: My answer to you will never be no, to anything you ask…or want.

Footsteps echoed down the hall, and I tried to will away my blush, tucking my phone into my shoe and trying not to focus on the alluring man on the other side of the conversation.

Reid paused as he walked through the doorway, his eyes dropping to where my pants were perched around my knees. I'd been so flustered I'd forgotten to pull them off.

"Need some help?" he asked, amusement lacing his tone.

"Shut up," I hissed, watching as he plugged in the heater and walked over to me, dropping to his knees and tugging at one of the elastic bands covering my ankles. My eyes locked with his as I tried not to stare at his now bare chest and the swirling ink that covered one of his firm pecs.

"Hey, I'm just trying to help." His steady gaze made my cheeks burn hotter, and I tried not to hyperventilate as his fingers tugged the fabric free from my legs. One large palm cupped the back of my calf, his thumb dragging across the rough skin of my scar. I nibbled on my lip and fought off a shudder while his other hand pulled the last bit free. He tossed my sweats on top of my shoes and held out his hand. "Up you go, I need to lay this down if you want both of us to fit. It'd be a little tight if we set up like this."

Do not think dirty thoughts about things being a tight fit...

"Can I touch your camera?" I asked, trying to step around him.

He caught my elbow, his bare chest pressing against the side of my arm. "You can touch whatever you want."

Trying not to take his statement literally, I escaped across the room while he busied himself pulling the futon away from the wall and laying it down flat. I took his camera out of the bag, attaching the small zoom lens to the front and checking the settings while he opened the tripod a few feet away.

Once he was done, he held out his hand, quickly fastening it to the top of the mount and looking through the viewfinder.

"Come look," he said, gesturing with his head for me to come closer. He hovered next to the tripod while I looked at the image it would capture, trying to picture him laying down on the mattress.

"Can you go lay down? Face away from me."

"Bossy little thing," he chuckled, and I opened my mouth to apologize, looking over at him. "I was kidding. You're in charge here. Tell me where you want me."

He laid down, and I tried not to focus on the way his abs rippled while he got situated. It really was unfair how handsome he was.

"Hmm," I hummed, and he arched his neck to look back at me.

"You're directing this show, Haz. If you need me to move, you gotta say the words. Or just come move me into position."

I closed my eyes, my pulse pounding as I squeaked out. "Take off your pants."

"Haz," he coaxed when I still hadn't opened my eyes a few moments later. "I still have briefs on. Not naked over here. Well, unless that's what you want me to be."

Shaking my head almost violently, I tried not to let my face go entirely nuclear as he chuckled at my reaction.

"Grab the remote from the camera bag and get over here. Not going to get what you need hiding from me over there."

I knew I wouldn't get what I needed right now, especially not from Reid, or anyone else, for at least a few weeks. Hopefully.

Blowing out a breath, I turned and opened my eyes, reaching into the camera bag until my hands closed on the tiny remote shutter button. At least I didn't have to set a timer with my hands shaking like they were.

Reid was watching me as I walked toward him, one hand extended back in my direction. "Climb on up."

"Easy for you to say," I mumbled under my breath, but of course, he heard me and his deep chuckle filled the air as he grasped my hand and urged me onto the futon with him.

"You got this," he responded, settling his hands on the sides of my waist and urging me to straddle his chest. "Take what you need from me."

I expected him to be looking at me with one of his usual cocky smirks, but his eyes were hooded, focused entirely on me and softer than I'd ever seen them. He wasn't doing this to use as ammunition to ridicule me. He'd volunteered to help. And I needed to let him.

"Keep going," he whispered, his thumb dragging along my side in a way that had me wanting to sit somewhere a little lower than his face. "I won't bite. You have to ask nicely if you want that."

Shaking my head, I scooted forward, straddling his arms and hovering above his strong shoulders. The edge of his beard tickled the inside of my thighs, but I was trying not to focus on how good it felt. Or the fact that it was inches from my...

"Deep breath. You're in charge. Tell me where you want me."

But I didn't feel in charge as I looked down at his face between my legs, I felt out of control. And wildly turned on, which was so fucking wrong. He wasn't doing this for me to rub up against him like a scratching post. He'd probably throw me out of the shop if I shoved my crotch into his face like my intrusive thoughts wanted to right now.

But I needed to fake it, or I was going to have a panic attack and embarrass myself even more if I didn't calm down.

"Wrap your hands around my thighs from behind, pretend like you're pulling me against you. I need your biceps to be flexed."

I knew I'd literally just told him to do it, but I still squeaked embarrassingly when his large hands grasped my thighs and pulled, seating me directly over his mouth. His warm breath seeped through the thin material covering my wildly aroused lady parts, and I tried to keep as much weight off him as I could to keep from suffocating him while I got my act together.

Running the pose through my head, I tried to remember how she had her arms in the drawing, positioning mine in a way where I was cupping one breast, and the other was buried in my hair. The subtle click of the electronic shutter engaging from across the room was the only thing keeping me grounded as I shifted my hips. But I was gone when Reid groaned, the vibrations of the sound sending a wave of heat licking up my spine.

"I'm sorry, I'll hurry. You probably can't breathe."

A low rumbling growl escaped from his chest as I tried to pull myself up, but his fingers digging into the skin of my thighs had me rocking against him once. And then again, as his nose pressed into just the right spot. And before I knew what I was doing, I tilted my pelvis forward, gasping at how good it felt.

He wasn't even really doing anything, but clearly my inexperienced body hadn't gotten the memo as a whimper escaped me, answered by another deep groan from between my thighs. And I couldn't stop myself, undulating again, and again until tingles shot up my body, my nipple tightening against my palm as I tried to remember what I was even doing.

Swaying forward again, I gasped as my knee slipped on the slick leather beneath it, my hips suddenly dropping all my weight on Reid's face.

"Fuck." The muffled word in his deep grumbling voice had my eyes darting open as I came back to reality.

Oh shit, this was bad.

Fumbling with the button in my hand, I pressed it multiple times, hoping I got the shots I needed before I flung myself backward and scrambled off the futon, watching with horrified eyes as Reid's chest rose and fell in rapid succession.

The poor guy hadn't signed up to be suffocated or to have his best friend's little sister hump his face.

"Are you okay?"

God, I was so embarrassed. I was supposed to be pretending to sit on his face, not actually do it. And with how hard I'd landed on him...*oh my God.*

"Haz, I'm fine," he chuckled, looking up at me while he gingerly held the bridge of his nose. I averted my gaze, but not quick enough to miss his other hand reaching down to adjust his...*ahem.* "Are you sure you got what you needed?"

"Yup, mm hmm," I hummed, turning toward the camera and pretending I was checking the images on the screen.

"Did you actually get them, or are you just saying that?" Reid rose from the futon, stepping in close behind me as he adjusted the dial on the back of the camera. I couldn't even concentrate on the images as he scrolled through them, my body too focused on the way it felt to have his warm, bare chest pressing against my skin.

He kept talking in an indistinct murmur in my ear as I tried not to imagine how it'd feel to have him wrapped around me from behind, his large hand pressed against my throat as he ground his hips into mine, his large coc...

"Does this one work?" His warm breath directly against my ear made me shiver, halting my brain's detour down dirty lane.

"Yeah. It's what I was looking for."

"Because if we need to change the angle, we've still got plenty of time. I'll do whatever you need."

But that was the thing. He wouldn't. Reid couldn't give me what I needed, because what I needed right now was his head buried between my legs for real. His tongue lapping at where I was wet for him, his deep groans a product of how much I turned him on, not because of an inability to breathe because I was a klutz. I needed him in ways I couldn't even describe, but it'd never be like that for him.

"I should go. I've already taken up enough of your time. Thank you for helping me. I understand if it was too weird, and you don't want to do this again. I'll just get dressed and walk back over to the bar. Can you email me those this morning? I mean, if it's not too much trouble before you need to open..."

"Haz." His tone was almost scolding as he spun me to face him. My palm landed on his pec—dangerously close to one of his piercings—as I tried to balance myself. Realizing how close my thumb was to the tiny metal bar, I pulled my hand back like I'd been burned, but a firm palm to my hip kept me from escaping. "You don't have to run away from me. It's fine. It was just a pose for a picture. As long as you got what you needed, I'm not worried about the brain cells I lost when you tried to suffocate me."

"Oh, my God." This was mortifying.

"I'm joking. It's fine. I'm fine. If accidental death by pussy is how I go out, at least it was a nice one."

Flattening my palms against his chest, I pushed, breaking his hold on my waist. "Quit screwing with me. I'm embarrassed enough as it is."

"You'd know if I was screwing with you." He didn't let me escape though, banding his arm around my back and hauling me into his warm, bare chest. "I'm serious, kitten. Going out between those thighs would not be a bad thing. The man lucky enough to have his face between your thighs for real better not squander the opportunity."

Reid stared down at me and my finger twitched, brushing against the fine hairs covering his chest. His answering rumble vibrated against me as I grazed the very end of the barbell running through his nipple. The way he was looking at me lit something primal inside of me, and I pushed up to my tiptoes, my eyes locked in his gaze. His head dipped down, eyes flickering to my mouth as our chests heaved against each other. I was convinced he was going to kiss me, but...

"Hey, Harding, you here?" A booming voice echoed down the hallway like a gunshot, but it was enough to clear my foggy brain.

"I should go," I whispered, breaking free from his hold and rushing toward my sweats, yanking them on as he continued to stare at me.

Guilt flared through me when I thought about how close I'd come to... I couldn't even say it in my brain, the thought was too startling. There was no way in hell he was about to kiss me. That was just crazy.

"Haz," Reid's voice was low, almost imploring, as I threw my things back into my bag while avoiding the enormous elephant in the room.

"Reid?" The voice was closer, almost to the break room, and my skin crawled as I thought about the repercussions of getting caught in here with Reid only wearing a pair of boxer briefs and me half dressed.

Most of the guys in the shop were tight with Hudson, and my brother would have lost his shit if a rumor got back to him I was messing around with Reid. Nothing had happened, but we lived in a small town and the rumor mill was alive and well. Half the town would know I was in here with Reid doing...I don't even want to think about the things they'd make up that Reid and I were doing.

"Gimme a sec, Grayson," Reid shouted through the door, pulling my attention in his direction. He'd somehow managed to dress himself in athletic shorts and a loose T-shirt and was currently leaning over to tie a pair of sneakers I hadn't even realized were in here.

God, he had a nice ass.

No, bad Hazel. You need to get out of here.

"Dude, why is the door locked?" the voice asked, and my face flamed as the handle jiggled.

Reid looked in my direction, motioning toward the back of the room where the coat cabinet was. One door was open, but I could tell that if I stepped into the corner by the window, you'd never see me hiding back there.

Grabbing my coat and bag, I scanned the area quickly to make sure I hadn't left anything incriminating out. When the door handle jiggled again, I hurried into the corner, flattening myself against the wall with my heart hammering.

"Hey, man. What's up?" Reid's voice was strong, completely nonchalant, and I wished I could be that unaffected by stressful situations.

"What are you doing in here?" Grayson asked, the tattoo artist's gruff voice laced with amusement. "You start an Only Fans, or something?"

"No, you wish," Reid joked, and I stared at the window, debating on whether I could throw myself out the back and make a run for it before Gray and Reid noticed. I didn't even want to think about Reid doing something like that. But he'd probably make a killing if it he did. Still, an irrational flare of jealousy flowed through me at the thought of other women seeing him naked. I mean, I knew some had—probably more than I wanted to acknowledge—but it made my temper flare with jealousy.

Reid wasn't mine, and I couldn't tell him what to do with his life, but it didn't stop me from wanting him.

"I was testing out this new lens on my camera, making sure it'd catch the details in client photos I needed it to."

"You have a girl in here modeling for you?" Gray chuckled and my eyes widened at the idea of Gray seeing any of the pictures on that memory card.

"Nah, that's what the remote is for. I was taking pics of my chest piece."

"You ever going to let me finish it?" For a tattoo artist, Reid really didn't have a lot of them. Only a spiraling mandala piece covering part of one firm pec and a partial sleeve of interlocking geometric shapes that covered his shoulder and extended down his bicep.

"Someday. Don't have time to let it heal properly right now. I'm backed up for months at this rate."

The longer they stayed in this room, the more amped up I became at the thought of being caught. And it didn't help I had a nervous bladder that was making itself known from the adrenaline rush.

"You mind taking this to my office?" Reid asked, and I breathed a sigh of relief. "I've got some paperwork I need to go through before people get here for appointments. Then I need to go get changed."

"Yeah, just wanted to touch base about the new equipment that…" Gray's voice drifted off as they left the room, and I peeked out of my hiding spot, sighing in relief when I saw they were gone.

Rushing to the camera, I popped open the compartment that should've housed the memory card, but it was empty.

Fuck, he'd taken the pictures with him.

The sound of Reid laughing from down the hallway spurred me into action, and I pulled my bag tighter against my shoulder as I moved toward the doorway. Once I'd verified the coast was clear, I rushed to the back exit of the building, gently pushing the door open and closing it quietly so I didn't draw attention to my sneaky escape.

Scanning the parking lot for cars as I rushed across the gravel, I was thankful it was too early for any of the staff to show up to prep for tonight's shifts. I'd never been so grateful that Charley had managed to get Hudson to stop spending every waking moment at the bar.

When I got inside my apartment, flicking the lock on the door and resting against the hard wood as I tried to regulate my breathing, my phone buzzed from my pocket.

Pulling it out, my heart raced at the text message on the screen. I desperately wished it'd been another flirty text from Seven, but it was not.

> *Reid: When is our next session? That was fun.*

We clearly had very different definitions of the word fun.

Beneath the text was an image that had my pulse jumping. It was me, with my head thrown back while I was perched above Reid's face, looking positively aroused. But that wasn't the part that left me breathless, it was the way his fingers dug into the flesh of my thighs and his biceps bulged as he held me there, seemingly desperate to keep me attached to him.

It was perfect for what I needed to capture for the commission, and I should have been relieved, but it just had me thinking about things I shouldn't want.

Chapter
Ten

I SHOULDN'T HAVE BLIND carbon copied myself the pictures and saved them to my phone when I'd emailed them to Hazel before I deleted them from the memory card. But as I sat in my bed later that night, flicking through the images Hazel had captured earlier in the day, I couldn't resist staring at them.

Despite the tender bruise now forming across the bridge of my nose, this morning had been a rush. Even though nothing had happened, and I knew she was getting into character and doing what she had to do to capture the shots she needed, I'd been rock fucking hard as she ground that tempting pussy across my face.

Even though it was muffled with her thighs covering my ears, I'd heard the gasps and whimpers she made, and it'd made me desperate to rip off her tiny shorts. And I might've if Gray hadn't cock blocked me.

Well, that wasn't entirely true. There was no way Hazel would have let things get that far, but I'd almost slipped and kissed her before he interrupted our tense moment.

I'd wanted to try to get information from her about the text exchange I'd initiated while I got the heater from the storage room, but there hadn't been enough time. But judging by how pink her cheeks were when I came back into the room and found her with her pants around her knees, she'd been into it.

Which was exactly where I wanted her. If we kept doing this picture thing, I needed to behave myself, because I couldn't afford to complicate things before I'd let her see the real me hiding behind bachelor number seven. She still thought I was a fuck boy, and Gray's sarcastic comments about an Only Fans and having a girl in the break room didn't help my case.

Pulling open the text thread from earlier, I scrolled through her replies, my chest warming at how flirty she'd been. It was a side of her I was desperate to bring out. She was still jumpy around me in real life, and I wanted to make her comfortable being playful with me. To see me as someone safe in her life. Someone who wanted to keep her safe, and four little letters drifted through my brain when I thought about what other feelings I was having for her.

It was way too early to even be thinking that, much less acknowledging it.

Hesitating, I typed out a message, hoping she was home from her shift and would be available to chat with me.

> Seven: Are you ever going to show me these illustrations? As a fellow creative, I'm curious about the detail in your pieces.

Her response didn't come right away, but I eagerly devoured it when my phone buzzed a few moments later.

> Fourteen: Good evening, my mysterious suitor. How was your day?

She was so fucking cute.

> Seven: It was good. Busy, but I kind of like the longer shifts because I feel accomplished at the end of the day. Although my fingers are a little sore.

And my nose, but I wasn't telling her that because then she'd figure out the identity of her anonymous texter.

> Fourteen: So, you work with your hands? When you're marking things for others?

> Seven: I do. But you're still avoiding the question. Are you comfortable sharing your work with me? If you're not, that's okay, but I'm kind of desperate to see it. I kept thinking about it, and you, all day.

Fourteen: Actually, I just finished doing the line art on a piece I was having some trouble with. About to start the color rendering. But I'm not sure it's appropriate to send you.

Fuck, that was fast if she'd already finished the drawing. I knew she worked quickly, but she must have really been motivated. I know I'd felt almost inspired all day with how it had begun. Spending any amount of time with her lately seemed to get me amped up.

Seven: Screw appropriate. I asked. If I wasn't prepared to see it, I wouldn't have asked.

Fourteen: Why does everything seem to revolve around sex with us?

God, how I wished that were true. I'd been imagining what might have happened this morning all day when I had any kind of break.

Seven: Does that bother you? That we seem to have some intense chemistry? You can tell me if I'm making you uncomfortable.

Fourteen: I'm just worried when you meet me, you'll be disappointed at how inexperienced I really am. I may talk a big game, but I don't have the record to back it up.

Seven: Experience doesn't always make you more attractive to someone. I'm okay with taking things in the real world at your pace, but I find I have trouble holding back when we're chatting like this. I wish we didn't have to wait to meet.

Fourteen: Maybe it's better this way. Because I feel the same urges toward you. This level of attraction without even seeing you seems dangerous. I don't want to get hurt by investing too much into this and then getting burned when you realize I'm not what you're thinking.

Seven: I won't hurt you. Not intentionally, at least.

But I couldn't promise that. Because I had no idea how she would take *me* being the man she was talking to at the reveal.

> *Fourteen: Don't judge me.*

> *Seven: Never.*

The three little dots showing she was typing danced across the screen while I waited for a response, stopping briefly, but then starting back up again. She was second guessing herself, and I hated that I'd made her feel that way. She was so closed off sometimes it made me ache.

Maybe that was why I was throwing myself into getting to know her like this. I *missed* her. The way things had been before she caught me with that girl. Back when we spent late nights sketching together and talking about our futures in her parent's basement while everyone was asleep. Before she froze me out of her life, and I became a spectator when I'd once been considered a friend.

My phone buzzed, and I picked it up, my cock surging to life when the image she'd sent me loaded.

The first image I'd seen on her tablet was a sketch—a hot sketch—but it was unfinished and unrefined.

This...this was not that. While it was uncolored, crisp black lines outlined a woman who was in the throes of passion, with one hand holding a bare breast and the other digging into her flowing hair. But between her legs and extending behind this sensual woman was a man with shaggy hair like mine, with his face buried between her legs. The detail on his hair, despite the fact it was line work, was kind of insane.

My eyes eagerly traced every outline, from the subtle peek of his tongue to the way his knee was bent in the background, his hard cock protruding from between his legs. As I scanned the detail of his fingers flexing against her thighs, I couldn't help recalling how it'd felt to have Hazel hovering above my face—the overwhelming scent of her driving me insane—and the way I'd instinctually dug in my fingers when she'd tried to pull away from me.

Despite the throbbing pain when she'd slipped and put down her entire weight, I'd wanted to keep her there, nuzzling her until she couldn't take it anymore, and begged me to rip off those tiny fucking shorts.

Fourteen: That bad?

Fuck. Just the opposite. How was I supposed to resist telling her I was currently palming my cock and convincing myself it was a wildly bad idea to go bang on the door to her apartment right now so I could give her some proper source material to work from?

Seven: You're insanely talented. Thank you for sharing this with me.

Fourteen: That was a very polite response.

Shit. Even through text, I could tell she was disappointed with me.

Seven: Fine, you want the impolite response?

Fourteen: Well…

Seven: Your work is incredibly arousing. I'm sitting here palming my hard cock, trying to resist the urge to fuck my hand while I stare at your artwork. You've got a gift. Seriously, this is fucking hot…

The dots danced again, and I tried to think unsexy thoughts.

Fourteen: I may have made myself aroused by drawing this…

Seven: And what did you do?

Fourteen: I got out my vibrator and fucked it in my tiny bathtub while I thought about you.

Goddammit.

Seven: You shouldn't say things like that to me. My willpower is not that strong.

Fourteen: Should I go back to asking you more innocent questions? So we can get to know each other?

Seven: As much as I want to say no, and have you send me a detailed account of your time in the tub today, we probably should. I don't want you to think I'm only messaging you because I want to fuck you in a few weeks.

Fourteen: You don't want to fuck me in a few weeks? How disappointing…

Seven: You're a bad girl, Fourteen. What am I going to do with you?

Fourteen: Should I start a list? I might be inexperienced, but I have a very active imagination.

Seven: Fuck, yes. Save that list for me. I want to check every damn item off it.

Fourteen: What's your favorite color?

Seven: Well, that was one way to jump topics. Blue. You?

Fourteen: Aubergine.

Seven: Mine sounds awfully plain next to yours. You like eggplants?

Fourteen: Now you have me giggling. Trying to keep my mind out of the gutter.

Seven: I was asking about the vegetable, naughty girl. Aubergine is the English name for an eggplant.

Fourteen: Yes, I'm aware. And no. Ew. Even breaded and fried, I'd rather have a piece of meat. Put all the meat in my mouth instead.

Seven: Now I'm the one trying to keep my mind out of the gutter.

Fourteen: Do you want to put your meat in my mouth, Seven?

Seven: Desperately. Would you like a pink, meaty hunk?

Fourteen: Of what?

Seven: Steak. Do you like steak? Or are you more of a chicken girl?

Fourteen: Give me your pink meat, you hunk. Lol. I like my meat medium rare. Are you going to cook for me?

Seven: If that's what you'd like. How does a quiet night in with steaks and wine sound?

Fourteen: Sounds like a…date?

Seven: Definitely a date. I wish we didn't have to wait. I'd bring you home with me tomorrow if I could.

Fourteen: Maybe we could both make the same meal and eat together? Have any favorite recipes?

Seven: I like your style. We can still date without seeing each other. I'll text you a recipe in the morning. Maybe we'll run into each other at the grocery store. I go to the one on Fort Street. Would that be cheating?

Fourteen: I'll just steal the ingredients from my brother. I live above his bar.

Shit, she'd expect a response to that.

Seven: *Dangerous for you to tell me that. Now I'm going to be hunting down every bar in town trying to figure out which ones have apartments above them.*

Fourteen: *Not that many bars in town.*

Seven: *It's not time yet, Fourteen. Despite how much I want to see you, it's better if we wait. I'm sorry if I started this with talking about running into each other at the store. I was just teasing.*

Fourteen: *I don't want to cut you off, but I'm yawning. I'd rather say good night to you than accidentally fall asleep and leave you hanging.*

Seven: *Sweet dreams, Fourteen. Mine will be filled with you.*

Fourteen: *Night.*

My heart soared, and I felt like a fucking sap, but I couldn't help it. I was down bad for this girl, and she didn't even realize her effect on me. But a vibration showing another text came through, and my heart flipped as I read it.

Hazel: *If you're serious about helping me, I'm going to need your motorcycle. And you to be wearing leather pants. Do you own any?*

Reid: *Yes, to the pants. And in what context do you need my bike in?*

Hazel: *Is there somewhere indoors we can set up with it? It's supposed to be freezing for the next week, and I can't wear what I need to for the shot outdoors.*

Reid: *Color me intrigued. And yes, I can use Jayden's warehouse at the distillery. What time?*

Hazel: He won't be there, will he?

Reid: He skis with Colette most mornings. He's usually gone until noon. But I can make sure.

My cousin was best friends with her cousin, who was a ski instructor at a resort in the next town over. Those two had been joined at the hip since middle school. But their relationship was completely platonic, because he'd been fucking Annie, the bartender at Hudson's, on and off since high school. We really did live in a small town where everyone was connected to each other.

Hazel: Is eight too early?

Reid: Not for you. Are you sure that's enough time for you to get a decent night's sleep? You looked tired this morning.

Hazel: Thanks for reminding me how unattractive I was when I answered the door.

Reid: That's not what I meant, and you were adorable.

Hazel: Just what every woman wants to hear.

Reid: Eight is good. You riding with me?

Hazel: Can I? I don't have a helmet or anything.

Reid: I've got an extra one from when I first started riding. Should fit you. You gonna be my backpack in the morning?

Hazel: I don't know what that means.

Reid: A backpack is a passenger on a motorcycle.

Hazel: Gotcha. Then yes, I'll be your backpack.

I liked how that statement looked entirely too much.

Reid: Dress warm and wear boots.

Hazel: Can't wait. Thank you again.

Reid: My pleasure, trust me.

She didn't respond, but that didn't matter. I needed to get some fucking sleep so I could survive whatever setup she needed my bike for. I had a feeling that it was going to be one I dreamed about for a long fucking time.

Chapter
Eleven

R EID WAS RIGHT, I was exhausted last night, but with one more Seven—and Reid if I was being completely honest with myself—round with my vibrator and I'd been out for a solid six hours before my alarm woke me at seven.

Rifling through the top drawer of my dresser, I shifted the pieces of lace and satin to the side as I tried to find the bright pink lace bustier I'd stashed in here last year. I'd never worn it, but I couldn't resist it on the lingerie website when I'd found it on sale.

I wasn't sure how comfortable it'd be to wear pressed against Reid on the back of his motorcycle, but I knew I needed it after listening to the chapter of the audiobook my latest commission was based on. The heroine had been stretched out across the handlebars of the hero's motorcycle in only a thong and a lace bustier while he sat shirtless in his helmet and leather pants with her perched on his lap, his thumb strumming her into an explosive orgasm before he bent her over the side of the bike and fucked her.

My author had wanted that moment captured, the one right before the frantic fucking when the hero was worshipping her lace clad body. And while I'd been listening, I imagined the same scene, but with me in the heroine's place and Reid running his hands over every inch of my body while he whispered dirty praises and coaxed an orgasm out of me.

Quickly donning it and the matching thong, I ran to my closet next to pull out jeans and a loose sweater. My black leather combat boots were next, and once I had them on, I paused in front of the mirror, studying my chaotic hair, deciding a sleek ponytail at the base of my neck was the safest way to wear it.

By the time I had my backpack ready to go, a knock sounding from my front door caught my attention, and I yanked it open, expecting my handsome model, but it was my best friend instead.

"Hey." She smiled, stepping around me and plopping herself down on my couch as I followed her back into the apartment. "You look cute this morning. Got plans you didn't tell me about?"

"Um...not that I'm not happy to see you, but why are you here so early? I didn't think you and Hudson came up for air before noon most days."

"It's Sunday," she said, like the answer should have been obvious. "Hudson is downstairs unloading the produce shipment with Reid and then he needs to do inventory and place next week's order."

I'd completely forgotten that was his usual weekly routine. At least Reid regularly helped him, and he wouldn't be questioning why his best friend was in the bar this early.

"Why do you look guilty? And weren't you on until midnight last night? Shouldn't you be sleeping?" Normally, I would be. This girl loved her sleep, but I also needed to keep the momentum going on my commissions queue, so I didn't fall behind. With Reid helping, I wouldn't have to spend hours combing the internet for reference photos for the poses. We could create them in real time, and I could keep taking on new clients that I'd turned down before and keep up with my online coursework at the same time.

"I'm going somewhere this morning. Why didn't you tell me you were coming over?"

She smirked, slowly assessing my outfit. "Where are you going dressed like that at eight on a Sunday? There isn't really anything open for another few hours."

"Donuts?" I asked, like an idiot, because the bakery was the only place I knew was open this early on a Sunday.

"Okay...and why was it so important for you to get donuts today?"

"Does anyone really need an excuse to need donuts any day? I mean, donuts and potatoes need to be their own food groups in my opinion. But I digress."

"Haz, are you okay? You've been a little jumpy lately. You're not getting burned out, are you? I can talk to Hudson about cutting your hours if you need me to. He won't get mad if he knows you need the time for your classes."

"No! No..." I tried to lower my voice. "It's fine. I've got plenty of time to keep working at the bar while I do my commissions and course work during the day. I promise I'm not getting burned out."

She nodded, looking around the apartment, probably noticing that since she was gone, it wasn't quite as neat as it'd once been. Despite her bad girl persona, once she'd started dating Hudson, his neat freak ways had rubbed off on her. "So, how have other *things* been going?"

"Things?" I asked, but we both knew what she was asking about. She wanted to talk about if either of the guys I'd left numbers for had texted me.

"Don't play coy, Haz. Have either of them messaged you?"

"And the *them* you are referring to are?"

She narrowed her eyes, and I tried not to fidget. While I told her nearly everything, I wasn't sure I wanted to share anything about Seven with her yet. "I'll give you points for evasion, but you know I'm gonna keep asking until you give me more details."

"Ten has not."

"But...?" she asked, knowing he wasn't the only person I left my number for.

"Seven has."

"God, this is like pulling teeth," she laughed, but I was still trying to figure out what to tell her without making him sound bad. She hadn't designed the experiment for the singles to start immediately sexting each other, but it wasn't like I'd even done that with Seven. Things with him were...complicated. They were beyond just innocent flirting, but not quite to R-rated territory. Not that I was opposed to it heading in that direction.

"He's...nice?" God, now I was making him sound lame.

"Sounds like a dud," a deep voice coming from the stairwell startled me, and I turned toward my open front door, trying not to gasp as I got an eyeful of Reid wearing the fuck out of a pair of black leather pants.

"Yeah, Haz. He sounds kind of lame," Charley replied, giving Reid a pointed look over my shoulder. I could tell she was irritated he'd crashed her mission to get intel on my interactions with bachelors' number seven and ten. "Maybe you need to cut Seven loose and focus on Ten. I can get his number so you can text him if you want. I know it breaks the rules, but we both know I'm not that great at following them, anyway."

"Hey," Reid cut in, stepping in behind me and resting his hand on the middle of my back. Even through the lace and my sweater, along with the leather glove covering his palm, it still sent tingles racing up my spine. Tingles I should not be focusing on. "Maybe Seven is still warming up. I wouldn't count him out yet, and if Ten hasn't messaged her, that's his loss and she should chalk it up to him not being interested enough. If he wasn't eager to send her a message right away, he's not the right guy for her."

"Maybe Seven is coming on too strong and Ten is just easing his way into things."

Charley and Reid were staring at each other like I wasn't in the room, or the person who these mystery men were supposed to be texting.

"Hey," I interrupted as they opened their mouths to start another verbal volley. "Seven is holding his own. And I'm not cutting him out of anywhere."

"See, told you." Reid shot a satisfied grin at Charley, and she bit her lip as she raised an eyebrow back in response.

"And Ten hasn't shown any interest at all, so I'll pass on getting his number. If he couldn't be bothered to send a text, then I don't want to talk to him until he does."

"But..." Charley argued, but Reid cut her off.

"I'm sure Haz is more than capable of running her own dating life. Maybe her best friend should butt out of it, especially when she is suggesting trying to undermine the setup of her own event."

"Oh, I'm the one undermining the integrity of the event, huh?" she asked Reid, her eyes briefly cutting to mine. I frowned as I tried to gauge what she meant by that. "What about—"

"*Anyway*," Reid said loudly, cutting her off. "I'm borrowing Haz to come help me work on the logo concept and design for Jay's new restaurant plans this morning, so maybe you should go drag your boyfriend out of his office before he spends all day in there. I think he's wrapping up the supply order right now."

"Donuts, huh?" Charley asked, calling me out, but Reid was quicker.

"Yeah, I know the way to this girl's heart. Gotta feed her donuts, so she'll agree to help me."

"You sure you want him to put you to work on your day off? I thought Jay was already working with the architect on all the designs for the expansion. He was talking to Annie about it earlier this week," Charley commented, clearly fishing to see if Reid's cover story was true.

"That's just the architectural work. He's still figuring out things on the marketing end himself, right, Reid?"

"Right," he confirmed, shooting me a wink when Charley turned to grab the sweatshirt she'd thrown on the coffee table when she'd barged in earlier.

"Well, I guess I'll let you two work on those *marketing plans* this morning." She squinted as she looked at Reid, tilting her head to the side. "Do you have a black eye?"

"Um." He cleared his throat, his eyes briefly darting toward me. "No. It's just a bruise on my nose. I was working in the breakroom yesterday and something fell on my face."

"What fell on your face?"

I definitely shouldn't say, *"I did."*

"Oh, uh. A case of sterile gauze pads. Box turned, and the corner caught me right on the nose as it came down. It'd been rocking above me precariously, and I thought I could balance it before it fell. Guess I was wrong."

"Ouch. Looks like it caught you pretty good. Did it hurt?"

My cheeks heated as I tried to keep myself from recalling the brief moments before my knee had slipped when I was perched above Reid yesterday. As the blush spread, I looked away, knowing that Charley would be suspicious if talking about how Reid bruised his face was making me turn into a tomato.

"Nah, it's fine. Made it hard to breathe for a second, but I'll get over it. I like a little pain sometimes."

"Freak," Charley responded with a giggle, shaking her head.

"Yup, that's me. I kinda like the rush I get when things land on my face. You should see how excited I get when someone tries to smother me."

His shoulder nudged mine, and I fought the urge to break out into a nervous giggle. Or focus on Reid commenting that he liked a little pain. That'd only make the blush worse.

"On that note, I think I'm gonna go." Charley pushed Reid out of the way when she got to the doorway, pulling me into a hug. "You know I love you, right?"

I nodded, and she squeezed a little tighter. "Go with your heart, whoever you choose. But make him work for it. He doesn't deserve you either way, but he needs to earn your attention."

"Couldn't agree more," Reid commented once Charley let me go and headed down the stairs. "He's never going to deserve you, but make sure he shows you how much he wants you. Don't take it easy on him."

Smiling as I looked over at him, I realized maybe Reid wasn't as emotionally stunted as I'd once thought he was. "Definitely don't intend to make anything easy for him."

"The hard way. I like it." He grinned, and I tried to push away how seeing him smile like that made me feel. I needed to keep reminding myself Reid wasn't an option. But Seven was.

Chapter Twelve

I'D ALMOST FORGOTTEN HOW I was going to get to Jay's warehouse until Reid was leading me across the parking lot to his sleek black bike and motioning for me to wait as he ducked back into his shop. He came out after a few moments, his helmet on with the face visor open and another one tucked underneath his arm.

"You gonna tell me about the scene we're recreating when we get there?" he asked, smoothing my ponytail over my shoulder and tucking it into the back of my coat before he lowered the helmet onto my head. He flipped the face screen open on mine, his grin widening when he saw I was blushing again. "Now you've definitely got me intrigued if you're blushing that hard. These blushes kill me, Haz."

"I can't control it. It just happens. It's so annoying."

"Nah." He reached down to zip my coat, pulling it up until his knuckles brushed my exposed neck. "I kinda love the way you look when you're blushing."

"And now you've made it worse."

"You ready to go?" he asked, mercifully changing the subject.

"Yeah, I'm ready."

"I'm gonna help you up first, just hold on to the back of the seat and then once I'm settled, you can wrap your arms around me." He didn't even wait, turning me sideways and effortlessly lifting me up while I awkwardly tried to throw my leg over the bike to straddle it. God, I was such a fucking mess. He slipped in front of me in one clearly practiced motion, and I tried to breathe as he reached back toward me with one of his gloved hands.

"Don't be shy. Wrap yourself around me and hold on tight with your head against my back. When I lean, just move with me and you'll be fine. Rest your boots on the pegs, so it's easier to keep your balance."

He waited for me to get into position, reaching back to squeeze my thigh as he flicked his face screen closed. I did the same to mine and rested my covered cheek against his shoulder blades, trying not to let the vibrations between my legs once the bike purred to life make me do anything embarrassing. I'd already humped the poor guy once; he didn't need me to do it again.

I was sure he could feel my heart beating wildly as he pushed up the kickstand and walked the bike backward. He definitely heard me squeal when he rotated the throttle and the engine revved, the vibration of his laugh carrying through the material of both our coats.

Trying not to freak out, I closed my eyes and held on tight when he pulled out onto the main road that led toward Butterfly Ridge. It wasn't a far ride, but it felt like an eternity with my stomach in my throat as he sped up, leaning into turns and winding down the side of the mountain before he dipped toward the valley where our neighboring town was nestled.

Jayden's whiskey distillery was perched on the edge of town, hovering next to a ridge that overlooked the sprawling valley, the ski resort on a neighboring ridge a few miles away. I'd spent a lot of time there as a kid, learning how to ski with my cousins. I'd never been as good at it as Colette, who was now an instructor, but I wasn't as terrible as I thought I'd be at it.

When the bike slowed, I took a deep breath, hoping I hadn't been a terrible first-time passenger for Reid. I'd done what he asked and held him tightly around the curves, but hopefully I hadn't made it hard for him to breathe, wrapping around him like a koala.

He slowed, stopping near the loading dock at the back of the building and engaging the kickstand. The bike tilted as he climbed off and he held his hand out for me. I guess I'd never taken the time to appreciate it before, but Reid in full riding gear with his helmet on, was kinda fucking hot.

And there was something seriously wrong with me that that was the first thing I thought of as I stumbled off the side of the bike and into his arms. I could feel his laughter more than I could hear it, his hands bracing my arms until I gained my balance.

Once I was steady, he pulled off his helmet, laying it gently on the ground at his feet before he pulled off mine.

"Vibrations throw off your balance?" he asked with a chuckle as he reached back, pulling my ponytail from beneath my coat and giving it a playful tug before letting go.

"Something like that," I replied, still a little breathless from how much I'd liked it. Both the vibrations between my legs while we rode, and him pulling my ponytail. I wasn't sure which one was causing the blush to creep up my neck again, but Reid caught it, grinning as he brushed a gloved knuckle over my pink cheek.

"Let me go open the doors and I'll be back for you and the bike."

Nodding, I tried to muster the courage I needed to tell Reid about the setting for this scene. Although... Maybe it'd be easier to let him listen to the audiobook and hear it firsthand, instead of me bumbling through an explanation.

He came back a few moments later, leading me into the dark warehouse space, the door clanging shut behind me as I followed him, holding onto both our helmets. My brain was hazy as I stopped when he did, watching him get the bike situated by the back windows that overlooked the snowy woods behind the building.

It was almost romantic, the dark, quiet building, and the man dressed in way too much leather not to be hazardous to my libido. Watching him, I could envision how the heroine in the book was taken by her mysterious rider, seduced by his words and the way he touched her body. How the cool metal against her naked back would have made her desperate for him...

"You okay, Haz?" Reid asked, coming up beside me and reaching down to unzip my coat. I'd completely forgotten I still had it on.

While I'd been off in imagination station, Reid had already gotten the tripod and camera set up. He pressed the remote into my hand once he'd pulled my sleeve loose, tossing my coat on top of his next to our helmets.

"Oh, uh. Yeah. Good. I'm good. Why? Do I not look okay?"

He shook his head, an amused chuckle escaping his lips as he grabbed my free hand and tugged me toward the bike. "Spill. What are we doing here?"

Ah, the moment of truth. Reaching into my pocket, I pulled out my phone and the case with my earbuds, extending the headphones toward him while I tried to get the audiobook queued up to where the scene started. I'd already listened to it an obnoxious number of times, so I didn't need to, but clearly Reid thought otherwise when he put one earbud in his ear and smoothed the flyaway hairs that'd escaped my ponytail before pressing the other one into mine.

"You ready?" I asked, my voice cracking which made my cheeks flare hotter.

"Go for it."

As the deep male narrator's voice started setting the scene, I was almost transfixed by the look in Reid's eyes as he listened. He only broke my gaze momentarily when the narrator detailed the hero pulling his shirt over his head.

It was like Reid was being led by the audio, stalking toward me and removing my hair tie, running his fingers through my hair moments after it was happening in our ears. When it got to where he slowly unbuttoned the heroine's jeans, peeling them down her legs before he pulled them and her boots free, Reid followed suit, smoothing his palms up the backs of my legs as he stood back up, pausing briefly to rub his thumb against the scar on my calf.

But I didn't have time to focus on how it felt to have his hand there, Reid only hesitating for a moment when the narrator described taking off her shirt in the audio before he pulled mine over my head in one smooth motion.

We both listened, staring at each other as the narrator cursed when he took in what the heroine was wearing, Reid following suit with a rumbling, "Fuck, look at you."

The heroine looked away, embarrassed, and I did the same, Reid's thumb on my chin stopping me from breaking his gaze entirely.

When the hero picked her up with his hands clasped on the backs of her thighs and carried her to the bike to rest her on the seat, Reid did the same a few moments later. He tipped me backward toward the handlebars, urging me to straddle the bike. The leather seat was still warm underneath me as his rough palm traced down the center of my chest. When the hero's hand slipped beneath the lace of the heroine's tiny thong, Reid didn't follow suit with that one, but he effortlessly lifted my hips before he straddled the bike and settled me onto his lap, my legs draped on either side of him.

Closing my eyes tightly, I tried not to hyperventilate as Reid's fingers traced my body, lingering on the edge of the lace covering my breasts, and tracing the boning down the front of the bustier to tickle the sensitive skin near my belly button. I shifted, sighing as the lace of my thong pressed tighter against where it was barely covering me, the firm leather of Reid's pants providing just enough friction until I was almost as aroused as the moaning heroine in my ear.

Reid's fingers dipped just beneath the edge of the lace, pulling back and snapping the elastic to get my attention. My eyes flickered open to meet his, the pupils almost blown as he stared down at me. I wondered if he was as aroused as I was simply by listening and *almost* reenacting the words playing in our ears.

But then I noticed his lingering look at the remote clenched tightly in my hand, and it was a rude awakening that yet again I'd gotten distracted by the moment and wasn't taking pictures like I was supposed to. Using my thumb to depress the button, I watched Reid as he continued following the motions of the man in my ear, touching me where he touched her, pressing his hips into me when the hero pressed his into hers.

"*Good girl*," he whispered, moments before the hero echoed the same words, but there was no way he could have known that he was going to say them.

This suddenly felt way more complicated than it'd felt even yesterday, because it didn't feel like Reid was faking the way he touched me, especially when his thumb settled over the damp panel of my panties, pressing in and making me gasp, my back arching at the same time the heroine's did in the story.

Rocking my hips into his subtle movements, I tried to keep myself from spiraling, but I couldn't help it, my pulse racing as I barreled toward a very familiar yet also unfamiliar sensation. Not that I hadn't come before, I wasn't *that* inexperienced. It was that I'd never come *with* someone.

Fumbling high school boys and my only boyfriend in college had never actually gotten me there, and I'd been too embarrassed to tell them they hadn't quite completed the task with their mediocre attempts at third base. That was probably why I'd never let things progress further. What was the point of them stealing home if they were only going to be scoring a run for the home team? Okay, maybe my baseball metaphors needed a bit of work. But who could blame a girl when an extremely hot, leather pants wearing, tattooed God was between her thighs going where no man had gone before.

Reid was getting me there embarrassingly quickly, with only a few strategically placed motions of the pad of his thumb on top of my panties. I wasn't sure if he knew what his thumb placement was doing; he was just listening to the directions in his ears. But when I gasped, my back arching and my hair flowing out behind me over the handlebars like a waterfall of fire, there was no way he didn't realize that he'd just given me a very real—very unexpected—happy ending.

When I came back to earth, my eyes widened as the narrator was about to bend the heroine over the side of his bike, the sound of him unbuckling his belt pushing me into action. Ripping the earbud out of my ear, I threw myself forward and grabbed the one out of Reid's, clasping them both tightly in my hand.

"Hey," his deep voice whispered, a certain amount of mirth in his tone. "That was just getting to the good part. Maybe I wanted to finish."

My eyes widened even further at the thought of him *finishing*.

"Not like that. I wanted to finish listening, dirty girl," he teased, his laughter jostling me against his chest.

"Not gonna happen," I giggled nervously, enjoying it entirely too much as his long fingers danced up my spine and dug into my loose hair. They massaged my scalp, and I fought the urge to rub up against his chest like a cat. It was bad enough I'd just rubbed my *kitty* all over the pad of his thumb until I came. "I think we're done here."

"Do we have to be?" he asked, tracing his nose along the side of my cheek and resting his lips on the sensitive skin behind my ear. He wasn't quite kissing me, but this didn't feel like how friends should touch each other. And that's all we were.

Friends. We were friends. Friends don't hump other friends, right? Well, except friends with benefits, but judging by the last two encounters we'd had, Reid wasn't getting any benefits.

Not that I hadn't imagined giving them to him.

"*Reid*," I whispered breathily, my fingers creeping up his chest and brushing over one of the piercings I'd discovered were sensitive yesterday.

He growled, his fingertips digging into my skin. "Don't say my name like that, kitten. It makes me want to do bad things to you. And you're not mine."

"I'm not anyone's," I replied softly, enjoying the way he shuddered as I played with the ball on the end of the barbell beneath my thumb.

"Not yet." It was so quiet I wasn't sure if he meant for me to hear it, but it had me disentangling myself and sliding off the side of the bike anyway. He'd been right. There was someone else. And it wasn't fair of me to be behaving like I had been. But I didn't want to stop. With either of them.

Reid was quiet behind me as I got dressed, and when I turned around, I figured out why, because he was nowhere to be seen.

The scene of the crime was still there though, the tripod with the camera still aimed at his bike, the sunlight streaming in the window backlighting the tableau. I pressed the button still clasped in my hand, the camera beeping instead of making the quiet click it normally did.

Growling under my breath, I stalked to the camera, flicking open the compartment for the memory card, but I already knew it wouldn't be there. Reid had stolen it before he escaped, sort of like he was stealing my will to resist him with every moment we spent together.

Part of me wished I'd never decided to stop avoiding him, but the other part was reminded why I hadn't when he walked toward me a few moments later.

We were both quiet as we picked up the equipment, packing things away and putting on our coats. Reid brushed my fingers away as I tried to line up the parts of my zipper, pulling it up for me and running his thumb along the side of my cheek before he turned and walked back to his bike.

I held the back door open for him as he wheeled it outside into the parking lot. Quietly taking his hand after he'd gotten his equipment strapped to the back of the bike, I climbed on behind him before we each put on our own helmets.

Wordlessly, I wrapped my arms around him, and he took off, his bike navigating the trip back over the ridge much quicker than I would have liked.

Reid was silent as I climbed off the back, pulling off his extra helmet and handing it to him before I made a beeline for the back door of the bar without a backward glance.

The engine revved behind me, and I turned in time to see him gun it out of the parking lot and toward the mountains, clearly eager to get away from whatever had happened between us earlier.

I knew we were skating very close to the line of taking things too far, but I also didn't really care.

Which wasn't like me. I over thought everything. I should have been freaking out, but I didn't want to. I wanted to do something fun for once. And it'd been a hell of a lot of fun to strip down and have Reid lay me out over his bike as a very naughty audiobook played simultaneously in our ears.

Trying not to obsess about it, I escaped into my studio, sketching out the rough outline of the scene we'd made earlier. I'd have to fine tune it once he sent me the pictures. *If* he sent me the pictures this time. Maybe he was regretting volunteering to help me with this project after all.

But as I laid down my digital pencil and opened my email app, the pictures were waiting for me. There wasn't any witty commentary in the subject line or body of the email, but knowing Reid, I unlocked the screen of my phone and opened our text thread.

> *Reid: Stop overthinking things. Just needed to clear my head earlier, so I didn't follow you back into the bar and do something we'd both regret. Let me know when you need my services again.*

I didn't hesitate to type out a reply.

> *Hazel: If you regret helping me, then maybe we should just stop while we're ahead.*

> *Reid: I don't regret helping you. Not for a moment, kitten. I would regret taking things farther than you're ready for, even if you think you are.*

> *Hazel: Things that are freely given shouldn't cause regrets.*

> *Reid: But sometimes they do. And I never want you to regret being my friend again.*

My heart sunk at his choice of words. Being Reid's friend wasn't all I wanted to be, but sometimes you needed to focus on the things that were possible, not things that would never happen.

Opening my text messages, I composed one to a man who *was* a possibility for me.

> Fourteen: Anything fun happen today while you were marking things for people?

> Seven: Not anything as fun as thinking about you all day. I missed you today.

> Fourteen: So much same. How many days left?

> Seven: Twelve, not that anyone is counting.

But I was. And despite the disappointment at how the afternoon turned out, I was going to focus on getting through twelve more days until I could meet the man who wasn't conflicted about wanting me.

Chapter
Thirteen

Reid

HAZEL WAS ICING ME out. I hadn't heard from her in two days. I knew she was probably working, but it hurt that she was ignoring *me*, yet still actively seeking out Seven. Which was the truly fucked-up part. I was jealous of myself. He'd talked to her in the last two days. *I* hadn't.

I wasn't even sure what had happened the other day. She'd been so nervous but playful once we left the bar, and then something had come over me when that audiobook had started playing out a dirty fantasy in my ear. My hands just automatically followed the movements of my counterpart, and I couldn't have stopped if I tried. It was like my body was on autopilot, and any worry about crossing boundaries went out the window when I stripped her down to that fucking pink lingerie.

But I came to when she was driving me crazy by thumbing my nipple piercing, all glowy and looking freshly fucked after she'd come against my thumb with very little input from me. Don't get me wrong, I knew how to please women, that was why my reputation was what it was. But it usually involved a little more work than a strategically placed thumb for her to wiggle against.

After, when she'd told me she didn't belong to anyone, it'd been like a punch to the gut. This entire situation wasn't fair to her. And the deeper I got into playing Seven and fighting my genuine attraction to her as myself, the more I knew that it'd crush her once there wasn't a screen between us any longer.

But I was finding it hard to stop when another text from her finally came on my real phone number.

Hazel: You done hiding from me yet? I need help.

Reid: Wasn't hiding. Just swamped with clients this week.

Hazel: You haven't been over here after hours in two days. Your regulars were asking where you were.

Fuck. The last thing I needed was her dealing with other women asking about me at the bar. She'd probably had to deal with it more than just the past few days when I thought about it. And it made me feel like a total dick for how I'd behaved until now.

Reid: Just tell me where you want me and I'm yours.

Hazel: Is your place tomorrow morning okay?

Reid: I'll leave the back door unlocked, let yourself in when you get here.

Shutting off my phone, I tossed it on my nightstand, deciding to take a night off from pretending and trying to get some sleep before I had to face her in the morning.

This was getting way more complicated than I ever expected it to be.

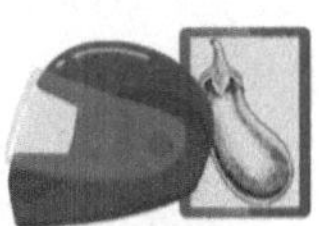

H AZEL HAD BEEN DIFFERENT ever since she let herself into the shop. Not that she was distant, per se. She was just detached. Friendly, but not overly so. And I had no fucking clue how to behave around her. So, of course, I'd been a jackass.

"Why are you here if you don't have a new pose to work on?" I asked, glancing at her out of the corner of my eye.

"Because you said you'd help me with shading if I needed it."

Taking a deep breath, I tried to turn my inner asshole down a notch and pulled the tablet out of her hand. The image on the screen was wildly different from the last piece I'd looked at on it, but no less impressive.

A detailed grayscale illustration of the inside of the distillery was practically jumping off the screen, my bike at the center of the piece, but the sprawling mountain landscape out the window was what she'd asked for my help on.

I hadn't even realized one of us had taken this picture. It had to have been an accidental press of the shutter button when she was getting dressed. Right before I'd taken the memory card out of the camera because I was a sick bastard and wanted control of the pictures we'd been taking. I knew if Hazel took the memory card, she'd erase it before she gave it back, and I didn't want to risk her erasing our time together. Not when my days with her like this were probably numbered.

After I'd pocketed the card, I'd escaped to the bathroom to take care of things that had arisen during our encounter on the bike. I knew I'd never be able to ride with how turned on I was, so I'd shamefully beat off in the bathroom stall at my cousin's distillery while I bit my fist to keep from groaning loud enough that she'd hear me on the other side of the wall.

To be honest, once I'd finally come back to my place, I'd saved the photos from the memory card into a folder on my remote drive and emailed her the link without looking at them. I'd never stay away from her if I saw how she looked in those pictures.

It was bad enough I carried the memories of how it'd felt to touch her like that. And don't even get me started on the sexy as fuck lingerie she'd almost been wearing. The entire time, I kept thinking about how easy it'd be to snap the thin satin material holding the thong together and pull down my pants far enough to be inside of her. But I couldn't let myself lose control. Not yet. And especially not like that with her.

So, for now, I'd focus on helping. "To get the texture on the mountains, you need to focus on layering the shading, not trying to get it in one pass. The dimension comes from varying the length and angle of the strokes. It takes a while, but it really makes the image jump out at you."

It was true when working on shading with a needle, too. Mountains were tricky to render realistically, but I'd drawn enough of them on people's skin over the years I'd perfected the technique. Seemed kind of cliché to get a mountain tattooed on your body when you were surrounded by them, but tourists loved to capture the beauty of Colorado while they were here.

Hazel took the pen back, mimicking my movements, the peaks of the snow-capped mountains slowly coming to life as she worked.

"Perfect," I murmured, keeping watch over her shoulder. It was mesmerizing observing her draw. I'd never noticed how expressive her face was when she was concentrating. Every moment I spent with her, she became harder and harder to resist. And I was almost afraid that once my restraint had hit its limit, I'd do something to fuck this up entirely.

I'd never *wanted* a woman to reciprocate my feelings until now. It'd always seemed inconvenient to involve feelings when I hadn't been looking for more than temporary companionship, but the embers of the flame that was growing for Hazel inside my heart weren't showing any signs of going out. And if she decided I wasn't worth returning those feelings, I was afraid they'd consume me.

"What's the weirdest thing you've ever tattooed?" she asked, never looking up from the tablet.

Maybe she wasn't only here to work on her homework. "Hmm. Probably teeth marks."

"How do you even draw that?" Her nose scrunched while she continued working, and I wondered if maybe I shouldn't go into the details of that particular tattoo. But I knew her curiosity was piqued, and she'd keep asking if I didn't tell her.

"You don't. Skin impression is the best method to get accurate shading."

"Like they had to be bitten? Did they bring their significant other or something? Is that even sanitary?"

Fuck, I should have never opened my big mouth and told her that. I should have said something lame, like someone's weird exotic pet. I'd done a few of those.

"Clear film and being careful not to break the skin works really well, actually." And a lot of hope that you didn't accidentally bite the wrong spot.

"You never answered my question. Who bit this person?" she repeated, glancing back at me. Her eyes were almost penetrating, one delicate eyebrow arched as she waited for my answer. But we both knew she'd already figured it out.

"I bit her."

Her eyes narrowed, and something that looked an awful lot like jealousy hardened her gaze. "Seriously? Isn't that like crossing some ethical boundaries or something?"

Shrugging and pretending I was unaffected by her stare down, I answered honestly. "It was mutually consensual."

"Ew. Why would you..."

I lifted an eyebrow. She was a smart girl; she knew exactly why I'd done it.

"You fucked her? Like during...?"

A blush crept from the side of her neck up her cheeks as she stared at my lips and the teeth peeking out beneath them, and my mouth watered at the thought of biting her. I knew she didn't have much experience, but I wondered if *she* would like to be bitten.

The thought of marking her soft, fair skin had me shifting under her appraisal. "That came after, but yeah. She might have gotten a little turned on by the entire process."

Haz's nose wrinkled, clearly not liking the thought of me with another woman. "You're disgusting. I can't believe you did that."

But the way she kept staring at my mouth didn't look like disgust. Maybe she was thinking about me biting her, too. "Sounds like someone is jealous."

"Gross. It wasn't on this couch, was it?" she asked, moving to stand.

"No," I chuckled, pressing a hand against her thigh to keep her seated beside me.

"At least you had the decency to take her home with you, I guess," she muttered, returning her attention to the tablet in her lap. The once delicately placed marks had become angry, dark streaks, and I placed my hand on the back of hers to keep her from ruining the piece.

"First of all, I never take them to my place. Second, I said we didn't fuck on this couch, not that we left the building."

"Ew, ew, ew. Not on the couch in your office? I've sat on that."

"Not exactly," I laughed, knowing that I should shut this down before too much damage was done, but something about seeing Hazel jealous was a little addictive.

"But it was in your office?"

I nodded in confirmation.

"On your desk?" she asked, glancing down the hallway.

"Not with her," I replied. But there had only been a few I'd taken in there. Considering my track record, there could have been a lot more. Most ended up pressed against the wall in the hallway after everyone had gone home for the night. Although, I should probably think about replacing the couch in my office.

"You're a pig."

I used to be, was what I wanted to tell her, but of course I goaded her instead. "It was all consensual. It's not like I came onto any of these women."

"Just into them."

"Not that either," I laughed. Accidentally putting my random partners or myself into a precarious situation had me pulling out half the time and coming into the condom outside of them. While I was kind of indifferent about having kids, there was no way I wanted to raise one outside of a committed relationship. Not that I'd ever had one of those.

"I don't even want to know."

"Yet you're the one asking for details about my sex life." And I was dumb enough to tell her about them. But it was bound to come up, eventually. She knew I was far from innocent.

"I asked about a tattoo. Not for a blow by blow of your sexcapades," she laughed, shaking her head as she smiled at me.

"Now that *has* happened on my couch. And my desk, and on this..."

"Stop!" Her hands covered her eyes, and she shook her head as her giggles filled the air between us. While I knew she didn't like my history, I also wouldn't hide it from her. I was who I was, and I couldn't change my past.

"She had her hands braced on the back of my office door. I didn't want to disturb the fresh ink on her shoulder."

"What is with you and standing up during sex?" She uncovered her eyes, staring straight at me with expectation. She probably didn't want to know the real reason that it was easier to keep things casual if I didn't spend time with these women in a bed. Most of the time, we weren't even undressed all the way.

I'd certainly never felt the need to worship a woman like I'd done to Hazel a few days ago. And my fingers itched at the knowledge of what she felt like underneath all those bulky sweatshirts she wore around the bar.

"Don't knock it until you try it, Haz."

As she stared at me, clearly thinking about it, I shifted my hips, fighting the urge to pick her up and pin her to the nearest wall to show her exactly how enjoyable it could be. But she deserved so much more. And it wasn't the right time either. I was supposed to be trying to win her heart—not give her orgasms, but I'd already failed at that part.

She held mine in the palm of her hands. She truly didn't know how hard I was falling for her the more time we spent together. Both as Seven and during whatever it was we were doing in real life.

And Hudson could never, ever find out how hard I'd fallen for her before I figured out how to win her for good. Because I knew my best friend. He would hold this against both of us if things fell apart, no matter how platonic the arrangement was for her.

Chapter Fourteen

STARING AT THE DIRECT message that had just shown up in my Instagram account, I blinked, trying to figure out how in the hell I was going to pull this off. I couldn't ask Reid to do this.

I wasn't even sure I *could* set up shots to capture exactly what this author was asking for. Logistically, I could, but yeah...this scene might be a little much for my determination to resist my brother's epically sexy best friend. Although since it didn't require us being in the same room, I might be able to just ask him to send me his part—minus the whole actually showing certain parts of his anatomy—and take care of fumbling through trying to get mine.

> Reid: Did your instructor appreciate your truly impressive shading skills?

He had, but I wasn't in the right frame of mind to deal with playful Reid right now.

> Hazel: He gave me an F. Straight to jail.

> Reid: Feeling a little snarky today, kitten?

> Hazel: Quit calling me kitten. I am not soft and cuddly.

He immediately started typing, but I sent off another one to cut him off.

> Hazel: Or adorable.

And it made me feel even more insecure since he still didn't see me as anything but *adorable.* I was starting to hate that word every time he used it.

Reid: You are after you've used an unsuspecting thumb to get yourself off.

My mouth literally dropped open at his brazen text. I could not believe he just went there. But I also wasn't letting him think it got under my skin.

Hazel: Maybe I was just faking it.

Reid: That was not fake. Neither was the way your chest flushed or how your eyes rolled back when you let go. I couldn't take my eyes off you. Not fake at all.

Hazel: I'm sure it's hard for you to recognize what a real one looks like.

Reid: Don't fucking test me, woman. I will come over there and prove it to you if you need confirmation that I know what it looks like when a woman comes all over my hand.

He didn't even realize that he was kind of setting up the scene I needed for these pictures. But there was no way I could have asked him to simulate having phone sex with me. The motorcycle pictures had crossed a line, and I couldn't bring myself to cross back to the other side where things were safe.

And his increasingly suggestive texts were showing me he didn't want to cross back either. But I was also treading into dangerous waters by letting myself get invested in a man who didn't really want me. I wasn't sure what kind of game Reid was playing.

Reid: Too much?

More like not enough. But I could never tell him that either. I still wasn't sure if things between us were just a case of unresolved sexual tension, or something more. And then I felt guilty whenever things got flirty with Seven, because it felt like I was cheating. I just wasn't sure which one of them I was cheating on.

> *Reid: I'm sorry. That moment will go back in the vault. I won't bring it up again. That wasn't fair of me to use to tease you. No matter how many times it's run through my mind on repeat.*

Mine too. But I resisted texting him that because it wouldn't help keep things under control.

> *Reid: Got any new commissions you need help with?*

I didn't respond, trying to search the internet for photos I could use for source material. It seemed anticlimactic to go back to my previous methods when I'd been able to get exactly what I needed to get to work from on my last few projects.

> *Reid: I have tomorrow off, and you're not on shift at the bar because I don't see your smiling face down here. If you keep ignoring me, I might come knocking.*

> *Reid: And if you're wearing anything remotely close to what you did to the last photoshoot, I'm not sure I can keep my hands to myself.*

> *Hazel: That's kind of exactly what I need. You to keep your hands to yourself.*

> *Reid: Are we talking about in general or for your commission?*

> *Hazel: Both.*

> *Reid: Really giving my self-restraint a workout, aren't you?*

> *Hazel: Don't even need you in the same room with me for this one.*

> *Reid: Alright, I'm intrigued. Details, please.*

> *Hazel: I could probably find a video online for his part.*

> *Reid: The fuck you are. I'm too invested in these now for you to get rid of me that easily.*

> *Reid: Speaking of, you never sent me the final product of the last one.*

That might have been intentional. Not only had the piece turned out amazingly well, but the author had paid for additional licensing to use it as a special edition cover.

But that didn't mean I wanted to show him. The picture I'd used for the final pose had to have been taken at the moment I fell apart against his hand. I'd almost told the author I wasn't able to finish the piece, but it helped that her character looked nothing like me in the finished product. It'd also taken a tremendous amount of effort to draw the male character with a helmet on instead of Reid's expressive face.

> *Reid: I'll come up there if you keep ignoring me.*

> *Reid: Did Hudson tell you he gave me the extra keys to the building in case of an emergency?*

> *Reid: I think one of those keys is to your apartment.*

> *Reid: Might need to do a wellness check, you know, to make sure you're alright. Just in case it's an emergency. I know mouth to mouth.*

> *Reid: Hudson and Charley headed home since I have these keys to lock up. The cooks just left, and Mikey left a while ago.*

> *Reid: You have five minutes to respond to me or you're about to have a visitor.*

Reid's texts had been background noise as I watched a video on my phone that might work for the scene I needed to draw. To be honest, I hadn't even really read them as they came through, swiping them out of the way as I watched the movements of the man on the screen.

In all my deep dives into studying male anatomy, I'd never actually watched any videos like this.

And certainly never ones this graphic.

It was mesmerizing to watch his fingers flex while he gripped himself, his forearm muscles flexing and biceps bulging with every quick movement as he shuttled his fist up and down his...

"Haz," a muted, but very familiar deep voice carried down the short hallway leading from the front door to the living room, and I froze, my eyes wide as I watched Reid just let himself into my apartment without a knock. Or maybe he had, and I'd been so focused I hadn't heard it.

I was so busy staring at my uninvited visitor that I hadn't even realized that my headphones had come unplugged, a very masculine grunt emanating from the speaker and making Reid's eyes widen.

Holy fucking shit...

My wireless earbuds were still charging after I'd forgotten to put them *in* the case before I had placed it on the charger earlier today. I'd grabbed my old over-the-ear ones and plugged them in while I did my research and had clearly forgotten that the reason I'd stopped using them was because the connector had a habit of wiggling loose.

Reid stalked toward me while I frantically tried to close out of the window in the browser on my phone, but he was too fast, gently grasping my wrist and pulling the phone out of my hand.

He watched the screen; the grunts getting louder and louder as the guy clearly got closer and closer to finishing, Reid's expressive eyes flickering briefly toward mine with a look I couldn't quite place.

This was so embarrassing. It'd be one thing to get caught masturbating by the person who starred in way too many of your fantasies, but it was an entirely different thing to get caught watching someone else do it on your phone.

Reid reached forward, pulling the headphones from my head and tossing them toward the coffee table while he sat down next to me.

My pulse hammered as he scooted closer, his knees pressing up against mine. He was dressed more casually than I would have expected him to be if he was downstairs earlier, wearing a pair of loose mesh basketball shorts, a fitted dark gray T-shirt, a pair of beat-up Converse sneakers and a backwards cap.

Either he went to change after all the texts he'd sent me, or he wasn't downstairs to pick up women like he usually was. Not that he looked any less attractive than he did in his usual attire of dark wash jeans, leather boots, tight graphic shirts that hugged his biceps in a way that was practically obscene and his artfully messy sex hair.

"What kind of research are you doing here, kitten? Is this for one of your projects, or is this for something else?"

His smile widened when I shook my head, clamping my mouth shut. I was so mortified. Not that watching porn was shameful or anything, but getting caught watching it by your brother's best friend—who you had a very unhealthy crush on—was not exactly great. I was sure my cheeks had gone full on nuclear in the few minutes since he'd let himself in and crashed my little viewing party.

"Is this what you like…watching?" he asked, studying me with half-lidded eyes. His voice sounded lower somehow, and I glanced toward his shorts, my eyes widening when I realized I was staring at his dick. Not his actual dick, but where it was located.

"Eyes up here, sweetheart." The teasing in his voice only made the blush worse, because the smug bastard knew exactly what I'd been doing.

"Give me the phone." Thrusting my hand into the space between us with way more confidence than I actually possessed, I lifted my gaze and stared him down. I'd dealt with his teasing more than enough when I was a teenager and knew cowering would only make it worse.

"Tell me about your commission," he shot back, pressing the phone into my hand, but instead of moving away, he wrapped his large palm around the back of the phone, holding it captive between our hands.

"No. I don't need your help anymore. I found what I needed." I did still need his help, specifically because the scene I needed to illustrate was from a side profile of what I'd just watched, not a front view.

"Yes, you do."

"You don't even know what I'm working on. I was doing just fine before you inserted yourself into my business. And I'll be fine doing this by myself."

He chuckled, leaning forward and tucking a loose piece of hair behind my ear, but instead of backing off, he just wrapped his hand around the back of my neck. His warm breath fanned over my face, and I fought the urge to whimper audibly. I wasn't giving him the satisfaction of knowing how much his proximity affected me.

"I don't *want* you doing this by yourself. And I don't think you really want to do these commissions alone either. I think you've enjoyed the last week, and I *know* you've been thinking about what other kinds of projects we can *collaborate* on."

"Reid..." I warned, pressing on his shoulder with my free hand, but he responded by flexing his fingertips against my head and pulling my face even closer, which made my heart pound.

"Hazel..." My pulse skyrocketed for an entirely different reason when his eyes briefly flickered to my lips.

"If I tell you what I'm working on, you have to promise this is the last time. I can't keep doing this with you." It was too hard to be in these tense situations like this when I knew he didn't really want me.

And things with Seven had been progressing, too. He was still vague about his job, but he'd told me other things about himself. He was the eldest of three siblings, and he had a shitload of cousins.

His family growing up had struggled, but it made him that much more determined to make something of himself. He owned a small business, and he had just finished paying off both of the business loans he'd taken out while he was starting up.

I hadn't sent him any more NSFW sketches, but he asked how things were going with my illustrations. He'd thought the drawing of Reid's bike in the distillery was insanely good and reiterated he wanted to teach me to ride when we met in person. I didn't bother telling him that Reid had already taken me on my first ride as a passenger. Or what had happened on that bike in a dim warehouse earlier in the week.

"Where did you go?" Reid's voice was almost distant as I stared at the wall over his shoulder, clearly disassociating again because my brain was so overstimulated. "Haz…come back to me."

It was easier to manage in the mornings when I got stressed out, but in the evenings, when my meds had long worn off, it was difficult to focus on things when I was nervous…or being turned on against my will by my brother's entirely too charming best friend.

Taking in a deep, shuddering breath, I closed my eyes and tipped my head back, trying to calm my thoughts. Reid couldn't keep playing with me like this. It wasn't fair to me, and it wasn't fair to Seven. I had developed big feelings for a man I'd never even seen, while a man who'd never really seen *me* was playing with my emotions.

I knew Reid probably had no idea his behavior was having this effect on me, but the more I let myself see him as a possibility, even for a fling, the harder it'd be when he inevitably moved on.

"I'm sorry," he whispered, pulling me against his chest. "I know I keep blurring the lines here. But I want to help you. I can't seem to make myself stay away from you anymore."

His fingers combed through my hair as he held me, and I tried to breathe through the drowsiness that was suddenly making itself known.

"Things aren't supposed to be like this between us."

"I know, kitten. I know. But I've missed you so much over the last two years that I've been greedily taking anything you'll give me at this point. I know I fucked everything up, but I never want to lose you like that again."

My chin quivered when his words sunk in. I wasn't sure until now if he'd felt the gaping hole in his life for the last couple of years that I had. It'd been shocking to find him like that, especially because I had a crush on him, but that wasn't why I'd withdrawn from our friendship and pushed him away. He was always going to be Hudson's first. And I had Charley, so it wasn't like I'd lost my *best* friend, but it made me realize how different our lives were.

I was sheltered and inexperienced, and he was the opposite. We were too different. Even though our lives were lived parallel to one another, and he was always around, I wasn't sure what exactly we had in common. He was confident and charismatic where I was not. He was established in his career and successful, where I was only starting out. He had women lining up to spend time with him, and I definitely did not have men seeking me out.

Seeing him fucking that girl had made me question everything about my life at that point. The physical recovery from my accident had been horrible, and to a certain extent, every bit of pain I felt had further fractured the way I looked at him. And he had just gone on like nothing had happened. Like his behavior hadn't literally caused me physical harm. He didn't push me over that crate or stab a piece of glass in my leg, but sometimes it felt like he had.

"Please talk to me," he whispered, leaning back and wiping his thumbs beneath my eyes. I hadn't even realized I'd been crying. And I hated myself for doing it in front of him. I vowed back then to never let him have that much emotional power over me again, but here I was practically swooning because he'd finally noticed I was more than just Hudson's boring little sister.

"You can't keep hurting me," I whispered, clearing my throat before I continued. "I know you're trying to help me, and I appreciate it. I really do. But when you toy with my emotions, it hurts. This is my life, my business. And I can't keep doing this when you act like..."

He nodded, brushing his fingers through my hair before letting go and scooting away from me. "I know, we...*I* got carried away, and I let things go too far. But I don't think you realize what kind of power you have over me."

Scoffing, I pushed him back, and he settled halfway down on the couch, pulling my legs into his lap in the process. He gently pulled off my slippers, dropping them to the floor before he rubbed the arches of my feet, laughing when I failed to hold in a groan. While my life as an artist had me relatively sedentary, I spent a lot of time on my feet downstairs in the bar.

As his fingertips crept up my ankles and dug into the muscles on the back of my calves, I winced, trying to pull my leg out of his grasp.

"Hey," Reid whispered, drawing my attention toward his face and away from the scar his palm was currently covering. "I'm sorry."

"It wasn't your fault." I knew that; I did. But I'd held onto an unhealthy amount of resentment over the last few years. Wearing shorts was rare because of the long scar that wrapped around the back of my calf and crept up toward my knee. Even though the scar had faded over time, it was still there for the entire world to see.

"Yeah, it was. I know I didn't push you, but I was the reason you were back there to begin with. Hudson asked me to bring that case to the bar, and I'd gotten distracted and left it on the floor there. So yeah, it was my fault. And I never apologized to you for what you walked in on, either."

Closing my eyes, I avoided looking at him, trying to push the images that still haunted me to this day out of my mind. How mesmerized I'd been at how his body moved while he'd been...

"You're blushing again, kitten." Reid's murmured voice startled me, and my eyes popped open, locking with his. Caught in his gaze, I couldn't look away. Every part of me was acutely aware of the feeling of his hands on me as his fingers traced the raised skin on my leg, burning a path up my calf and behind my knee.

"I'm sorry too," I whispered, trying to blink away my clouded emotions. Embarrassment and shame enveloped me for months back then, and every time Reid had tried to talk to me after I'd been released from the hospital, I turned around and walked away. I'd run from him at every opportunity, and until Halloween a few months ago, I would have been perfectly content to continue to do it for the rest of my life. "The way I've treated you for the last two years wasn't right, either. We *did* used to be friends, and I just threw that out the window because I was..."

Shaking my head, I looked away from him, but I should have known he wouldn't let me off that easily. Reid lifted my legs, scooting closer until I was practically sitting on his lap. Gentle fingers traced along the side of my face and caused my lip to shake. I wasn't even sure why, but I had the sudden urge to cry.

"Come here," he whispered, wrapping an arm around my back and encouraging me to wrap my arms around him. I tucked my face into his neck and tried to sort through my thoughts. Last week I'd been fine. I'd been minding my own business and working two jobs, taking my courses and keeping to myself.

A little lonely since my best friend had shacked up with my brother, but I had other things to focus on. And now I had Reid pushing his way into my life and my heart while this other man, whose name I didn't even know, was opening me up in a whole new way.

"Is this where you want to be marked?" Reid asked, his thumb rubbing across the scar, just barely grazing my skin. I nodded and his fingers dug in, massaging the damaged skin. Goosebumps raced up my legs, making him chuckle as he tucked his face next to mine, his breath warm on my lips. "You don't need to hide this from the world. I think every part of you is beautiful. But if you want it, please let me do the cover up?"

He didn't wait for an answer, because he knew I'd tell him yes. Urging me to lie down, Reid lifted his hips, pulling a marker out of his shorts pocket, using his teeth to pull off the lid. I watched him from my place against the couch pillows, his brow wrinkled in concentration, and the pen cap still between his teeth while his fingers deftly maneuvered the fine tipped marker against my skin.

"You better not be drawing anything inappropriate with that permanent marker on my leg," I warned, and he grinned, flashing me a wink before he returned his attention to whatever he was drawing.

"Just give me a minute, woman," he mumbled around the pen cap, continuing to shift my leg as he worked. Leaning up, I tried to look, but he narrowed his eyes at me, nodding to indicate I needed to lie back down. "No peeking."

Closing my eyes, I tried to focus on breathing and not how much it turned me on to not only have Reid's hands tracing all over my leg, but to hold this much of his undivided attention. In moments like this, when he reminded me we did have things in common, like our love for drawing, it was hard to convince myself we were so wildly different.

"You still awake, pretty girl?" he teased, the sound of the cap clicking into place on his marker drawing me back into reality.

"Can I look?" Sitting up, I scooted my hips back so I could study my leg, the intricate black lines wrapping around my skin in stark contrast to the paleness of my calf, and the slightly pinker skin of my scar. But you could barely make it out through the design, a flowing vine that was impressively shaded considering what he'd been drawing with, wrapping around the back of my leg and flowing down the front of my shin to just above my ankle.

"*Reid*," I breathed, a little stunned by the design, very similar to the calf wrap that I'd tried to draw, but so much more detailed. "Did Charley tell you about my design?"

He frowned, shaking his head as he casually rested his arms along the back of the couch. Again, looking as if he belonged here. "No, I didn't even know you had a design." He paused, tracing the outline of the flower on the side of my calf with his fingertip. "I mean, I know it's not penises, since you apparently seem to really enjoy looking at those. But I know how much you love peonies. And..."

He nodded to the large painted flowers on my living room walls. When we'd moved into this once boring dark gray apartment, I'd immediately set to work turning it into something not quite so dreary, starting with painting the walls a pale peach. Then I'd spent days hand painting huge reddish pink peony blossoms across the space. My hands had hurt for weeks afterward since I'd spent so many hours detailing the intricate parts of the flowers I easily could have left out. Charley had told me I was hyper fixating, but once it was done, I'd just sat and stared for hours at what I'd created.

The large blooms made me happy, and staring down at the outlines on my skin, a warm feeling blossomed in my chest. Reid's flowers made me happy, too.

"It's okay if you don't like them. This is just a temporary tattoo marker. The lines will fade after a few weeks. I guess I should have asked if I could draw on you before I did it, but ever since Charley mentioned someone else inking you, I haven't been able to shake the idea. I was trying to be patient and let you come to me, but..."

Reaching up to place my fingertips over his mouth, I shook my head. His hand grasped my wrist, his thumb rubbing across my pulse point while he waited for me to talk.

"It's beautiful. I'm not sure if I'd ever have the guts to actually let you put a needle to my skin, but you drew exactly what I wanted."

Reid pulled my fingers away, interlacing his with mine and placing our joined hands in my lap. "This wasn't to pressure you. I know how much it bothers you. I see how you wear pants most of the year to hide it. Every time I get a glimpse of your scar and know that I was part of what caused it, I feel this intense regret that I made you feel unsafe in your own home. And that my actions damaged this beautiful body. Not that the scars make you any less beautiful, but—"

"Stop." Pulling my legs up, I scooted away from him, running my fingers across the lines, imagining them being permanent. I knew it'd take hours being in his chair next door to complete. Hours I was forced to spend with him, but not *with* him. "I'm not saying no. I'm just saying not right now. But you'd also better take pictures, because when I do finally muster enough courage to let you near me with that tat gun, I want this."

"You know how I feel about taking pictures of you." His voice was a low grumble, and I knew I needed to start asking for what I really needed. And I shouldn't be second guessing his help on my commissions. Things may have been weird between us, but I knew his heart was in a good place. It was just the rest of him that my brain kept taking to a very, very naughty place.

"Well, I hope you brought your camera when you came on this breaking and entering mission, because I need your help."

"And I am more than willing to give it to you. Whatever you need."

Raising an eyebrow, I turned the tables on him, intentionally sweeping my gaze over his tight T-shirt and lingering on his shorts. "Oh, really?"

"You sure you wanna go there, kitten? Because if you ask for it, I'm going to deliver. Now that I know how much you like looking at *packages.*"

"Well, not all packages are created the same. Not sure yours can help with this project. I need to see it in the pictures to sketch it, and we aren't the kind of friends that get naked together, so…"

Reid shifted, moving my legs to the side so he could slide out from under them. His biceps flexed on either side of my head as he planted his hands on the arm of the couch behind my back, looming over me.

"I don't need to get naked for you to see what you need to sketch, Haz."

Chapter
Fifteen

Reid

"WE'VE GOTTEN CREATIVE WITH our posing so far without taking off too many clothes. Now I need you to tell me exactly what I'm trying to capture, and then we're going to set it up. Where's your camera stand?"

Hazel's doe eyes stared up at me, her lips parted slightly, and a flush creeping up the side of her neck. It seemed someone enjoyed being bossed around. Which was good, because I wanted to be the one telling her what to do right now.

Not in real life, of course, because I was all about her newfound confidence in the last few months, but when we were alone working on her commissions, I had no problem taking the lead. At least until she decided it was her turn. I could be a good boy when I needed to be.

"Um, I, uh…" she stuttered, her cheeks bright pink. I fucking loved that she had a tell, and I had been fantasizing way too much lately about what she'd look like with nothing on and exactly where that flush would spread when I made her come.

Leaning back, I offered her my hand, helping her sit up on the couch. Her eyes widened when she looked at my shorts, and I had a feeling that my compression shorts weren't doing too much to conceal my reaction to her.

"Can you…" She shooed me away, and I took a seat on the coffee table, leaning forward and bracing my forearms on my thighs.

"Spill. I'm not letting you back out on me now."

But my courageous spitfire had suddenly clammed up again, refusing to open those gorgeous lips.

"Since you have decided to go silent on me, let's see if I can guess." Raising an eyebrow, I watched as she leaned back against the cushions, banding her arms around her knees in a defensive posture. I rubbed my hands together, grinning as I continued. "Earlier, you mentioned something about me keeping my hands to myself, and then I caught you watching...what you were watching. Does your commission have something to do with self-pleasure?"

"Maybe," she mumbled, tugging on her lower lip with her teeth.

"And you also said that you didn't even need me to be in the same room to catch the picture you needed. So that leads me to believe that at least one character is touching themselves while the other one is listening...or watching."

A tiny nod was all the confirmation I got, but without her explicitly telling me, I was forced to imagine my own version of the scene she'd been commissioned to draw. And while the thought of watching something like that was really fucking tempting, I was going to let her lead on how she wanted to stage this.

"The real question is...do you want to fake this scenario, or do you really want to act it out?"

Her eyes widened, her delicate mouth opening, but the pink hints on her cheeks gave her away. "Like with you... And me..." she stuttered, hugging her arms tighter around her legs.

"That's up to you. Since what you were watching seemed self-explanatory, I'm assuming the male character is touching himself. But you never told me what the female character's role is while he's doing it."

Hazel's curious eyes continued staring at me, and I could tell she was clearly still having issues talking to me about anything sexual without getting embarrassed, so I pushed the envelope a little.

"Here's what I think we need to do. You help me set up your camera in your bedroom to capture the angle you need, and when I go home, I'll do the same thing. Then you're going to call me, and we'll talk things through while we get the images you need."

"And the things we'll be talking through are...?"

Scooting forward again, I pulled Hazel's arms loose and leaned over her, bracing my hand on the back of the couch. "That's up to you, but I'd be more than happy to tell you exactly how I think you should touch yourself. Because I might keep things covered for taking the pictures you need, but while I'm on the phone with you, I don't think I can keep myself from taking things into my own hands while I imagine the sounds you make while you're touching yourself."

"You're blurring the lines again, Reid."

Standing up and holding my hand out toward her so we could get started, I said what had been on my mind for weeks. "Maybe there shouldn't be any lines between us, Haz. Not anymore."

AN HOUR LATER, I was still waiting for Hazel to call me. After helping her set up her camera next to her bed and leaving her with a suggestive wink that'd made her blush again, I'd rushed home to duplicate the same setup.

While I waited, I'd worked on getting the side profile shots of myself she'd described, sheets pulled low on my hips. My fist was wrapped around the white material, grasping the erection I hadn't been able to control while I pretended I was doing something a little more salacious.

You couldn't really see any details, just my exposed hip at the edge of the sheet, but I hoped it was close enough that Hazel could fill in the rest of what she needed using her imagination. Or the memory of the man she'd been watching on her phone. Because she'd better not have been looking for more videos to watch when I would have gladly sent her one.

Now I was lying on my bed, my briefs pulled back on, staring at my phone like the desperate man I'd become around her. I was also waiting for a response to the last text message I'd sent her as Seven before I'd come over to the bar tonight to help Hudson put up some new shelves in the storeroom after last call.

Seven: What's something you've always wanted to do, but never told anyone about?

But she'd left my alter ego on read all evening as well while she was online looking up naughty videos.

I'd even been thinking about what to tell her once she finally answered me. I was trying to be more open with information about myself without giving too much away regarding my identity. She hadn't asked again for more specifics on my job, but I'd revealed things—or wanted to reveal things—that I didn't even share with Hudson.

And I wanted to tell her what I'd been thinking about more and more lately, because once my identity was revealed, I wanted to bring her on to help me. If she was still talking to me, that is.

Deciding to torture myself more, I navigated to my external file hosting service, clicking on the link I'd sent her from the time we'd spent together at the distillery. I knew it was stupid to look at them, because it'd just make me feel more frustrated, but I couldn't help myself.

Before the images could load, a text came through, making my pulse skip and I closed out of the window.

Fourteen: Sorry, was distracted by something earlier and didn't see this come through.

Yeah, I'm sure you were, dirty girl, was what I wanted to reply, knowing that she'd been looking at porn when I'd sent that message. But I behaved myself because Seven didn't know what she'd been doing.

Seven: No worries, you're here now. Anything I can help with? Need someone to talk things through?

Fourteen: No. It's fine. Just a project that I was working on. A friend helped me get things figured out.

But had I? She hadn't called me after I'd left, and she hadn't sent a response to my email with the pictures I'd sent her. Maybe I *had* come on too strong.

Seven: You going to answer my question from earlier, or do you want me to go first?

Fourteen: Gasp. You mean you'll share something with me, and I don't have to drag it out of you?

Seven: I've given you answers about myself.

Fourteen: Begrudgingly. But sure, you go first. Although from what I know about you, I have a hard time believing you don't go after what you want. I can't see there being much you would want to do that you wouldn't make happen.

Seven: Sometimes even assertive people have things they keep to themselves.

Fourteen: Like specific details about their jobs?

Seven: Touche. But this has to do with my job in a roundabout way.

Fourteen: I'm intrigued. Go ahead.

Seven: I've been thinking of holding workshops at my shop during summer break. For kids whose parents can't afford to send them to summer camp.

Fourteen: What kind of workshops?

Obviously, I couldn't tell her outright that I wanted to teach kids how to fine-tune their illustration skills and tell them what kinds of jobs they could use those skills for that didn't require more than a high school diploma, because then she would have asked questions about what professional experience I had in that area. But I knew if anyone would understand the need to encourage kids to pursue artistic endeavors, she would. I also had a few other local business owners I thought might be good to partner with because I knew they had similar backgrounds to mine and applied their creative talents to practical businesses.

If it hadn't been for my art teachers in high school, along with Hudson's parents, seeing my artistic skills and encouraging me to find a way to use them without needing a college degree, I wouldn't have become a tattoo artist. I'd probably be working in construction with my dad and uncle. Which wouldn't have been nearly as fulfilling as the career and life I'd been able to build for myself over the last decade doing something I was passionate about.

> *Seven: Helping them learn how to do things with their hands. Actual skills they could develop without having to rely on going to college.*

> *Fourteen: You didn't go, did you?*

> *Seven: No. Wasn't in the cards for me. We didn't have a lot of extra cash growing up, and I wasn't the best student academically, so I found a way to harness my other skills.*

> *Fourteen: And those skills would be?*

> *Seven: Nice try. But I want to be a safe place these kids can come to where they don't feel pressured to conform to what some guidance counselor thinks they should do. Not everyone is cut out for college, and there aren't enough adults that encourage kids to go into other trades.*

> *Fourteen: Carpenter? You like polishing your wood?*

I couldn't hold in the smile because of our interactions earlier in the evening, but I wasn't budging on keeping some things to myself.

Seven: Nope.

Fourteen: Plumber? You going to come snake my pipes?

Seven: While my snake would love to be introduced to your pipes, no.

Fourteen: Mechanic? You want to check my fluids?

Seven: Wow, you're really giving this your all to figure it out. But, no. And last I checked, plumbers and mechanics don't mark things for people. You'll just have to be patient.

Fourteen: Fine. I'll behave.

Seven: We both know that isn't true.

Fourteen: I think you secretly like me feisty.

Seven: Not a secret.

Fourteen: Have you told anyone else about these workshops? I bet there are lots of people (me included) who would love to help you start some kind of summer program for kids like that.

Seven: No. It's just an idea at this point.

Fourteen: You haven't told anyone but me?!? What about your friends? I'm sure they'd help where they could if they knew how much you wanted to make this happen.

Seven: No. My best friend probably wouldn't get it. He never had any doubts about his future like I did as a kid. His family

Which was something I never held against Hudson. He'd been tagging along to spend time at the bar—learning the ropes from his dad—since we were kids. Then, once he was old enough to work there, he'd jumped right in and never even considered doing something else with his life.

He'd also had parents who could afford to send him to college to hone his skills in restaurant management. So, while I'd taken the long route to making my dreams come true, he'd had a level of privilege I'd always been a little envious of. But his family had never judged me for taking a different route. His dad had even worked with me to develop a business plan when I'd been trying to get the loan to open my shop after I'd moved back to Sage Springs.

This was why I was falling so hard for her, because no matter who I was when we talked, she seemed to get it. Get *me*. And she didn't judge.

Hudson meant well. He'd always been there when I needed him, and I never doubted for a second he had my back. But sometimes I felt like he used my recreational activities as a justification that I couldn't take things seriously.

I knew he'd use the same lens to judge my feelings for Hazel. He wouldn't look at the fact I adored her for who she was. Every part of her, even the ones she hid from her brother. He'd focus on how adamant I'd once been that I didn't want to be in a committed relationship. But I'd always told him, if I found the right person, I'd do it in a heartbeat. I just hadn't realized that the right person had been literally hiding under my nose for years. Only she hadn't been ready yet. And neither had I.

But I was ready now. And there was a very real possibility she was going to hate me in a week when I walked into that reveal and told her I loved her. But I was still going to try.

Fourteen: To answer your question, I guess you could say I'm doing what I always wanted to do right now.

Seven: How so?

Fourteen: I'm creating art on my own terms.

Seven: With your commissions?

Fourteen: Yeah. I know my family wouldn't understand what I've been doing. But I really enjoy it. Bringing these characters to life. I know I'm not writing the books, or planning the scenes, but I feel like I'm breathing life into these author's creations.

Seven: I said it before, and I'll say it again. You're insanely talented. And even if you were drawing less racy things, I'd still think your determination was sexy as hell.

Fourteen: I know you can't see it, but you're making me blush.

Seven: I want to tell you to take a picture. Even though I know I shouldn't and it's breaking the rules, it's killing me not to see it.

She didn't respond right away, but I watched the little dots dancing on the screen with rapt attention until I had to put my phone down because I was having dangerous thoughts of using my keys to go back over there.

After ten minutes of staring at the television across the room that I wasn't really watching, my phone pinged.

The image waiting for me almost made me blow my cover and follow through with my fleeting thoughts to throw everything out the window and confess who I really was to her tonight.

She was laying against her pillows, a hint of cleavage peeking above the neckline of her white tank top. Her red hair fanned out around her on the pillowcase and an enticing pink blush splashed her cheeks and traveled down the side of her neck. A peek of pink mesh panties, just barely visible at the bottom of the frame, made my arousal from earlier roar back to life.

> **Seven:** You're making it very difficult to be a good boy and stay away from you.

I probably should have phrased it differently, because I wasn't supposed to know where she was, but she didn't seem to pick up on that.

> **Fourteen:** Maybe I want you to be a bad boy. But we've only got a week left. Do I get a picture now? Seems only fair that you reciprocate since I sent you one of me.

> **Seven:** And I don't think I'm going to be able to stop looking at it. I was right; you are a sexy little thing.

> **Fourteen:** You can't even see my entire face.

> **Seven:** Not looking at your face right now.

> **Fourteen:** You can't be impressed by my tiny boobs.

> **Seven:** Nope. You're not doing that. You're breathtaking. It's literally taking all my self-control right now not to call the event coordinator and figure out how to get my hands on you before Valentine's Day.

> *Fourteen: I like the idea of your hands on me. You going to send me a picture of them?*

Fuck. I'd wanted to send a picture of them holding onto the one thing that was hiding under my sheets earlier, doing something similar to the video she'd been watching, but Seven would not be sending her dick pics, and neither would I.

> *Seven: Fine. I'll send you a picture, but we both know this is breaking the rules, naughty girl.*

Trying to decide what to include in the shot that wouldn't give me away, I glanced around my room. The reflective visor on the motorcycle helmet sitting on the bench by my door gave me an idea. I hopped up and placed it on my dresser, framing the shot, so it captured what I wanted it to without being too obvious.

> *Fourteen: That's a motorcycle helmet. You were supposed to send me a picture of you.*

But clearly, she hadn't realized I *had* technically sent her a picture of me. It was barely distinguishable in the small screen on my phone, but on the visor was the reflection of a shirtless man holding a phone.

> *Seven: Very good. Such a clever girl.*

I was waiting for her to give me shit for not doing what she asked. But I wasn't going to send her something revealing because I was afraid with my piercings and tattoos, she'd figure it out if I sent her a picture right now. I should have known my secretly naughty girl would still find a way to flirt with me despite my continued evasions.

> *Fourteen: I can imagine you whispering that in my ear in your deep sexy voice.*

> *Seven: Good girl.*

Fourteen: I want to hear you whisper that too. Hold on, brb. Gotta go change my panties. The thought of your voice is making them wet.

Seven: As long as you tell me what color they are before you take them off.

Fourteen: You're naughty.

Seven: I think you are too. Or at least you want to be.

Fourteen: Light pink mesh, if you squint at the bottom of my picture, you can see them.

Seven: :growls:

Fourteen: So, does that mean you're teaching me to ride once we meet?

Seven: Huh?

Fourteen: The helmet. You told me during our date that you ride. Are you still going to teach me?

Seven: Are you a good listener?

Fourteen: I promise to be good.

Seven: You'd have to listen carefully to my instructions. Maybe it's safer if you ride with me first. I'd bet you'll be a warm little backpack.

Fourteen: I'd happily ride you.

Seven: Somehow, I don't think you're referring to my bike.

Fourteen: Now who's naughty?

Seven: You're the one with their mind in the gutter. I'm just over here coming up with a lesson plan to teach you how to ride.

Fourteen: I'm more of a learn by doing kind of gal.

Seven: Then I guess I'd better be ready for you to do me.

Fourteen: Seven more days and you'd better be.

Seven: I thought the whole point of texting like this was to get to know each other better and not make everything physical.

Fourteen: Then you better get to know me quickly. Because if your body matches the voice that I hear in my bed at night, then you'd better clear your calendar.

Seven: What's your favorite color again?

Fourteen: Not even going to acknowledge that I hear your voice in my head when I touch myself?

Seven: No, because I'm never going to make it through the next week if I do.

Fourteen: What color are your boxers?

Seven: Blue.

Fourteen: Then blue is my favorite color to see on the floor next to my bed.

Seven: Well, it's now on the floor next to mine.

Fourteen: Does that mean you're touching yourself?

Seven: It means I'm about to get in the shower.

Fourteen: So, you're texting me naked?

Seven: There's a good possibility.

Fourteen: Want me to join you?

Seven: Killing me…

Fourteen: Have fun in the shower. I know I will. My shower head has 12 settings.

Fuck. Well, now I knew what I'd be imagining while I stroked myself in the shower. Picturing what Hazel did with those 12 settings was going to have to tide me over until I could see it in person.

Seven: Goodnight, naughty girl.

Fourteen: :picture of a pair of light pink mesh panties on a gray bathroom rug:

Since she was going there, I didn't see the harm in sending her another picture.

Seven: :picture of a pair of dark blue boxer briefs on a gray tile floor:

Fourteen: My dreams will be very sweet.

So would mine.

The night may not have turned out how I'd wanted it to, and I was insanely jealous that Hazel had initiated this kind of conversation with Seven and not me, but I'd shared something with her I hoped would make my case later. Even if it was unconventional, I had faith she'd see our conversations as Fourteen and Seven as a way to get to know each other. That wouldn't have happened as Hazel and Reid.

The history that had driven her away from me in real life wasn't there when she was talking to me as Seven. And while I was still holding some things back, there were other parts of myself I'd never revealed to anyone but her.

But that didn't mean I was backing off in real life. Especially when I opened our text thread after my shower, a rough sketch of the poses we'd taken pictures of earlier filling the screen.

Reid: You never called me.

Hazel: I managed to take care of things myself.

And I tried to keep my mind off other things I knew she was taking care of by herself. Things I desperately wanted to be doing for her.

Reid: I see that. What's next in the queue?

Her next text was a link to an mp3 file that I didn't hesitate to download. As the scene she sent played out the speakers of my phone, I wasn't sure I had the willpower to wait until tomorrow night to act this one out.

Chapter Sixteen

ATTACHING THE FINAL IMAGES to an email, I sent them off to my client, hoping the author was getting what she needed with what I'd drawn. Because I wasn't sure how much longer I could keep my clothes on if I spent any more time with Reid working on reference photos.

And whatever weird Valentine's Day vibes were in the air blurring the lines with Reid, were also steering things back into a naughty place with Seven. We'd continued texting every evening, learning more about each other without divulging too much that might potentially reveal our true identities. I was sure Charley would be more than willing to spill details on any information I asked her about him, but I was trying to let things play out without an unfair advantage.

But we'd also continued sending pictures to each other. Not quite breaking the rules, and most of them weren't that revealing, but a few had me thinking some very dirty thoughts. After some coaxing, he'd finally sent me one with his body actually in the frame, showing a sliver of his stomach with a fine trail of dark hair visible above the waistband of a pair of the blue boxer briefs that seemed to be his favorites.

In a moment of pure desperation, I'd zoomed in on the bottom of the image, hoping to catch a peek of what might be inside them, but he'd clearly cropped it in a very specific way that still left a lot of things up to my imagination. It was a good thing I had a very active one.

But that imagination was simultaneously getting me into a very precarious situation with my brother's best friend. My latest commission was almost worse than the previous ones, because it wasn't Reid touching me this time, it was me touching him. And after listening to the scene in the audiobook and sending the clip to my very willing posing assistant, I was afraid that this would be the scenario to finally tip both of us over the edge of the cliff we'd been toeing for a week.

Without coming out and explicitly saying it, we were both clearly fighting a potent attraction to each other. He'd become more blatant in revealing his feelings about me physically the more time we spent together, but I knew he was letting me lead. I'd never outright told him I was a virgin, but I wasn't exactly hiding it, either. He had to know I wasn't even on the same level as him with experience because of my annoyingly persistent blush when he was anywhere in my vicinity.

Reid: Finishing up with my last client now. When are you done?

Hazel: I just got home. Annie convinced your cousin to help her finish up downstairs. There wasn't much to do tonight.

Reid: Judging by the annoyingly loud diesel engine I just heard pull out of the parking lot, they're gone.

Hazel: You coming over here?

Reid: Unless you want to come over here.

While it might be easier if I could make a quick getaway after we were done, I also didn't want to think about how many other women had been in the same position with him over there...or where...or how many times.

I knew it wasn't fair to judge him based upon his past, but I could feel the jealousy bubble up inside me when I was reminded of his antics. Even knowing he'd seemingly been trying to change his ways over the last few months. Something had shifted for him, because I hadn't seen him picking up women at the bar, and I hadn't noticed any cars still in the parking lot next to his shop long after the bar was closed. Not that I checked out my window before I went to bed at night.

Hazel: Pass. I think I'd feel more comfortable over here.

Reid: Have you eaten anything?

Pausing, I tried to remember when the last time I'd eaten was. Half the time I worked on food service downstairs, I forgot to eat. Not because I was too busy, but because when you spent that much time around the smell of fried food, you didn't want to eat anything remotely similar to what you were serving. And sometimes my brain forgot it needed things to fuel it, like water and food.

Hazel: Honestly, I don't remember what I ate today.

Reid: I would use right now to make a poorly timed sausage joke because of what we'll be staging later, but I'll spare you.

Hazel: I happen to enjoy a plump sausage now and then. But not too plump, don't want my jaw to ache once I finish.

Reid: ...

Hazel: Have I actually rendered you speechless for once? I didn't know that was possible. I thought you were unflappable.

Reid: Yes, kitten, you have. I want to be simultaneously proud of you for stooping to my level in bawdy humor, but also a bit horrified that I've corrupted your innocent mind.

Hazel: Hate to break it to you, mister. My body might be innocent, but my mind is not. At all.

A flush ran through me at the thought of him whispering those words, but when I ran it back through my head, his voice mixed with Seven's. Shaking my head to clear the unwelcome thought, I realized that I never answered him.

Fifteen minutes later, I'd run through my apartment, making sure there weren't any stray incriminating sketches lying around. I'd moved on from my hyper fixation to perfect my illustration skills of the male anatomy, but you could never be too safe when hiding your dick pics. Even if they were just drawings.

The dirty clothes I'd piled on the chair next to my bed were now inside the hamper. I'd also collected the plethora of half-finished drinks from around my workspace and either poured them out or drank them—depending on the contents.

Charley would be proud that my frantic cleaning had gotten me to my hydration goals for the day. She was constantly reminding me to drink and eat things. And it seemed that Reid had decided to fill in since my best friend had been busy planning the party at the end of the week.

The party that made glee and dread flow through me in almost equal measure. I was excited because I'd finally get to meet Seven. To find out his name, explore the spark I felt when he texted me and see if it translated to real life. But then I was disappointed because it'd mean the end of my time with Reid.

If I hit it off with Seven, then whatever was happening with Reid had to be over. It was bad enough I was entertaining dangerous thoughts of what would happen if Reid made a move to take things further than the heavy flirtation that had been happening since he offered to help me.

Part of me wanted to chalk it up to getting carried away because of the context of my commissions, but when I opened the door a few moments later, I realized that what I felt for my brother's best friend had morphed from a childish crush into a full-blown attraction to the man standing in my doorway with a pizza box in his hands.

"Sausage delivery."

Resisting the urge to take the bait, since, of course, he knew Italian sausage was my favorite pizza topping; I asked the more important question. "It's after midnight, how did you get that?"

My stomach, apparently suddenly ravenous, decided to growl. But as I took in his casual attire, I realized it wasn't the only part of me that was hungry.

Pushing down my lustful thoughts, I stepped aside, shuddering slightly when Reid dusted a kiss at the edge of my jaw on his way past. His footsteps faltered, his eyes flashing to mine, but I shook my head, trying desperately not to let my blush take over. I wasn't prepared to answer his questions about my reaction to a barely there brush of his lips.

"I have my methods." Following along behind him to my living room, I resisted the urge to push him out of the way and steal the box. But I was also enjoying the view because his collection of mesh basketball shorts was growing on me. "Also doesn't hurt that the owner was my last client of the day, and he had one of his drivers deliver it to the shop for him when I asked."

Without looking away from the mesmerizing view of his ass flexing underneath those shorts, I absentmindedly commented. "You knew I would forget to eat."

He turned, his smile widening when he noticed where my gaze had been focused.

"Do I have something on the back of my shorts, kitten?"

"Quit calling me that."

"Never. I love it when you bring out the claws." He opened the box, pulling out the paper plates he'd apparently thought to bring with him, carefully lifting a piece from inside and placing it on one—the cheese stretching enticingly—and then turned, holding it out to me.

Narrowing my eyes, I took the plate, almost expecting him to tease me and pull it away, but he didn't. His smile only widened when he realized I was blushing yet again.

"It's warm in here."

"Mm hmm. Not sure your nipples would agree with you." Instinctively, I pulled my arm up, trying to shield my chest, but Reid just laughed harder, holding his hand to the edge of my plate to keep my piece of pizza from sliding to the floor.

"Nervous about something, Haz?" he asked, averting his gaze back to the pizza and piling two slices onto his plate. His chest grazed my arm as he passed me, moving to take a seat in the middle of my couch. When I didn't move, he nodded to the empty cushion beside him.

"No, why should I be nervous?" I asked, reluctantly taking a seat. The warmth of his leg seeped through my leggings, and I fought the urge to move away from him, but I knew he'd call me out on it. Not that I wanted to get away from him.

If I was being honest with myself, I wanted to curl up in his lap like the pet name he kept calling me, but that would be an epically bad idea. Because if I acted on the urge to touch him like I wanted to, I'd never want to stop.

And I had a feeling he wouldn't want me to either. Which was something I hadn't expected a week ago—that he would encourage my affection and look at me like he wanted what I had for so long. What I still did. Even if it was a terrible idea.

Even if it meant risking something real developing between me and a man I'd never met.

"Spill. Because the nervous lip chewing you're doing over there is driving me nuts. It's going to bleed if you keep it up. And I like your lips how they are."

"What?" Eyes wide, I shoved the rest of my pizza in my mouth and turned to face him.

"You heard me, you have pretty lips, and I'd hate to see you destroy them because you're nervous about something."

"I have pretty lips?" He'd made fleeting compliments in the last week that had surprised me, but this one was the most jarring.

"Yes, you do. And I'd rather you stop abusing them and just tell me why you're nervous instead of getting yourself worked up over there. Lips like yours should only be abused for one reason."

I wasn't even sure how to respond to that. No one had ever called my lips *pretty* before. And I hadn't realized Reid had been paying enough attention to mine to notice that they were.

Reid finished chewing and tossed his plate near mine, scooting closer and draping his arm along the back of the couch behind me. "Please tell me what's bothering you? I promise I won't tease you."

Turning toward him, I blinked hard, not realizing his face was quite so close, but I also didn't want to move away. "I don't know how to get into character for the next picture."

His warm breath coasted over my lips, and I should have been worried about both of us having pizza breath, but I was also enjoying the affectionate gaze currently aimed in my direction.

"I'm not going to be judging your form, if that's what you're worried about. All of my clothes will stay on the entire time, and you can just focus on recreating the scene based on the book. Or maybe you can channel some memories of the last time you..."

He trailed off, swallowing hard before he glanced away. Maybe Reid was having just as hard of a time talking about specifics with me as I did with him.

"That's the problem. The last time..." I hesitated to finish the sentence, because there hadn't been a last time.

"I'm sure your technique is fine, kitten. It's always more about the enthusiasm than the handiwork. Just try to look like you're enjoying yourself."

But that was the problem. I had zero personal material to draw from. Reid's dick was the only one I'd seen in real life. Which was a complete accident and slightly mortifying considering what else happened that night. And if he found out the truth, I was pretty sure I'd die of embarrassment.

"But I don't know—"

"You need to quit second guessing yourself. Most guys don't care what you do as long as you—"

"Stop, Reid," I cut him off, my voice rising. "Just stop. I wasn't kidding when I said I didn't know what I was doing. I literally don't know what I'm doing."

He blinked, tilting his head as his brows furrowed. He stared at me for a long minute before his eyes widened in realization.

"Like you've never...?"

Shaking my head, I looked away from him, hating that I was this inexperienced, because I was sure he felt sorry for me. And having the guy you wanted to do naughty things with feel sorry for you because you were an inexperienced virgin was a new kind of humiliation.

"Are we talking that you've just never given a blow job, or...?"

Clearing my throat, I tried to find my words. No matter how hard this was to confess, I wanted to tell him. I needed to tell him.

"The only one I've seen not on a video screen is yours."

Chapter Seventeen

THE LOOK HE GAVE me in response was priceless. A heavy dose of confusion mixed with curiosity flittered across his features, and then he pinned me down with the one he settled on.

Determination.

"Explain. Because I think I would remember if somehow over the last few weeks I showed you my dick."

"It wasn't recently."

"Wha...*oh shit.*"

Pressing my lips together, I gave him a jerky nod, confirming the conclusion he'd come to a lot quicker than I'd expected.

"That night."

Nodding, I tried to look away, but he shifted, holding my gaze. I flinched as he raised his hand, gently grazing my jaw with his fingertips until I relaxed. His warm palm cradled the side of my face, and I tried to remain calm, waiting for him to process this new kernel of information.

"I guess I'm not exactly sure how that's true. You've had boyfriends before, Haz. I've met a few of them. They didn't deserve you, but it's just not computing in my head that none of them wanted to..."

"It was me. *I* didn't want to." And until recently, I was happy with my decision not to jump into bed with the men I'd dated just because it was expected. I'd wanted it to mean something. And I knew Reid hadn't shared the same sentiments about intimacy, but this was about me, not him. His past was just that. In the past.

And he'd never once pushed me during the last week to do or take part in anything I wasn't one hundred percent a willing participant in.

"You could've told me. I would have toned it down. If I made you uncomfortable, you should have sai—"

"Nothing that has happened in the last week has made me uncomfortable. At least the bad kind of uncomfortable. I feel safe with you, Reid. Scared shitless half the time, but safe. That's part of why I agreed to let you help me with this. I knew you would respect my boundaries."

He closed his eyes, shaking his head momentarily, but the pad of his thumb tenderly stroked my cheekbone.

"Please don't start treating me differently."

"Haz, I…"

"Please. This can't make things weird between us. Because I don't know what I would do without you. I spent so long running from the things you made me feel, and I decided after Halloween that I wasn't doing that anymore. I missed our friendship more than I was embarrassed, and after you helped defend me, I…"

"That was all you, kitten. I wasn't the one with the pink bat in my hands. My job was solely as moral support while you put Viv in her place."

My brother's ex had come after me at the bar's Halloween party shortly after he'd accidentally fake kidnapped my best friend. Things with Viv had gotten nasty quickly, with her accusing me of trying to bad mouth her to ruin her relationship with my brother. But she didn't need my help. She did that all on her own, I was just tired of taking her shit. When she'd tried to physically assault me during the party while she threatened me, I'd grabbed the closest thing I could reach and rammed it into her stomach.

Only I missed and she got the blunt end of a bright pink bat shoved straight into her crotch. Once she started howling and carrying on about assault, Reid had dragged her out with Mikey, the guy who worked the door at the bar.

"So maybe I should thank her for you finally talking to me again?" It felt good to hear him laugh, but the way he was tenderly stroking my cheek had my brain going fuzzy and warm.

"I don't think we should go crazy, but I'm not sad you're back in my life. Even if you push me way out of my comfort zone."

"If I'm coming on too strong, or…"

"You're perfect, Reid. Seriously. You haven't crossed any lines I wasn't inviting you to cross. But I'll understand if this changes things for you. Because—"

His fingers plunged into my hair; his face suddenly much closer than I was expecting. "Fuck that, Haz. You're the one who is perfect, and your experience or lack thereof doesn't bother me."

"Yeah, cause I'm such a fucking catch. Flighty, sarcastic, built like an adolescent, has two public personas… complete silence or never shuts up and has no social awareness. But, yeah, I'm great."

"Well, you were right about one thing…" he whispered, leaning in close to my ear. "You are pretty great."

"You have to say that," I mumbled into his cheek, wishing I saw myself the same way he saw me.

He pulled back, releasing my face, but he scooted in close, his arm draped across the back of the couch again. "And why is that?"

"Because you're Hudson's best friend. You're supposed to be protective."

He nodded, pursing his lips, but I could tell he wasn't buying into that reasoning. "You're right, I do feel protective of you. But it's not because you're Hud's little sister."

"It's not?" I asked, and he chuckled, looking amused at my reaction.

"No. It's not. It's because this is pretty much all I can focus on lately."

"I'm sorry. This project is taking up too much of your time, I…" My voice trailed off as he started shaking his head again, but it was hard to keep myself from babbling more apologies as my anxiety spiked.

"Don't even say it. You're not getting rid of me that easily," he warned, placing his hand on my thigh. He wasn't even touching my bare skin, but my pulse hammered as I tried to keep focusing on what he was saying without spacing out. "Nor do I want you to let me off the hook. In fact, I want you to sink all your hooks into me."

"Even if I have no idea what I'm doing half the time we're setting up these photoshoots?"

"Especially when you don't know what you're doing. You could have told me earlier, and I would have approached things with a little more finesse. No wonder you were so jittery the first time. You've never done that either, right?"

His smile widened, and I was glad that laid back Reid had returned. I was worried telling him all this would change how he acted around me. It had whenever I'd confessed my inexperience to past boyfriends. Most of them had run in the opposite direction and promptly lost my phone number.

"You couldn't tell?"

"Well, there was the whole attempting to suffocate me and the bruise that's just now fading, but I was chalking those up to nerves and you being a klutz, not inexperience."

"I'm not that much of a klutz."

He cocked a brow and nodded at my leg, his drawing mostly covered by my leggings, but the tip of the vine peeking out was easily visible, trailing toward my ankle.

"What was I supposed to do? You told me you were the one who left the crate there in the middle of the floor. It's not like I tripped on purpose. It wasn't supposed to be there."

My previous friendship with Reid had become strained and almost nonexistent after I'd walked in on him having sex against the storeroom wall at the bar with some random hookup a few years ago.

At first, I hadn't realized what was going on, but when she started moaning and I noticed his pants around his ankles, I'd caught on pretty quickly.

Only I'd tripped over a case of whiskey bottles while trying to get out without being noticed and ended up with a piece of glass bottle sticking out of my leg.

"I was just trying to escape before you realized I was there!" I exclaimed, narrowing my eyes at him when he started to laugh at me.

"Yeah, and apparently you got an eyeful instead."

"Well, I don't know about that. Maybe just a smidge of an eyeful. Not a full one. It was dark, and you'd already finished, so I'm sure that affects the size. Then there was the condom, so I really didn't see much..."

"Not much, huh? Is that what you think I'm packing? No wonder you haven't fallen for my charms. Maybe I shouldn't have hidden it underneath that sheet in the last photos so you could at least have an accurate depiction. I thought about asking you to video chat while we took the pictures, but someone never called me last night."

My eyes widened at the blatant flirting he'd been holding in coming back in full force. "What happened to you not wanting to make me uncomfortable?"

"Does the thought of me showing you my dick make you un-comfortable, kitten?" he asked, leaning in to whisper in my ear. "Because it makes things uncomfortable for me too, but only because thinking about your reaction is getting me hard."

"Right now?" I squeaked, looking down at his shorts.

"Does that bother you?" His voice was quiet, but I heard him despite the pounding in my ears from my racing pulse. "Because if it does, I'll stop. Do you want me to stop, Haz?"

"No," I breathed, my movements shaky as I shook my head.

"Do you like the idea of me getting hard because of you?"

A jerky nod was my only response, but Reid somehow knew I was giving him the go ahead to lead as he continued talking to me.

"Because every time I've been near you this week, this is how hard I've been." He picked up my hand, softly stroking my fingers before he placed it on the part of his anatomy we'd been talking about. My fingers twitched, and he groaned softly, leaning close to whisper in my ear. "Why don't we get the camera set up before I get too carried away?"

"This isn't getting carried away?" I asked, wrapping my hand around him. He hissed and my adrenaline soared at the thought of how much I'd affected him.

"Not yet." Gently pulling my hand free, he placed it in my lap, standing up from the couch like he hadn't just put my hand on his dick and let me feel how hard he was.

Reid tidied up the pizza, throwing away our trash before he calmly walked to where he'd dropped his camera bag. I watched as he set it up, carefully lining up the shot before he came back over to the couch and grabbed a pillow, holding out his other hand to me. "You ready?"

"No. Not really," I laughed nervously, but I took his hand and followed him to the wall in the small hallway leading to my bedroom, where he'd set everything up.

He tossed the pillow to the floor before he turned me to face him, bending his knees so he could look me in the eyes. "I'm not expecting anything from you, but I'm also not going to stop it if you decide you want to touch me. What happens next is entirely up to you. We can take the pictures, and I'll pack up and go home, but—"

"And if I want to do more?"

"Then you can see exactly how much you affect me every time we're together while I tell you how I like to be touched. But guys are easy, Haz. It doesn't take much to turn us on, and we're very visual. Any guy who is lucky enough to have your hands or lips on him won't stand a chance."

My eyes were laser focused on the pillow he'd thrown on the floor, touched he was worried about my comfort, but also wildly turned on at the thought of getting to touch him. To feel the evidence of how much he wanted me. Never in my wildest dreams did I imagine he'd return my attraction, but my fingers itched with the memory of how warm and hard he'd been beneath the soft material of his shorts.

"And you're okay if I tell you to keep your pants on the whole time? Like you won't think I'm a tease and get mad later if I…"

It'd been years, but my boyfriend in high school had broken up with me when I wouldn't do anything other than teenage over the clothes fumbling. I hadn't been ready back then, and when I'd told him, he'd bailed instead of waiting for me to be comfortable touching him.

Reid's fingers tilted my chin up, forcing me to hold his gaze as he stood to his full height, looming over me. "I will never get mad at you for taking things at your own pace, sweet girl. And I wasn't just saying it when I told you that you're in control here. You have my consent to explore however you want to, and I'll follow your lead. Just do whatever feels natural to you. I promise it'll all feel good for me."

Laughing humorlessly, I shook my head. "You're not what I expected, Mister Harding."

He grinned, leaning down to coast his lips against my cheek, his warm breath fanning across my ear. "You're not what I expected, Miss Rivera, but I have to admit I really like you showing me this side of yourself."

"The side that is an even bigger hot mess than you expected?" I laughed, the sound morphing into a gasp when his lips pressed against the skin beneath my ear, ghosting a barely there kiss and making my pulse soar.

"The side of you that is honest and feisty. I love that you're not afraid to be authentically yourself. It's sexy as fuck."

"We'll see if you're still saying that a few moments from now," I whispered, pushing against his chest and closing my eyes briefly, trying to muster the courage to kneel on the pillow at his feet. "Because I am authentically a disaster."

Reid's intimidating gaze was focused on me as I settled into place and then looked up toward him. My heart skipped as he took a few steps forward, bracing his palms on the wall far above my head, essentially trapping me there with his hips directly in front of my face.

I should have been terrified, feeling completely out of my element and self-conscious, but I wasn't.

The look in his eyes made me feel empowered and sexy. With this man looming over me completely at my mercy despite our positions. He'd turned over the control to me, and that was what had me pulling him closer, my fingers skating along the hem of his shirt and lifting it, a clear demand to remove it.

As his toned chest was revealed inch by tantalizing inch, I tried to focus and zeroed in on the waistband of his shorts, playfully slipping a finger underneath the elastic and tugging on it.

"If you want them off, take them off," Reid whispered. I gulped, slipping my thumbs beneath the material, his warm skin sending a rush through me as I started shifting his waistband lower. Looking up at him, I tried to figure out what to do next.

Absently, I could hear the click of the camera a few feet away every so often, Reid doing a much better job of documenting this scene than I'd done with the others, but I wasn't in position to capture what I needed for my reference photos just yet, and he knew it.

Reid was capturing these pictures so he could look at them later. And the thought of him stroking himself to the memory of me on my knees for him had me leaning in, grasping the back of his knees and ghosting my face along the outline of what he'd put my hand on earlier.

"Did you just nuzzle my dick?" Reid chuckled, his body vibrating as I watched his cock flex beneath the material of his briefs.

But he'd told me I was in charge, and that he'd let me lead. It wasn't time for him to distract me. Looking up, I pinned him down with an unimpressed look. "What happened to me being in charge here? If you don't like what I do, then I'll stop right now."

His mouth dropped open, but he didn't laugh again before he spoke. "I'm not sure how to deal with this mouthy version of you."

"Well, then I guess it's a good thing you're keeping all your clothes on tonight. Then you won't have to live through the torture of my mouth on you."

His earlier shock turned into a naughty grin, his eyes flashing dangerously as he leaned forward, bracing his forearms against the wall and growling while he looked down at me. "Fuck, feisty Hazel is a little bossy, and I'm here for it."

"Are you going to keep talking or are we going to take a picture of me fake blowing you?"

He couldn't hold in the laughter, his body shaking inches from my face. "Sorry, kitten. Shutting up. Do your worst."

"We both know I don't settle for mediocrity," I teased, holding his gaze as I tipped my head back.

"What has gotten into you? Maybe I should feed you sausage more often."

"Do you not like it?" Suddenly I was afraid that I was ruining the moment by not taking this more seriously. Bantering with Reid was instinct for me, but if it was killing the vibe, I could try to keep my mouth shut.

He shook his head slowly, a mischievous grin drawing across his lips. "No, I fucking love it."

Nodding, I took a deep breath and mustered my earlier courage. "Good. Then keep your mouth shut. I need you to behave like the good boy I know you're not and quit distracting me from pulling off your shorts."

Reid just watched as I tugged the material lower, leaving it pooled at his ankles while I appraised the package in front of me. There was something familiar about the waistband of the boxer briefs suddenly inches from my face. But when I grazed my fingertip down the hard ridge inside them, Reid's answering groan was enough to distract me from any thoughts about his underwear purchasing habits.

Chapter Eighteen

Reid

T HERE WERE ONLY TWO options to describe what was happening. I was going to hell for corrupting my best friend's little sister. Or she was about to put me through hell. Either way, I was fucked because the sight of Hazel Rivera on her knees for me was about to be my undoing.

All she'd done was graze her nose along my shorts and run a finger down my length, and I was hard as fuck. You'd have thought I was a teenage boy with a girl touching his dick for the first time with how I was responding to her curious exploration.

It was intoxicating, trying to remain still while her gentle hands traced my thighs, when her fingers experimentally ventured between my legs, playfully cupping my balls as I tracked her every move with rapt attention.

Maybe there was something to slowing things down and exploring each other. Usually, my encounters were over as quickly as they began. Fast and hot, both of us parting ways after an exchange of orgasms without much fuss. It was just as much about the women getting what they wanted from me as it was about me getting off.

But as Hazel's explorations progressively became more brazen—her bolder touches leaving my cock pulsing as she caressed it through the thin material—I was too caught up in what she was doing to me to want to rush things.

It'd be fucking torture, but she could play with me all she wanted. Despite her admitted inexperience, she seemed to instinctively know exactly how to touch me, an obnoxiously loud groan escaping my mouth as she finally wrapped her hand around my length, gripping hard and experimentally pulling upward.

"Fuck, kitten. Keep going," I begged, my arms shaking as I looked down at her.

This didn't feel like her using me to satisfy her curiosity. This felt like her wanting me, every movement of her hands showing me exactly how much she wanted to bring me pleasure.

"Look at me," I gasped, flexing my hips as she leaned in and nuzzled my erection again.

Her eyes flashed to mine, filled with heat as she gripped me harder, drawing her hand upward while she kept eye contact and then leaned in to playfully bite the end of my dick. I groaned when her teeth grazed the ring at the tip and she gasped, moving her thumb to explore what she'd just accidentally discovered.

"You've got…" she breathed, her chest heaving. I watched the flush on her breasts spread enticingly up her neck as she realized my dick was pierced.

"Don't stop," I moaned, closing my eyes briefly and trying to focus on not finishing too early as she pressed harder, her thumb rubbing maddeningly against the ridge below the tip and then harder against the ring that protruded from the end of my cock.

"How did I not know you had a cock piercing?" Her voice was a nervous whisper. But it didn't stop her from looking up at me as she leaned in, using her teeth to grab a hold of the little ball at the end, watching to see what I'd do when she tugged on it.

"Not exactly something I should be sharing with my buddy's innocent little sister, Haz," I rasped out, groaning again as she leaned in, sucking the tip of my dick through the material of my boxers, her tongue playing with the ring running through it while she firmly gripped the rest of me in her palm.

"Don't talk about my brother when I've got your dick in my mouth," she growled, stroking her hand roughly against me, my brain going fuzzy from the pleasure. For a virgin who'd never seen a dick in real life, she was doing a really fucking good job of knowing what to do with mine.

"I'm sorry," I groaned, whimpering when she moved closer, flattening her tongue against the material covering me and tracing it firmly against the outline of my cock. It pulsed against her, and she grinned when it flexed, a bead of precum seeping through the material. Her eyes lit up at the sight, clearly realizing the wetness wasn't only from her mouth.

"You like this?" she asked before she did it again, following the movement with a rough stroke of her fist, squeezing when she reached the tip and rubbing her thumb across the ring again and again until I was panting and trying to hold off from embarrassing myself.

"Yes, *fuck*. If you keep doing that, I'm going to come."

"Good," she whispered, leaning in to suck me through the material as she repeated her actions, my balls aching as I tried to fight off the urge to finish too quickly with the movements of her hands and her fucking sinful mouth.

If I didn't know any better, looking down at her you'd think she had my cock down her throat with the motions of her head, and I pressed the button in my hand frantically, hoping I was capturing the images she needed for this commission before I accidentally destroyed the remote.

"Shit. I...I can't..." I panted as she roughly stroked, her tongue playing relentlessly with my piercing, while she drove me closer and closer to the edge. "Fuck. I'm gonna come. Haz, I..."

She didn't stop. Didn't let up as she continued what she was doing, making my entire body tense before she looked up at me, watching me fall apart as my cock spurted, cum seeping through the thin material, drawing her attention as my warm release trailed down the back of her fingers.

Holding my gaze, she leaned in, darting her tongue out and tasting me, her eyes closing before she swallowed hard, shuddering.

"Fuck," I growled, flexing my fists against the wall as I tried to tamp down the urge to haul her against me and kiss her hard.

Her chest heaved as she stared up at me, hand covered in the evidence of my desire for her, the taste of it on her tongue. My self-control was stretched thin as I watched her, eyes bright and a slow smile spreading across her lips when she realized she'd literally just tilted my fucking world on its axis. And it had me imagining her in this position with all our clothes out of the way, my cum dripping down her pink cheek.

"You liked that," she whispered, a naughty glint in her eyes.

Unable to help myself, I pushed off the wall, pulling up my shorts before I dropped to my knees, grabbing my discarded shirt from the floor and using it to wipe her fingers. She watched me while I cleaned her up, nibbling on her lower lip. Once I was done, I looked at her, realizing she needed self-assurance right now, not some animal desperate to fuck her.

"Yes, kitten. I fucking loved that."

She nodded, shifting to the side to sit down on the floor before she pulled the pillow into her lap, hugging it. But I didn't want her to seek comfort from a pillow, I wanted her to seek it from me. Tugging it from her grasp, I flipped it backward onto the couch behind me, reaching forward to haul her into my lap. Turning her with her back against my chest, I nuzzled her neck, breathing her in while my frantic heartbeat settled.

"And it was—" I covered her mouth with my palm, leaning in to whisper in her ear.

"Yes, whatever you were going to ask, the answer is yes. You fucking rocked my world. I haven't come in my pants since I was a teenager, and you had me so desperate I couldn't even last a few minutes. So yes, Hazel, it was fucking okay."

She nodded, leaning the side of her head against my bicep and wrapping my arms around her while she relaxed into my hold. Her hips squirmed against me, and I pulled her in tighter, nipping at her throat as I pressed my hips into her from below. It'd take me a few minutes to recover, so I wasn't hard, but it felt good to have her in my lap like this. Like she belonged there.

"Come here," I whispered, grasping her waist and urging her to turn around. Once she was settled facing me, I gripped her waist, pulling her in snug, and rubbing my hands along her back. She shuddered as I teased my fingertips at her waist, dipping underneath the hem of her tank top and teasing the bare skin above the waistband of her leggings.

Her eyes drifted closed as I touched her, my fingers trailing higher up her bare back, groaning when I realized she wasn't wearing a bra. My fingertips lingered where the band would be, and she tucked her face into my neck, her soft breaths turning into whimpers that had me desperate to strip her down and explore every inch of her soft skin with my tongue.

"Making you come made me wet," she exhaled, her hips pressing down against me. "I didn't know it'd make me feel like this."

"Like what?" I asked, my fingers creeping along her side, my thumb tracing the soft skin along the side of her breast. She shuddered and leaned in further, running her nose along my throat as her thighs squeezed the outside of mine. Taking her silence as a cue she didn't want to talk about it, I was surprised, and really fucking turned on when she whispered one word into my skin.

"Desperate."

After her confession, it was like a dam broke, my hands frantically pulling out of her shirt and grabbing her ass, pushing my hips up into her as she clawed at my chest, rocking against me.

My teeth dug into the skin on her shoulder, nipping at her as she worked herself into a frenzy, rocking against my hardening cock like her sanity depended on it. I was trying desperately to let her lead, to take what she needed from me without letting things go too far, but when she whimpered in frustration, I knew I needed to take control.

"I need to make you come right now, kitten," I groaned, holding her hands against my chest and tipping my head so I could see her face. Her eyes were frantic, her chest heaving as she nodded, licking her lips. "If I go too far, tell me to stop."

"Okay," she breathed, nodding in confirmation. I guided her up to her knees, pressing a hand between us. The material of her leggings was soft beneath my fingertips, not doing much to disguise how turned on she was when the material effortlessly slipped against her pussy underneath. But there were too many layers.

"Can I take these off?" My voice was a whisper, but she shook her head, practically vibrating in my lap. "That's okay, I can still make you feel good with them on, scoot for—"

"Rip them," she breathed, pressing my hand harder against her and whimpering when I crooked my fingers and grazed my fingertips against her clit.

"You sure?"

Another frantic nod had me settling her against my knees, my fingers grasping the soft material covering her with both hands and pulling until the stitches gave way with a ripping sound. She moaned as I pulled the hole wider, rubbing my thumbs against the wet panel of her light purple panties. For a virgin, Hazel had some seriously sexy underwear.

"Touch me," she whimpered, leaning back, but I hauled her forward, banding an arm around her back as she straddled my waist. The fingers on my other hand delved into the ruined material of her leggings, teasing the damp panel of fabric, my cock springing to life beneath her legs when she rocked into my movements, chasing her own pleasure in a way that made my blood soar.

"Fuck, you're so goddamn sexy," I groaned, my fingers slipping against the slick material barely concealing her wet pussy, desperate to be inside of her. But I didn't want to do something she'd regret later. Until she explicitly told me to fuck her with my fingers, I wouldn't go there. No matter how desperate I was to feel her clenching around them—and my cock that had turned to steel inside my shorts.

"Oh, god, Reid, yes," she gasped, arching backward, and I tucked my face into her chest, nipping at the exposed skin on her neck, dragging my lips down the column of her throat, and using my teeth to tug on her nipples through the thin material of her tank top while my thumb continued to rub her covered clit.

Hazel was frantic as she chased her release, instinctively grinding against my fingers with the same rhythm I was desperate for her to ride my cock. Having her like this felt natural, like she was meant to be in my arms, chasing her pleasure at my hands. And the thought of not being with her like this was a cold shock to my system as her body grew taut, and then snapped, her moans filling the air as she melted into my chest, trembling with her release.

"Just breathe," I whispered into her hair, combing my fingers down the length, my nose buried into her soft locks, inhaling the sweet honeysuckle scent of it while she came back down to earth. "Breathe. I've got you."

But I wasn't sure for how long. This could be the last time she let me touch her. She could raise her head and shatter my heart by telling me this was a mistake. By using this as a reason to push me away.

And then she'd torture me by seeking comfort in Seven. Her mysterious boyfriend who didn't even feel like me. I typed the words on the screen to her every night, but it was like she'd unlocked this part of me I'd forgotten for so long. The person who wanted to love someone and be loved. Who couldn't wait to hear from the woman he was obsessed with.

Seven was someone who could break if she rejected him. But I found that so was I. If Hazel decided she didn't want me, or that my betrayal had gone too far, then I'd lose her forever, and the mere idea of that happening had me hugging her tighter to my chest, not wanting to let her out of my sight until I could convince her I was the man she needed. Both sides of me.

I wasn't sure how long we sat there; her curled into my chest, delicate fingers idly playing with the barbell through my nipple and me memorizing the texture of her hair with my fingertips. But eventually her breaths evened out, her body becoming heavy as she fell asleep in my arms. She worked so hard, and clearly the tension of the last week was getting to her.

And that was my cue to let her get some rest.

Gathering her into my arms, I stood carefully, cradling her body against my chest. She stirred as I carried her down the hallway, mumbling into my neck, but she was asleep again as I pulled back her covers and laid her on the bed. She curled on her side as I tried to smooth out her chaotic pink sheets, sighing as I tucked her blankets around her shoulders.

Laying a whisper of a kiss against her temple, I returned to the living room.

Erasing the evidence of our evening, I packed up the extra pizza and put it in her refrigerator. Resisting the urge to look at the pictures was torture, my camera roughly shoved into the bag before I collapsed the tripod. Her apartment was quiet as I gathered the empty pizza box and my equipment, using the spare keys to lock her door as I left.

It felt wrong to leave her like this, sneaking off in the middle of the night without a word, but I wasn't sure what the next step with her was. How to move forward from here. Just like the events of the evening, everything was up to her. I was leaving the ball in her court, my heart in her hands, whatever cliché you could think of—the power was all in her tiny, talented fingertips.

As I braced myself to step out into the dark parking lot that separated my shop from the bar, I cast one last longing look toward her door, hoping the light of day wouldn't ruin things between us.

Chapter Nineteen

S TRETCHING, I GROANED, REACHING for the pillow I normally slept curled against, but my hands came up empty. And it was quiet—too quiet—as the sound machine next to my bed was silent and not playing the white noise I used to drown out my thoughts at night so I could actually sleep.

Normally, when I woke up and my sleep ritual hadn't been followed, it was because I fell asleep on the couch, but I was tucked under the covers that'd been half dumped on the floor yesterday wearing the casual clothes I'd put on after my shift last night.

Blinking again, I tried to remember how I'd gotten in the bed. The last thing I remembered was clinging to Reid on the floor in my hallway after we—*Oh fuck.*

I sort of, kind of, pretty much gave Reid a blow job last night in my hallway and didn't even get to see the package hidden beneath his boxer briefs.

As the reel of what went down—spoiler alert: it was me, I was what went down—in my hallway ran through my now wide-awake brain, my face flamed as I recalled how powerful I'd felt with Reid looming over me. The way he'd looked at me through half-lidded eyes, his forearms flexed as I explored. The rough exclamations that'd escaped his lips and the way his eyelashes fluttered as I tugged on what had felt like a ring piercing through the head of his dick.

Maybe I'd been doing my research into dick illustration all wrong. Because of all the kinds of cocks I'd drawn over the last few months, I had yet to detail any with a piercing. And if there was anything I'd learned during the last week, and this create your own commission reference photos project, it was that seeing things firsthand and knowing exactly how the body parts were positioned made it infinitely easier to complete my drawings.

But there was no way that Reid would agree to let me sketch his dick. We'd done a lot of things that skirted a very fine boundary line this week, but seeing him completely naked—whether in a photo or in person—erased that line completely. And while I was wildly attracted to my brother's dangerously tempting best friend, I wasn't sure if I was prepared to handle him. Or his pierced peen.

That I was now going to obsess about, because honestly, even through a layer of very thin material, the rumors about Reid were not fabricated. At all. And I honestly didn't give a fuck about his slutty ways because he felt like a different person lately, specifically the last week. Not that he was truly interested in taking things further with me. And I wasn't sure if I was ready to risk my heart on the chance that he was.

No matter how much he invaded all my waking moments.

Seven: You didn't say goodnight.

And that was another reason I couldn't get too invested in Reid. I was already invested in something—someone—else.

Fourteen: Was working last night and lost track of time. Then I fell asleep without my phone.

Guilt crept through me with each word that I typed out, but it wasn't exactly like I could tell him I'd been too busy fake blowing, and then sort of really blowing, my brother's best friend. Which brought out what I needed to do. I needed to erect some boundaries between Reid and myself, even though his erection seemed to want to cross every one of my boundaries last night.

My face flushed at the thought of the feral look in his eyes when he ripped open my leggings last night. I know I'd told him to do it, but it was epically hot.

Seven: What are you up to today?

Having a breakdown at the thought of talking to my brother's best friend, knowing what happened last night crossed too many boundaries.

My mother had been right when I was in high school, nothing good happens after midnight and the only things open *were* legs and the emergency room. Although as I recalled the way Reid had been looking at me, his hand doing maddening things through the now ruined material of my panties, I knew something very, *very* good had happened late last night.

I just wasn't sure what to do about it.

> *Fourteen: Sketching, still have 4-5 projects on my waiting list and I want to get them off my plate before Valentine's Day.*

> *Seven: Ambitious when you only have a few days left.*

> *Fourteen: I'll just trick myself into thinking something bad will happen if I don't finish them. I work best under tight deadlines.*

It wouldn't be the first time I'd tried to hack my ridiculous brain when I wanted to switch hyper focus onto something. I was a pro at lying to myself.

> *Seven: Got a hot date coming up or something?*

> *Fourteen: Or something. How about you?*

> *Seven: I hope I have a hot date for Valentine's Day. I might have to cry into my beer if she stands me up.*

He might have been joking, but I *had* considered calling the whole thing off. Between my budding feelings for Seven, along with my explosive and startling chemistry with Reid, I was having the sudden urge to escape from reality and hide under my covers until they both lost interest.

It's not like that wouldn't be the result eventually, anyway. Reid would lose interest as soon as feelings were involved, because he always did. I'd seen it enough times to know exactly how things would go with him.

And with Seven, I knew I'd never keep his interest when things weren't hidden under the veil of anonymity. He was obnoxiously charming through the barrier and, expecting him to be any less so in person, would be delusional. And once he realized I was more of a homebody than someone more exciting, he'd lose interest and walk away.

So maybe it *was* in my best interest to just let things fade away. Because taking a chance on either of them was setting myself up for heartbreak.

> Seven: Your silence isn't exactly reassuring. What's going on, sweet girl? Anything I can help with?

My heart lurched at the term of endearment that Reid had used last night. Another reminder that both only saw me in a way that was what I'd wanted to break away from. I didn't want to be the sweet, unassuming person I'd always been, and the last week I'd finally felt like maybe I could be different, but reality was bound to bring me back to earth, eventually. It always did.

> Fourteen: I'm sorry I'm not much fun today.

> Seven: Don't you ever apologize for being yourself.

> Fourteen: I've spent my entire life doing it. Why stop now?

He didn't respond the entire time I tried to convince myself that the sense of dread I felt in the shower was all in my head.

And he didn't respond as I spent the morning sketching the scene last night that had launched me into this spiral and sent it off to the author for approval before I started the color.

He also didn't respond when I headed down to the bar for my shift, ignoring the giant ball of nerves that had lodged itself in my gut at the thought of facing Reid after what we'd done.

But just like Seven didn't respond to my text message, Reid never showed up at the bar during my shift.

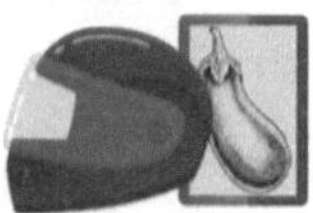

T HE NEXT MORNING, AS the guilt continued to build, I headed over to the tattoo shop at midday so I could get this over with before my shift tonight. It would only fester the longer I let it eat at me. And it was time to cut off the limb. Even if the limb was long, and deliciously hard, and I was dying to see exactly what the piercing on this limb looked like.

But I would be strong. I *had* to be strong and resist him, because if I didn't, my brother's charming best friend would steal my heart. And I was terrified if I let him take it, that it'd be his forever—long after he decided I wasn't as fun and bright and shiny as he made me feel.

"Haz?" I'd hoped to sneak in and get to Reid's office unnoticed, but of course, that was a stupid idea when there was a reception area in the front of the building I'd have to walk through to get there. Because while I knew my brother had a key to the back door, I wasn't explaining to him why I needed it.

"Hey, Gray. How's it going?"

Gray had been one of the first body piercers Reid had hired after opening, and much like Reid, for a guy who did piercings, he didn't have that many. Only a few plugs in his earlobes and a nose ring. Although he could hide them like Reid did, but I had zero desire to see him with his shirt or pants off. Gray had also been apprenticing with Reid to learn how to tattoo, but other than his professional relationship with Reid, I didn't know much about him.

Although, I wondered if he was the one who'd pierced Reid's dick. And how exactly did the process of getting one's dick pierced go? When had he done it? How much did it hurt? Did he have to abstain from dicking down entire sororities when he had it done?

But all those thoughts had my next question going to a dangerous place. Like, how did it feel moving inside you?

"You coming to see me today, gorgeous?" Gray's flirtatious voice drew me out of my musings, but I knew he was like that with everyone. I was glad Reid had hidden me after our first photoshoot because I knew my face would resemble even more of a tomato if I had to face Gray knowing he'd caught me humping his boss' face in that room down the hall.

"Does Reid have any openings in his schedule today?"

Gray's eyes flickered down the length of me, slowly appraising the dark wash jeans and loose off the shoulder sweater I'd thrown on after spending too much time deciding what to wear this morning.

What *did* you wear to break up with your brother's best friend who you weren't really dating? Could what happened over the last week be considered a situationship? And had making him come short circuited something in my brain?

Gray returned his gaze to my face, smiling. "He's wrapping up a piece now, and then he's got an hour or so before his next appointment. I'm sure he'll be happy to see your pretty face to break up the monotony. We've been slammed lately."

I wasn't so sure what Reid would be to see my face. Because I was probably making a much bigger deal out of this whole situation than I needed to. He wouldn't care that I was calling things off because we'd just gotten caught up in the moment.

His words from earlier had been running through my head. This project was all he could think about lately. I was becoming a distraction for him, and he'd probably be relieved for me to let him off the hook.

Being intimate with someone like I'd been with him this week—even though it wasn't anything particularly racy—wasn't new to him like it was to me. He didn't have the emotional connection to being vulnerable with another person that I did. Once this was over, he wouldn't obsess about it like I would. This wouldn't change the way he looked at me for the rest of his life. He probably wouldn't even look back on this whole situation with any strong feelings one way or the other. And I knew I would.

He'd ruined me in a few short days, and he didn't even realize it. Which was why it had to stop. Before my heart got more attached to a man I could never keep.

And when I walked around the corner, peeking into the room that I knew he worked in, I stopped in my tracks at the scene in front of me, and I knew what I had to do.

Chapter Twenty

Reid

THERE WAS A CERTAIN element to my job that I had once loved, but now dreaded.

As the woman stretched out across the chair next to me batted her long, fake eyelashes at me, I wasn't the least bit tempted to see what she looked like moaning out my name while those lashes fluttered. Honestly, I'd be content if she just stopped talking altogether. She was pouring on the charm thickly, complimenting how gentle I was with my hands, telling me I had pretty eyes for such a big, powerful man.

In my experience, there were only a few ways people reacted during a session. This woman was one of the nervous ramblers who would not stop talking—or, in her case, relentlessly flirting—the entire session because the adrenaline and endorphins turned them into motormouths. My favorite were the ones who came in nervous but then promptly fell asleep as soon as the initial rush wore off.

Then there was a special third type that turned the stress hormone rush into another kind of hormone rush and wanted to fuck me after we were done. Those were the ones I was most dreading because I didn't want to be that guy anymore. Unless I happened to be tattooing a certain feisty redhead that I couldn't keep from invading my every waking thought.

"Now that you're almost done, I was wondering if..." the woman in the chair's voice had suddenly dropped lower as I finished up the last few details on her piece, wiping away the excess ink and setting my equipment on the nearby cart.

"Oh, don't worry," I cut her off, knowing exactly where this conversation was going. "I'll send home a sheet of care instructions and some healing balm for you to use. As long as you keep it clean and dry so it can heal, you don't need to worry about coming back in here again."

"That's so kind of you," she cooed, placing her hand on my arm again and brushing her thumb across the edge of my wrist. And instead of my brain deciding it was horny and things perking up inside my jeans, I felt nothing. Not a damn fucking thing. "But I was hoping…"

A flash of movement outside the door to my private room had the hairs on the back of my neck standing up, and my eyes kept flitting between where my hands were smoothing the bandage over the fresh ink on this woman's hip and trying to figure out who was out there.

The door was cracked open since we weren't super busy this afternoon, but I also liked to leave the door partially open when I had women clients, so they didn't feel trapped in a small room with a strange man.

"I'm booked out several months in advance right now, but if you had any other pieces in mind, Gray would be happy to get you settled out front. I usually recommend waiting at least two months so this one can have a chance to fully heal before you get another one."

Her lips pursed and settled into a pout, which for a woman in her late thirties was not exactly a good look. Not that I had a thing against older women, but typically they were a little more mature than resorting to pouting when it was clear they were getting shot down.

"Oh, I definitely will," she replied, reaching out to press her hand against my chest as I cupped her elbow and helped her sit upright. "I really liked the feel of your hands on me."

Sometimes being in one position for a few hours and the letdown of happy chemicals tattoos usually sent roaring through your veins, made people a little unsteady, but as her hand crept up my shirt and settled on the side of my neck, it was clear she wasn't trying to steady herself.

Gently prying her fingers away from my skin, I squeezed her hand and gently settled it back on her leg.

"If my schedule is too full to fit you in, I also have several other artists on staff who are just as talented, if not more so than I am. Gray can set you up with an appointment if you feel like their style fits what you need better. We each have a portfolio available at the desk for clients to look at."

She grinned, biting her lip, but it only smeared her bright pink lipstick across the bottom of her teeth. Objectively, she was an attractive woman, and under other circumstances, I would have been encouraging her advances, but I didn't want that anymore.

"I appreciate that, Reid. But I have very specific tastes, and you fit them very, very well. I'm more than happy to wait for you. I enjoy the prolonged satisfaction of having to wait to get what I want."

Taking a deep breath, I stepped back, busying myself with getting my equipment sorted and disassembled so I could get it sanitized before my next client. I was hoping I could spend my hour break hunting down the woman who'd been on my mind all last night while I tried to get the payroll under control so I could be free for the weekend after Valentine's.

"That works. Like I said, Gray can get you booked when you check out. But you shouldn't need to see me again until our next consult as long as you follow your care instructions."

When I turned back around, her clothing was re-situated, and she was zipping up her coat...with her eyes focused squarely on my ass. I wanted to be flattered, I really did, but it also had me questioning all my life choices over the last decade. I'd created this impression of myself for the world, and unfortunately, I was now having to deal with the consequences.

"It's been a pleasure, Mr. *Hard*ing," she purred, standing in front of me and pressing a piece of paper into my palm. I clenched it into my fist as I watched her leave through the partially open door, stopping short when she saw the woman leaning against the opposite wall before she turned and headed toward the reception area.

Hazel's expressive eyes flashed to mine, her cheeks turning an enticing shade of pink as we stared at each other, but when her lip quivered and she looked away, I knew she'd been standing there long enough to hear what was going on with my flirty client. *Fuck.*

Pulling off the apron I wore when I worked, I tossed it toward the chair, dropping the crumpled paper in my wastebasket as I headed in the only direction my heart wanted to go right now. When I reached the doorway, I noticed how tightly Hazel's fingers were clenched in the material of her coat and knew I needed to do some damage control.

"Hey, kitten. Why didn't you tell me you'd be coming over? Got another project for us to work on?"

She shook her head, stepping away when I held my hand out toward her.

"No. No more projects."

Frowning, I stepped forward again, grasping her fingers and trying to tug her inside my room. "Let's talk."

"Not in there," she whispered, pulling free and balling her hands into fists.

"The new couch in my office hasn't been unwrapped yet, but if you don't mind waiting a few minutes, I can get all the plastic wrap off. They just delivered it this morning."

"Can we…" she trailed off, clearing her throat. "Can we go sit in the break room or something? I can't say this in your office."

Frowning, I watched her expressions shift from anxious to disappointment to sadness and I wasn't sure why the happy sarcastic girl she'd been around me for the last week was suddenly absent. She'd seen women hit on me before, and if she'd been out in the hallway long enough, she'd surely have heard that I wasn't encouraging it and kept things strictly professional.

Not that I needed to explain myself to her, but I wanted to.

"Or I can just go home, but…" she sniffed and reached up to wipe the corner of her eye.

Deciding I couldn't just stand here and watch her try to hold back her emotions, I stepped forward and grabbed her hand, guiding her down the hallway to the break room and ushering her inside. After flicking on the light, I locked the door behind me just in case we were interrupted, but since Gray and Priscilla were the only ones in the building, and I knew they both had appointments, it shouldn't be a problem.

"What's going on, Haz?" I asked, pulling her into my chest and wrapping my arms around her. The top of her head fit neatly underneath my chin, and I turned my face, resting my cheek on the top of her head. But my heart sank when she didn't hug me back, her body tensing after a few moments in my embrace.

When I reluctantly released her, she took a step away, casting a nervous glance at the futon and then back at me, before she took a purposeful step toward the small table at the side of the room.

"We need to talk."

Famous last words. Hearing a woman say that to you was never a good thing. It either meant she was about to break things off, or she thought she might be pregnant. And unless someone could magically get pregnant while not having sex, Hazel was about to tell me something I didn't want to hear.

Joining her across the table, I tried to gauge her mood, but the vulnerability she'd been displaying before we came in here was gone. It was replaced with determination. And I hated that my girl had decided to use her newfound confidence on something I would not like.

"The floor is yours. What's up?"

Her jaw clenched, and I fought the urge to reach out and rub the tension out of her hands that were balled in her lap so tightly her knuckles were white.

"I don't think I can keep doing this," she whispered, looking away from me. "If things go how I'd like them to, then I might be dating someone for real after the party. The lines between us have gotten so blurred that it feels like I'm cheating on him."

Oh, sweet girl. It made my guilt flare, feeling like I'd let things get too far with Seven and my feelings getting mixed up and confusing both of us. I opened my mouth to confess what I'd done when I saw how conflicted she was, but that wasn't what came out.

"Then I guess we've got the next few days to set up pictures for every commission you have on your waiting list."

She shook her head, still not looking at me. "Reid, seriously. That's too much. I can't ask you to do that."

"You're not asking. And I'm not taking no for an answer. You'd better figure out a schedule and a shot list, because we don't have a lot of time. I can move around clients if you need me to. Just tell me when you need me, and I'll make it happen."

"Okay, I haven't wanted to bring it up before now," she stuttered nervously, flexing her fingers under the table. I hated I knew all her tells; she was really freaking herself out about this situation I'd put her in. "Because I don't want to make things weird, but I feel like I should pay you for all the help you've given me."

I was the one who'd made things weird between us by not being honest, but this was enough.

"Haz, no. You don't need to pay me, I volunteered. And considering some things that have happened, I am not taking a dime from you."

"But I've been able to get the illustrations done so much faster since I'm not wasting time looking for source images—"

"Porn. Just say you're looking at porn, Haz," I tried to joke, and I got a smile out of it, but she still wasn't cracking.

"It's not *all* porn."

"I didn't say looking at porn was bad. I'm kind of curious what other things you've watched for *research*." And I wanted to watch them with her, preferably with no clothing on and in my bed.

"Focus, Reid. Please don't change the subject to distract me. How does ten percent of what I've made so far sound?"

"Sounds pretty terrible," I replied, crossing my arms over my chest. There was no way I was taking anything from her. She'd earned that money with her own talents; I was just her live action doll to move how she wanted. Only she'd discovered I wasn't smooth down there like a Ken doll.

"Okay...I can do more. But ten percent of the one with your bike was $80, so..." she trailed off and I was a bit flabbergasted once I did the mental math on that equation.

"You got paid $800 to draw an illustration of people fucking?"

This girl—this woman I was quickly becoming obsessed with—still continued to surprise me. I was fucking proud of her for charging what she was worth. That was a hard lesson to learn for most people who worked in creative fields. I know it'd taken me a long time to charge clients what I knew my time and talents were worth.

"Well, they weren't technically fucking yet in that one, but..." she trailed off, trying to fight off a smile as her eyes met mine, but then her expression suddenly hardened again.

"Haz," I tried to interject, but she held up her hand.

"They're custom, fully rendered illustrations, not coloring pages you break out the Crayolas for. And people pay you hundreds of dollars to draw on their skin with a needle. Why wouldn't I get paid that much? Do you think I'm charging too much? Because I—"

But it was just the opposite. I didn't think she was charging too much; I was impressed she knew how to leverage her talents to make exactly what she deserved.

"No, Haz. I admire the fuck out of your work ethic. You're doing exactly what you should be doing. This is why I offered to help you, because I could see how much you want this."

"I do," she whispered. "But I..." There was that damn lip quiver again and my heart broke at the thought I caused this. "It's not that I don't appreciate your help, but I'm taking up a lot of your time, and I know things have gotten a bit complicated the more time we spend together."

"Nothing we have done is complicated, Haz. And don't you, for one fucking second, think that I am not exactly where I want to be when I spend time with you—"

She sniffed again, wiping at her cheek. My throat felt tight as a tear slipped free. Balling my hands into my lap, I resisted reaching out to haul her into my lap and kiss away those tears. When Charley had begged me to be bachelor number Seven, I never expected things between us getting this twisted up.

"But I can't spend more time with you," she whispered, her voice cracking. "It's too hard. And I might be falling for the guy from the experiment, and I can't risk that for someone I know will break my heart when he gets bored with me."

Talk about a fucking knee to the balls. She didn't even hesitate to confess she thought I'd break her heart. Not that she was afraid of me hurting her—which I hadn't set out to do—but that she knew I *would* break her heart. Like it was a foregone conclusion for me to do it.

"Is that how you really feel about me? That it's inevitable I break your heart if things were to go further between us?"

She nodded, and I took in a sharp breath, wondering why I even fucking bothered. Because now I had a pretty good fucking idea how the reveal would go in a few days. She would find out Seven was me, and she'd shut me out like she was shutting me out now.

"I'm sorry. But I can't let myself fall further into this fantasy that you might actually want me like I..."

She stood from the table and my hand shot out, instinctually grasping her wrist. "Sometimes how people really feel might surprise you."

"And sometimes it's not worth the risk," she whispered, turning her wrist to pull free, and I immediately released her, not wanting to force her to be here if she didn't want to be.

Leaning forward, I dropped my head into my hands, realizing how epically I'd managed to fuck things up in a week and a half. If I could rewind time, I'd...

Fuck that.

If I could rewind time, I'd have followed her into that bathroom before the fucking experiment even started and shoved that chewed up pencil into her hand and told her she *could* keep the penis. And the man attached to it, because I didn't like the idea of her risking her heart on a stranger, even if I *was* the stranger on the other side of the wall.

Chapter Twenty-One

Hazel

The look in Reid's eyes when I'd confessed I thought he would break my heart did the breaking even before he had the chance to. I could tell I'd hurt him, and that was never my intention when I went over there. But it hurt too much to let things keep building like they had been.

Especially after witnessing that client—who was ten times more attractive and probably a billion times more experienced than I was—shamelessly hitting on him after he was done working on her tattoo. And that was his reality. He was a handsome man who had women throwing themselves at him, and he didn't need me doing the same thing.

Because they all ended up a fleeting memory to him, and I wasn't sure I could sacrifice our already fragile friendship to know what it felt like to be with him. I couldn't risk the chance of losing him for good. It was hard enough to know what he was like behind the mask he put on for others.

But I couldn't take back what I'd said to him, because I knew things had already gone too far for me to keep my heart safe. It hurt to walk away from the possibility of more.

As I walked across the cold parking lot, I mustered up what was left of my courage and sent the text I'd been plotting in my head since last night.

> *Fourteen: If you don't want to talk to me, please just tell me. I'm spiraling a bit today and I'm not sure if I should read into you not responding to my last text. And while you claimed you'd be*

Three dots danced across the screen, and my heart pounded as I punched in the code on the lock to the back door. Too busy staring at my phone, I wasn't paying attention to where I was going and almost dropped it when I crashed into someone turning the corner toward the back staircase.

"You okay, Haz?" My best friend's voice was concerned as she steadied me with her hands on my arms. I was sure my face was splotchy from my confrontation with Reid, but at least I'd managed not to completely break down in front of him.

"I'm fine," I muttered, looking away from her scrutinizing gaze. She was lucky, her face didn't give away all her emotions like mine did. And I was sure she wouldn't be freaking out if she was in my position, almost paralyzed by two men showing an interest in her. If she wasn't so obsessed with my brother, she would eat up the attention with a spoon.

"No, you're not." She cupped my elbow and steered me toward the staircase, following me to the top and closing the door to what used to be her apartment, too. I'd been so out of it last night and this morning and hadn't cleaned up the rest of the aftermath of what had happened with Reid.

Not that there was much, just a pile of pillows on the floor next to the couch in disarray. Staring hard at them, I wondered which was the one I'd been kneeling on.

"Why are you looking at your pillows like they've offended you? I thought you loved those things."

Turning away from Charley, I tried to keep the blush at bay, but she wasn't my best friend because she was unobservant. "No reason."

"Bullshit. Sit down and tell me why you are mean mugging a fucking floral throw pillow and moping around the bar like the world is ending."

I drew in a deep breath, trying to calm my heart, but I knew there was no way I was getting her out of the apartment without confessing what was bothering me. She eyed me from her seat at the other end as I nudged the pillows away from me and sat down.

"What do you want to know?"

"What do you think I want to know, Haz? We don't keep secrets from each other."

Raising an eyebrow, I pinned her with a look, because while she had texted me she was running off with my brother on Halloween with his psycho ex on the loose in the bar creating havoc, she also hadn't told me that her crush on him was more than just surface level.

There was no way she'd just fallen for him over the course of a single weekend and agreed to move in with him a couple of months later. That wasn't how Charley worked. She rarely had a second date, so the fact that she was so enamored with my brother after a few days meant her feelings for him had been building for a while.

"You don't want to know the secrets I keep about your brother, so don't even pretend whatever is going on with you is the same. There's a big difference between me not sharing details about my sex life and you keeping actual secrets about something that is clearly upsetting you enough you came in from wherever you were this morning crying."

"I wasn't crying."

"And I'm the virgin on this couch," she replied sarcastically.

"Okay. Maybe I was crying a little, but it wasn't a big deal. I cry all the time. You know this. Sometimes I cry when I'm angry."

"Then what are you angry about? Because as your best friend, you know I'm obligated to be equally angry if not angrier than you are about whatever it is you're hiding from me on your behalf."

And I knew if I told her to, Charley would march across that parking lot and beat my brother's best friend for playing with my emotions, but when I looked back on the situation, I wasn't sure he was the one who had done the hurting.

"I'm not angry. Just...conflicted. This week has been a lot and I'm all up in my feelings."

"Clearly. But you're still evading the question."

Glancing down at the phone in my hand, I swiped up to unlock the screen, my spirits deflating as I saw that while he'd once been typing, Seven hadn't replied.

"I'm not sure this experiment is going to work out."

She crossed her arms, her expression morphing into genuine concern. Charley may have pushed me into it, but I knew if I genuinely wanted to back out of it before the reveal, she'd let me. "How so?"

"Things with Seven were going great, and I was really looking forward to meeting him, but something changed in the last 24 hours and now I'm not sure I can go through with it."

Charley growled under her breath, muttering something I couldn't hear. "What did he do?"

"He didn't do anything, not really, but it's just this nagging feeling that he's losing interest or something. He isn't initiating conversations like he did previously, and then he's left me on read several times. He's probably just busy and I'm being paranoid. I've been so distracted working on my commissions with—" I trailed off, but judging by how her eyes widened, she'd heard my slip.

"Is that what you and Reid were really doing last Sunday? Working on one of your commissions?"

Closing my eyes, I tried to figure out what to tell her without revealing how embarrassed I was to have been taken in by his charm. She knew his reputation, and while I don't think she would ever discourage me from rekindling my friendship with him, she would also warn me against letting anything else happen between us. Especially knowing that there was someone else because of the blind dating event.

"Maybe."

"Hazel, what the fuck is going on with you?" Char didn't sound angry, just a bit startled that I'd been keeping something from her. But she'd been so busy, and part of me knew I shouldn't be doing what I'd been doing with Reid. I just hadn't told her because I didn't want her to tell me to stop.

"You've been busy, and he offered to help—"

"Oh, I'm sure he fucking did..." she muttered, looking pissed on my behalf. "Did he do something to make you this upset? I don't care if he's Hudson's best friend, I'll fucking rip off his balls if he hurt you."

"He didn't..." I whispered, recalling the look on his face right before I'd walked out of the break room. "But I may have hurt him."

"Why don't you just tell me what happened, and I'll decide whose balls I need to injure."

To her credit, Charley just waited while I word vomited everything that'd been happening over the last week with both men. The flirtatious behavior, the text messages, how things had escalated with Reid until what had happened the other night. How ashamed I felt the last 24 hours as I tried to reconcile my feelings.

"First of all, you should not feel ashamed about anything that happened. You aren't dating anyone exclusively, and until that kind of commitment has been talked about, you don't have to explain your behavior to anyone."

"I know, but..."

"I wasn't fucking finished," she snapped, but then took a deep breath. "Sorry, got a little carried away there. Second, there are no rules for how this dating experiment is supposed to turn out. If you want to have naughty show and tell with Seven, then get it, girl. On the flip side, if you want to sort of blow your brother's best friend because it felt good, then do that too. Seven knew going in that there was the possibility of you talking to other guys before the reveal. So, he can't be upset if you followed through on that."

"But I wasn't talking to another guy who was part of the experiment, I was talking to Reid, who didn't even participate."

Something flickered across her expression, but it was gone before I could interpret it. "Whatever. Same thing. Seven knew you didn't have any obligations to him, and he doesn't get to have an opinion on you talking to another guy—regardless of if he was involved in the experiment. Speaking of...has anyone else been texting you?"

"Like I could handle anyone else with Seven and Reid taking up all the available real estate in my brain." Although now that I was thinking about it. Christian, the baseball player who I'd been talking to after the Halloween party, had been sending me texts this week. I hadn't really thought anything about it because I'd been so distracted by other things, but...

"What's that look about?" she asked, amusement clear in her expression.

"Well, there has been someone else texting me, but I kind of blew him off."

"As long as you didn't blow him like you—"

"Shut it!" I interrupted her before she said it, because even though it was through his boxer briefs, I *had* given Reid a very unconventional blow job. Figures that I couldn't even give my first blow job like a normal person.

She mimed zipping her lips and reached down to snag one pillow off the floor, hugging it to her chest, but thankfully it wasn't the same kind that I'd used the night before last. Because she would definitely want to know why I was prying a pillow out of her arms and throwing it out the window.

When I didn't start talking right away, she made a rolling motion with her hand and gave me an impatient look. "Do tell. I shouldn't have to pry it out of you."

"You know that baseball player who I was talking to in the fall who things kind of fizzled out with? He started texting me, too."

Charley laughed, but I still didn't see why that was so funny.

"What? What is so amusing about this situation? I'd rather go back to being invisible. You know I don't like this kind of attention."

"Hate to break it to you, Haz, but you've never been invisible. Oblivious maybe, but definitely not invisible."

"Whatever. How do I make it stop? I don't like feeling like this."

Her expression sobered, and she nodded, seeing that the last few weeks had essentially ripped me out of my little bubble of solitude. "What do you want? Do you want all of them to leave you alone?"

Thinking about how each of them made me feel, I wasn't sure that was what I wanted either. "No, not exactly."

"Then you just let things unfold naturally. If Seven wants to pursue something with you, he'll step up his game. No amount of freaking out is going to help the situation until you have an actual conversation with him face to face."

I nodded, absorbing her words before she spoke again.

"And Christian?"

"I don't know. He's cute, and he was nice to talk to. He'd definitely be the safer choice if he really was interested and not just being friendly."

"Doesn't exactly sound like animal attraction going on there."

"Well, animal attraction has only managed to complicate things more than I'm prepared to deal with, so..."

"So, you're not planning to ride off into the sunset with Reid?" she asked, making me think of what it'd felt like to be on the back of his bike.

Being with him like that had felt right. Like I fit there. But it wasn't the attraction part I was struggling with regarding Reid. It was the feelings part. Like I was developing actual feelings for him, and he was only showing how much he wanted the benefits portion of our rekindled friendship.

"I don't think it really matters. It'd never work out, anyway. I'm me, and he's Reid, it's not like we're even in the same league."

Charley frowned, throwing the pillow in her hands at my face. I batted it away, but she was still giving me a look like I'd offended her.

"That's bullshit. If anything, he's not in your league if he doesn't realize how fucking amazing you are. And if he really wants more, he needs to man the fuck up because he's doing a shitty job of showing you how he feels about you."

"Pretty sure his feelings are clear. He wants to add a benefits package to our friendship."

She shook her head, not convinced. "I wouldn't go jumping to any conclusions just yet. See how things work out with Seven once you see him in person and then go from there. Sometimes people can surprise you with how they really feel."

"That's pretty much what Reid told me before I left his place."

"Then maybe there's hope for him yet," she mused, standing up from the couch. "Now let's go pick out what you're going to wear on Valentine's Day, because no matter who you end up with at the end of the night, you need to make every guy in that room regret passing on the opportunity to have your undivided attention."

Chapter Twenty-Two

CHARLEY'S WORDS STAYED WITH me all afternoon, and into my shift that night, but we were too busy to let them truly blossom and for the panic to set in. Instead, I focused on running food from the kitchen to the hungry patrons in the packed bar, completely ignoring my phone and all the men on the other end of it.

But I should have known I'd never escape it, or them.

Annie cornered me in the small hallway outside the kitchen after I'd finished running out the last set of orders that'd come in from the servers on the floor.

"I don't know what's going on, but Reid was just up at the bar getting a round for his table."

I hadn't even realized Reid was in the bar, but it wasn't like I could tell him to stay away. His best friend was the owner. Yet another reminder that I'd never escape him if I let things go further and they fell apart.

"...and this guy came up and started asking if you were on shift tonight, and I swear to God, Reid legit growled at him."

"Wait, what?"

"This college guy in a baseball team hoodie was asking if you were working."

"Go back to the part about Reid."

She grinned, seemingly entertained that was the part I was asking her to repeat. "Is something going on between you two?"

"What? No..." I denied, but it sounded like a lie even to my ears.

"Too bad. I always thought there was a vibe between you two."

"Nope. No vibes between us."

Just me requiring lots of a different vibe to deal with all the pent-up attraction I'd been carrying around for him since puberty.

"Anyway, you should probably get out there and talk to him before shit hits the fan."

"Reid asked to talk to me?"

"No, baseball hoodie guy. Reid went back to his table once I shoved a pitcher at him and pointed out he had a table full of thirsty guys waiting for their beer."

With Annie following me back toward the floor, I saw Christian standing off to the side with his back against the bar while he watched the crowd.

I'd forgotten how cute he was with his slightly curly blond hair and dimples. He was just the kind of guy I should be interested in. But as I looked toward the back corner and my eyes caught on the penetrating stare of my brother's brooding best friend, I questioned whether the clean-cut baseball player was truly my type.

Annie's hand in the middle of my back reminded me I couldn't just awkwardly stare at them all night. I reluctantly made my way toward the younger guy, trying to ignore Reid's stare while I did.

"Hey, you," Christian's voice was warm as he greeted me, leaning in to give me a half hug before I could step away. "I was wondering if you were avoiding me."

"No," I squeaked nervously, suddenly wanting to escape from what I knew would be an awkward interaction. "We've just been super busy tonight."

"I wasn't talking about tonight."

"Oh?" I knew I hadn't really put much effort into responding to his texts, but he'd made it seem like he didn't have time last fall to worry about a girlfriend. Not that I'd gone on any actual dates with him to be considered his girlfriend. We'd just shared a few flirtatious conversations at the bar and some text messages until he'd confessed he was too busy with school and conditioning for more.

"Yeah. You kind of left me on read a few times last week. I know I told you practices were kicking my ass when we talked last, but when I found out about you, I couldn't resist."

"Found out what about me?" I asked, but I wasn't looking at him. My eyes were locked with Reid's pissed off ones, trying to figure out why he was glaring at me.

Well, I had a feeling it had to do with the man next to me, but it wasn't like I'd told Christian to come to the bar tonight. I hadn't even seen him in person in over a month.

"...so anyway, I just wanted to stop by and see you before..."

My pulse raced as Reid's gaze never left us, his mouth pulling into a wry grin when he noticed I wasn't really paying attention to the man standing a foot away from me who was still talking.

Breaking eye contact, I tried to return my focus to what was being said.

"I'm sorry. You're busy. I should've waited and not interrupted you at work." Christian smiled that boyish grin—one that once made my stomach flutter, only now I felt nothing other than annoyance that those flutters were absent.

"Yeah. It was great to see you. Sorry we're too slammed to properly catch up."

"That's alright. I've got a feeling I'll be seeing you again. I can be patient."

I frowned, realizing I may have missed more of what he'd been saying than just a few words. But as the line cook motioned toward the orders piling up in the expo window, I didn't have time to find out what.

"I've gotta go."

"Of course," he said, smiling. Before I could anticipate his next move, Christian was leaning in for a hug, his lips grazing my cheek. "It was great to see you, Hazel."

I blushed furiously as he stepped away, a wink aimed in my direction before he made his way through the bar and settled at a booth full of his teammates.

A whistle from the kitchen startled me out of my daze and had me trying to focus on my job, but not before I glanced at the table in the corner.

It was empty. Reid was gone.

BY THE END OF the night, I was more exhausted than I'd felt in a long time, but I knew I'd never be able to sleep with worst-case scenarios floating around in my brain. I just wanted to shut it all off and sleep away this feeling of foreboding that'd lodged itself in my chest.

Annie and I were the only two remaining in the bar at the end of my shift, her flipping the chairs upside down on the empty tables and me wiping down the glasses coming out of the dishwasher so they were clean for tomorrow.

"Big reveal coming up soon?" she asked, throwing the soiled rags she'd used to wipe down the tables into the bucket below the counter that I needed to remember empty into the washing machine before I headed upstairs for the night.

"Yeah, I guess." Although I couldn't manage to muster any excitement about it right now.

Annie brushed past me, grabbing a couple of shot glasses from underneath the counter and a bottle of amaretto. While I rarely drank because of my meds, it seemed she knew I wasn't a fan of the hard stuff.

"I think you need one of these," she chuckled, using her fingertip to push one in my direction while she picked up the other. "What are we toasting to?"

"Fuck if I know," I muttered picking up the shot and holding it to my lips.

"To getting the good dick." The wink she aimed at me had a smile pulling at my lips, but I doubted I'd be getting any dick anytime soon, much less the good kind.

Tipping the shot back, I swallowed and shuddered at the burn as it slid down my throat, warmth spreading through me. "Pretty sure I'm never going to get *any* dick."

Annie laughed, grabbing the shot glass and refilling it, pushing it back in my direction as she leaned her hip against the counter of the bar. "Sounds like there's a story there."

"How did you know that Jay was the one?" They seemed to be close, and I knew that he spent a lot of time here hanging out with her when she was bartending.

"Oh, he's definitely not," she laughed, giving the shot glass next to me a pointed look until I finally picked it up and shot it back. "But what we have works for both of us right now. He's never really been emotionally available and that was part of what drew me to him. I'm not interested in something serious and he's too much of a man child to want to settle down. We're both getting what we want out of our arrangement, and if that changes, we end it."

Being an emotionally unavailable man child seemed to be a Harding family trait that he shared with his cousin.

"And you're okay with that?" Maybe I was expecting too much from both him and Seven. What had started out as me trying to divest myself of my unwanted virginity had turned into me daydreaming about companionship and commitment. Things I wasn't sure either of them could give me.

"Yeah, I mean, it works, and the sex has always been off the charts, so I guess I never really thought about looking for more than that. I know we won't end up together, but until one of us meets someone else, we enjoy spending time with each other. He's one of my best friends."

"Maybe I need to lower my expectations," I mumbled, my fingers spinning the empty glass on the smooth wood of the bar as I thought about taking a chance with Reid and not expecting something more than just friendship and temporary companionship from him. Maybe he wasn't capable of giving me more than that.

"Nah, he's down bad for you. I don't think you'd need to lower anything if you gave him a chance." Frowning, I looked up at her, but she just raised a knowing eyebrow. "I've never seen Reid fall for anyone, but judging by the way he looks at you, he's well on his way."

"No, he's not... I told you..."

"You can deny it all you want, Haz. But I can see how you look at him too. I guess what you need to ask yourself now is if you're willing to do anything about it."

But I wasn't sure that it was up to me.

Chapter
Twenty-Three

S TARING AT THE PHONE in my hands, I knew I shouldn't respond to her text, but resisting using this one last way I had to be close to her was a futile effort. I wasn't strong enough to walk away like she wanted me to.

> Seven: Talking to you is the best part of my day. I'm sorry I didn't tell you that sooner.

I was sorry I didn't tell her a lot of things sooner. Because now I was stuck in this situation where no matter what I did, I was hurting her. But after watching that preppy dipshit flirting with her at the bar earlier, there was no way I was backing off.

Now that she wasn't hiding behind her anxiety, she was bound to see the men who paid attention to her at the bar. And one of these days—if I continued to hide from my feelings for her—she'd fall for one of them and my heart would slowly turn to stone as I watched her blossom into the confident woman she'd shown me brief glimpses of this week.

> Fourteen: I don't need apologies, I guess I just need some reassurance that my feelings aren't one sided. If you couldn't tell, this is all new to me.

> Seven: Feeling like this about someone is new to me, too. I'm used to people judging me based upon their preconceived notions of who I am.

And until recently, those preconceived notions weren't far from the mark, but I was tired of letting them define me. Living up to my reputation wasn't something I wanted anymore.

Fourteen: I might know something about that. It's hard to break away from how other people think you should act. That's why I was so drawn to you, you've never made me feel like that.

My heart warmed briefly, fluttering in my chest when I realized she'd essentially done the same for me until she'd let her fears take over. Until she decided the risk of falling for me wasn't worth it.

Seven: Can you promise me something?

It was selfish of me to even think, much less ask her to promise, but I was going to do it anyway.

Fourteen: Depends on what I'm promising.

And there was my snarky girl.

Seven: Promise me you'll follow your heart, even if it's not toward me. You deserve the world, and while I want to be the one to give it to you, I don't want you to ever doubt that.

Fourteen: Why does it feel like you're trying to let me down easy?

Because I was terrified once I walked into that party and she discovered everything I'd been keeping from her, that she'd cut me out of her life without a second thought.

Seven: Maybe I'm a little more insecure than I've let on.

She wasn't the only one who doubted herself.

Fourteen: Well, don't be. You deserve love, too.

My heart ached at the thought she might love Seven. Because she'd made it pretty clear that love wasn't on the table with me. And that hurt more than I thought it would.

Seven: We'll see.

THE NEXT MORNING, I woke later than expected, rushing through my morning and barely making it downstairs before my first client showed up. Thankfully, my reflexes were still sharp, because I couldn't afford for a lack of sleep to make me shaky.

I'd only drank three beers before I'd left the bar, unable to watch Hazel talking to that guy before the jealousy started to fester. Then I'd had trouble falling asleep after the text messages, running the entire encounter through my head an unhealthy number of times before I'd finally passed out.

All I'd wanted to do was see if the feelings that had been building for her over the last year were real, but I'd been so short sighted when I'd forced my help with her commissions that I didn't realize I'd be putting myself in a position to lose it all.

After powering through my handful of clients, I was grateful to have blocked out my schedule for the afternoon so I could take care of paperwork. But no matter how hard I tried; I couldn't focus on anything but what would happen tomorrow night.

And when my stomach growled, driving me toward the pizza place a mile down the road, I knew what I needed to do.

HAZEL'S TABLET WAS SITTING on the bar when I let myself in the back door, but the rest of the room was deserted. I briefly wondered if she'd forgotten it here, but knew that couldn't be the case because she rarely let it out of her sight. Especially lately with the subject matter of her commissions.

A quiet thumping sound coming from the little alcove leading toward the kitchen had me leaving the pizza box on the bar and moving toward the noise. Although I barely held in my laughter when I saw what was causing it.

"Stupid, fucking stupid…" Hazel muttered, letting her forehead drop to the wall again, the sound echoing from the wooden panel.

After the third thump, I stepped into her field of vision, tapping my shoe against the baseboard to get her attention.

"Fuck," she breathed out, covering her chest with her hand when she realized I was standing there. "How long have you been here?"

"Long enough to see you literally beating yourself up with the poor, unsuspecting wall."

"I wasn't…" she trailed off, reaching up to rub the red spot on her forehead. Part of me was worried she'd hurt herself, but it faded quickly once she'd stopped abusing it.

"Yeah, you were," I teased, and thankfully, she smiled. Maybe things between us weren't completely ruined. "And now you're going to tell me why."

"It's stupid," she muttered, trying to walk around me, but I stepped in front of her, chuckling when she bumped into my chest and looked up at me with narrowed eyes.

"It's not stupid, kitten. Clearly, something has gotten you all worked up."

"Doesn't matter. We're not doing this anymore."

"Doing what? Talking? You gonna run away from me again? I thought we were past that. I thought we were friends."

I wanted a whole lot fucking more than that, but I wasn't confessing that right now. Right now, I needed to help her fix whatever was stressing her out.

"This isn't a problem you can help with anymore. We decided we weren't those kinds of friends."

Needing to remind her she was the one who made that decision, not me, I leaned down and whispered in her ear. "So, this is about a commission?"

"No."

"Liar," I teased, secretly enjoying it when her expression morphed from uncertainty to something a little more heated. "What's wrong? I thought things were getting easier once you started using the photos as references. Maybe someone shouldn't have pushed their photographer away so quickly."

"They are—were—I don't fucking know. I can't get the proportions right, and now I just want to erase the whole thing. But she needs it for a PR package going out in a month and it takes two weeks to get prints..."

I'd seen her like this before—moments where she let her nerves get the best of her. Deciding I'd deal with the fallout later; I pulled her into my arms and tucked her head underneath my chin.

"Breathe, Haz. Show me. I'll see if I can help."

After unexpectedly squeezing me back, she broke free of my hold, reaching to grab her tablet and clutching it to her chest.

"Come on, it can't be that bad. If you're in a tight spot, you can always take a picture of me and use it."

"No!" she shouted, her cheeks turning pink before she lowered her voice. "I mean, no thank you. Not this one. It won't work. I can't ask you to..."

Before she could plot an escape, I pried the tablet out of her hands, quickly typing in the passcode and studying the image she was drawing in her illustration software.

It was just as detailed as her previous works, but instead of it being a couple in the photo, the subject was a man sitting in a chair.

A mostly nude man sitting with his hand wrapped around a blank space where I was assuming a dick would go.

"Um. Is this dude human?"

While none of the commissions she'd shared with me were otherworldly creatures, I knew that fantasy romance was popular right now.

"Yes," she mumbled, her voice muted through the hands now covering her face.

"Does he have an invisible penis?"

She shook her head, still refusing to look at me. "Well, right now he does, but no."

Taking her distraction as an opportunity, I swiped up, studying the other windows she had open to see if she'd been watching porn again to draw this guy.

But instead of porn, I found a Google drive folder labeled *Peen Portraits*. Hazel was still refusing to look at me, so I clicked on the window, scrolling through the very detailed anatomical studies of the male appendage that filled the folder. There were dozens of them.

She'd been a very busy girl over the last few months. And I was a little jealous she'd been looking at this many dicks on the Internet but hadn't uncovered mine. I wanted to make a comment about Goldilocks finding just the right dick, but I had a feeling it wouldn't go over well.

"Looks like you've been practicing. A girl doesn't have a folder full of illustrated dicks and not know how to draw one."

She grabbed the tablet from me, narrowing her eyes, before she turned to walk away. "Laugh it up. Cause, apparently, I am that girl. I've tried like ten times and none of them look right."

"Show me."

Pointing to the counter between us, I waited until she laid the tablet down, navigating back to her current drawing.

She turned on the first layer and I winced, taking in the massive erection protruding disproportionately from between his spread thighs.

"That thing looks like it could dislocate a hip."

"I know," she whispered, using her finger to scale the size down, but it still didn't look like it belonged to the man in the chair.

Hiding the layer, she pulled up the next one, and I tilted my head to the side, trying to figure out why this one didn't look right. "Did you draw the head of his dick backwards?"

"Shut up," she growled, switching to the next one.

"Why is that one so shiny? Did Midas give him a hand job?"

"I hate you," she hissed, glaring at me as I tried to hold back a laugh. "I was trying a new brush, and it clearly didn't go well when I was trying to paint in the highlights."

Nudging her out of the way, I swapped the layer for the next one, snorting when it looked abnormally skinny and didn't fill the fist of the man attempting to hold it. The head was also oddly flat on top. "This one brings a whole new meaning to *pencil dick*. The head looks like an eraser."

Her little growl was back as her hand reached for the tablet, but I was faster, moving it to the side before she could take it away.

Pulling up the next layer, I tilted my head, trying to figure out what she'd done to make it look so...furry.

"Are you sure he's human? He looks like he's hiding a wild animal in his pants. Or maybe he's a secret werewolf."

"If you must know..." she trailed off, crossing her arms over her chest.

"Don't leave me hanging now," I coaxed, unable to hold in laughter at the next one. She'd somehow managed to make this one look limp against his hold, despite the size of it. "Not like you did to this guy."

"I told you they were terrible. They're either too big, or too veiny, or too shiny. And now I won't get more work because all these authors are going to figure out I'm an inexperienced virgin and don't even know what a penis looks like in person."

"That's not strictly true," I reminded her. Technically, she had confessed to seeing mine.

"Well, I don't know what an erect one looks like and it's not like I can ask you to figure model pose for this one, and..."

"Why not? You've drawn nude models before me." I'd seen her figure drawing sketchbook when she had taken a few courses in undergrad with nude models.

"They weren't hard with cum running down the back of their hand." Well, no. That they definitely were not... She'd left those details out.

"Did you draw that part, too?" I teased, an amused thrill running through me as her cheeks flushed. I shouldn't be teasing her like this, but I also didn't want to stop. "Where is that one hiding?"

"Reid, seriously. I'm just gonna tell her I can't do this and give her deposit back."

Shaking my head, a plan started formulating in my head. There was no way I was letting her give up on herself this easily. "No, you're not. Do you work tonight?"

She took in a deep breath and uttered the only word I needed to hear. "No."

"Then give me an hour and I'll be back."

Her hand darted out, grabbing my arm before I could walk around her. I should have felt bad at the fear clearly visible in her eyes, but I didn't.

"Reid, no. This is too far. I can't ask you to do this."

But she wasn't asking me...and I was doing it. Because there was no way in hell I was letting her give up on herself when I could do something about it. Even if it meant knocking down the walls she'd been trying to erect around herself.

"I'm volunteering. Send me the scene from the book and I'll make it happen."

Chapter Twenty-Four

O NLY THINGS COULDN'T POSSIBLY go that smoothly, because when I climbed out of the shower, my phone was full of messages from my cousin, begging me to cover him at the distillery for the afternoon because of a family emergency he'd tell me about when I got there.

Switching over to the text thread with Hazel, I fired off a message because I knew she'd freak out if she heard my motorcycle tearing out of the parking lot since I'd told her I'd be right back.

> Reid: Jay was blowing up my phone when I got out of the shower. Have to head to the distillery to cover for him. Don't you dare email that author. As soon as I'm done, we're doing this.

> Hazel: What's going on? Anything I can help with?

Of course, she'd offer to help without knowing what was going on despite the current tension between us. Because that was just who she was. Hazel may have avoided putting herself into potentially stressful situations when she could, but if she thought someone needed help—even someone she was hesitant to trust—she was the first person to jump in without hesitation.

> Reid: Don't know details. All he told me was it's a family emergency and that he needed to catch a flight to Wyoming. I'm assuming it has something to do with Tristan, but I really don't know.

> Hazel: Don't worry about me. I'll figure it out. Go help your family. They're more important.

> Reid: Hate to break it to you, Haz. But you're family too. You are just as important.

> Hazel: Even more reason for you to focus on your cousins and not me. Not sure family should be watching each other do…things.

> Reid: Not getting out of this that easily. Send me that book and I'm coming for you as soon as I'm done.

Three little dots danced across the screen, but as another frantic text came through from Jay, I shoved my phone in my pocket, tucked my helmet underneath my arm, grabbed my leather riding gloves and headed for the door. Gray was doodling on the tablet we kept at the desk while he waited for his next appointment, and I knew it wouldn't be long before he had a waiting list like the rest of the artists who worked here.

"Hey boss man, I thought you were doing paperwork all afternoon?"

He was right, I should be doing paperwork, because payroll waited for no man. But family was more important, and I could work on getting the numbers submitted to the spreadsheet remotely since I'd started using an outside accounting firm to do the business taxes instead of suffering through them alone.

When I'd been in Gray's position, learning the skills I needed for the job instead of the business behind it, I didn't know being a small business owner was in my future. It always looked easier from the outside looking in.

"Maybe I'll start teaching you how to input the numbers for payroll, so I don't have to do it anymore."

"And maybe I'll give myself a pay increase to offset the extra job duties you want to pile on me so you can go moon over your best friend's little sister." My footsteps halted, and I turned in his direction. I was met with a grin that told me he'd been setting me up and I had just walked right into it. "Don't worry, I won't spill your secrets, but my silence is going to cost you."

Narrowing my eyes, I tried to gauge his intentions, but he burst out laughing, holding up his hands.

"Not like in a blackmail kind of way. I meant maybe you'll start giving me bigger pieces when they come in. I'm ready to do something other than spend my days piercing belly buttons for college girls."

"You'll get there. Give it time. But maybe you can mock something up for the client I had yesterday. I can already tell she's going to be a frequent flyer and I don't want to spend the next year turning her down."

"So, there *is* something going on between you and Hazel?"

I didn't want to lie to him, and things were still precarious because I had no idea how things at the reveal would go, but I had zero interest in messing around with clients anymore. Unless that client was the devastatingly beautiful illustrator from across the parking lot.

"No, not at the moment."

"That wasn't a flat out no," he mused, raising an eyebrow. I knew he might give me shit about it, but he also wouldn't say anything to Hudson.

"I'll keep you updated if it changes anytime soon."

"I kinda hope she gives you all kinds of shit and doesn't take it easy on you."

Grinning, I nodded at him before I pulled on my gloves, opening the door out into the frigid parking lot. "I hope she does, too."

Because nothing worth truly having came from taking the easy route.

I T WAS DARK BY the time I got home from the distillery, the lights in the shop were dimmed and only a handful of cars parked outside the bar next door. It wasn't time for last call yet, but clearly people were waiting to come out to drink their sorrows away or find someone to hook up with until Valentine's night.

The reveal party tomorrow was invitation only at the beginning of the evening, but the bar would open a few hours later to the public. I was sure the parking lot surrounding the bar would be packed tomorrow, along with all the spaces around my shop.

Holidays had a way of making people lonely or horny, but either way, it was good for business.

I'd spent the afternoon rearranging disgruntled clients, because my cousin Jayden was going to be out of town for longer than just a night. His older brother Tristan—who was a smoke jumper employed by the national forestry service—had been injured responding to a planned burn by the park service that had spread uncontrollably. He was apparently stable but in critical condition, so I was covering all the tours and tastings on the books for tomorrow.

With plans for his restaurant in the works for next year, Jay didn't want to risk the negative feedback if he closed without notice. He was already under scrutiny from the chamber of commerce board since one member wasn't a fan of him expanding his business without her son doing the architectural planning. Politics in a small town could be wild, but I was proud of him for bringing in a commercial architect to run the project for him. Even if it was one of his friends from college.

Reid: Are you still awake?

It was late, but I also knew Hazel didn't exactly keep a regular sleep schedule. She never had. That was part of how our friendship had formed when she was still in high school. She'd sneak into the basement, where I often spent the night when I was back in town visiting. Quietly curling up into her favorite chair, she'd bury her face in a sketchbook until she drifted off.

After the first time she'd done it while I was there, I'd started keeping the door of the guest room open so I could go cover her with a blanket and save her sketches from being crumpled or smeared when she inevitably fell asleep on her work.

Each time, I'd tried to resist looking at what she'd been drawing, knowing sometimes a sketchbook was a very personal thing for an artist, but eventually I'd end up seated on the couch across from her, watching her sleep as I flipped through the pages. I'd been stunned each time as I took in the progression of her skills, and it still stunned me even when she shared her work with me to this day.

She didn't know it, and I never told her, but sometimes when I was feeling unsure of myself as an apprentice in someone else's shop with no formal artistic training, I drew inspiration from her determination and started sketching whenever I had free time.

They say practice makes perfect, and I could honestly say I wouldn't be where I was in my career—running my own shop with a waiting list of clients—if it weren't for a teenage girl with a sketchbook sneaking into a basement late at night to draw when her brain wouldn't quiet enough to sleep. She'd saved me in ways I'd never told her about, and once she'd realized I was the one covering her up when she fell asleep after her nocturnal drawing sessions, she'd started trying to stay awake to talk to me.

We'd spent hours sitting across from each other talking while we sketched, and while it had been completely innocent—at least on my part—I could honestly say that it had stuck with me in a way spending time with someone of a different sex never had before then, and still hadn't to this day.

My feelings for her hadn't shifted until last summer, but once I realized that the skinny teen with wild red hair, braces and huge glasses had turned into one of the kindest and most beautiful humans I'd ever met, I couldn't stop my feelings for her from developing.

Even when she fled the room whenever I stepped into it the last few years, I was still charmed by her from a distance, only now it was in a way that had me wanting to kiss her breathless.

It probably wasn't healthy how much time I'd spent watching her from across a room, but I was tired of just watching from a distance now that I knew what it felt like to hold her in my arms.

Hazel: What do you think?

Reid: Someone must be feeling better if they're resorting to sarcasm. I felt that eye roll through the phone.

Hazel: Quit pretending you know me.

Reid: Not pretending, kitten. I do know you. Gonna grab another shower and then I'll be headed over.

Hazel: Wasn't aware working in the tasting room required a shower afterward. Women throwing drinks at you instead of panties today?

Reid: Considering today was filled with lovers-themed couples' tours, no panties were thrown. At least not at me. And I don't smell like alcohol. I smell like mash. Not sure if you've ever smelled it, but fermented Barley isn't a stink I want to share.

Hazel: There are stinks you want to share? Doesn't being stinky make you want to not share it by nature?

Reid: Are you going to continue busting my balls or are you going to let me shower now so I can come put on a show for you?

Hazel: It's not for me. It's for my client.

Reid: You planning to film it and share? Not that I'm opposed to a little exhibitionism, but an introduction would be nice first.

Hazel: Maybe Gray accusing you of having an Only Fans wasn't far off the mark.

Knowing I shouldn't be sending it, I grinned as I typed out my response, locking the screen and leaving my phone on the counter while I stripped down so I could get the sickly sweet smell that had clung to me all afternoon off my skin.

> Reid: There's only one subscriber I want to watch that kind of private show. And I'm sure she's currently trying to figure out if that comment was aimed at her. Yes, Hazel, it was. You're the only person I'm interested in putting on a show for.

Unsurprisingly, she hadn't responded by the time I was dressed again.

After badgering her via text this afternoon, she'd reluctantly sent me the title of the book. Despite refusing to tell me what part of the book the sketch was based on, it hadn't taken long to find it. I'd skimmed through the eBook on my phone between tours and tastings, grinning as a plan formed in my head to get a little audience participation, like the hero in the book had from his mafia rival's daughter.

It wasn't playing nice, and I was sure she'd kill me come tomorrow, but if this was the last night I got to spend with her, I was going to make it one to remember.

Deciding not to bother with a tie, I buttoned my jacket, stepping into my dressier black leather boots.

Snowflakes drifted aimlessly through the air, giving the almost deserted parking lot an ethereal quality, but I was only focused on getting into the second-floor apartment without alerting the remaining patrons of the bar of my presence.

Hudson's car was absent from the back of the parking lot, which made things infinitely easier. I wasn't sure who was closing tonight since Hazel had the night off, but I really didn't care as I let myself in the back door and locked it behind me before I silently ascended the staircase.

Having spent enough time here when Hudson lived in the apartment, I knew exactly which steps to avoid keeping Hazel unaware of my presence.

But I didn't want to just let myself in like I had before when she'd been futilely trying to avoid me. She knew I was coming this time, so I was sure there was a lot of overthinking going on in there, not sneaky porn viewing.

Flexing my fingers and exhaling a rough breath, I knocked on the door, immediately getting into position with my hand braced against the top of the frame for the maximum effect of my willingness to drop into character for her. Despite her likely thinking differently, I was enjoying our role play sessions immensely.

"Gimme a second, I..." The door opened inward, and I grinned as Hazel's eyes widened, her eyes slowly drifting down the buttons on the dress shirt I'd put on.

"Good evening, little one." I greeted in a low voice, trying to embody the character I was playing.

"I..."

"Cat got your tongue?"

Hazel stepped to the side, using her hand to yank me through the doorway. She pushed me behind her while she stuck her head into the stairwell, clearly trying to figure out if anyone had seen me coming up to her apartment dressed in a suit. "What the hell are you doing? Did anyone see you like this?"

"I came in the back door," I whispered, placing my palm between her shoulder blades and ghosting my hand down her soft sweater and tapping her butt suggestively.

"Yeah, don't get any ideas," she hissed, quietly closing the door and flattening herself against it.

"It's cute you think I haven't already concocted an entire fantasy in my head about it already."

"What the fuck, Reid?" Her voice was a low growl, and I tried not to laugh as she narrowed her eyes at me. "If you're just here to fuck with me all night, you can go back home."

"That's another fantasy, kitten. But no. I'm here because Giovanni can't resist his rival's beautiful daughter, Serafina, anymore, and has come to collect on a little bet he made with her."

"Oh no," she whispered, ducking underneath my arm and escaping further into the apartment. "That's not what's going on tonight. This is about me getting a picture I can use to finish this drawing so I can get it rendered before I need to send it tomorrow, not about reenacting whatever you read this afternoon."

"Come on, Haz. Where's my brave girl who shoved an earbud at me and straddled me on my bike to drop into character for a commission? Be brave with me."

"If you hadn't noticed, that's the problem between us, Reid."

Frowning, I followed her toward the hallway where she was trying to escape, slipping an arm around her waist and pulling her back into my chest before she could avoid answering my question. "What's the problem?"

Her body trembled against me, and I fought the urge to spin her around and wrap my arms around her for protection against whatever was bothering her. But when you're the source of the apparent problem, that only makes things worse.

"I'm not brave," she whispered, pushing out of my arms and slipping into her bedroom, the door closing in my face.

"Yes, you are," I responded, loud enough she could hear it through the door, but when her answering whisper carried back to me without a problem, I knew she heard me.

"Not with you."

Chapter Twenty-Five

W HILE HE'D LOOKED DEFEATED when I'd left his shop yesterday and worried this morning when he'd cornered me in
the empty bar while I'd been figuratively—and then more literally—banging my head against a wall, tonight he had an entirely
different look to him. Stubborn determination.

And I was woefully unprepared for Reid to fight against my
wishes quite like this. He knew I'd drawn a boundary line to keep
things from getting more complicated between us, but apparently,
he'd decided to pole vault right over that line by offering to…show
me his pole.

This situation was so fucked up. And I was still having trouble
believing this was my life anymore. Between the unexpected connection with Seven, both aurally and then through sharing our
typed words—and some suggestive amateur photography—with
each other, and now Reid turning his considerable charms on me
at the same time, I kept trying to pinch myself to wake up from
whatever dreamland I'd been transported to.

"I can wait out here all night," he taunted through the door,
clearly waiting for me to come out of hiding.

"Or you can go home."

His deep chuckle made the hairs on my neck stand on end. "Not
a chance, kitten. We're doing this. Now come out and set up your
camera or I'll come in there and get it myself."

Part of me wanted to see how far I could push him until he broke,
but I also knew he'd push right up to the edge of my boundaries,

but never actually violate them. That didn't mean he wouldn't torture me in the meantime.

"Keep your pants on."

"Pretty sure you need them off for this," he laughed, his voice close like he was leaning against the door while he waited for me. "But I'll wait to take them off until you can appreciate the process."

"You're so full of yourself," I muttered, a smile pulling at my lips as his chuckle filled my chest with warmth.

He was quiet on the other side of the door as I gathered my equipment, getting the memory card loaded into my camera, glad he couldn't run off with it for once while I was distracted this time. Although I wouldn't put it past him to steal my memory card to use as leverage to keep the line of communication open between us.

When I finally emerged from the bedroom, I found him in the living room with my tablet in his lap, stylus in hand, sketching something on the screen.

"What are you doing? You better not have messed with any of my files."

"Chill, Haz. I opened a new one. I didn't jeopardize the integrity of your peen pics."

"Do you even know what you're doing?" I asked, grabbing the stylus from him before he could get into anything else.

He willingly offered me the tablet, winking as I looked at the screen. An abstract outline of a kitten was sketched in the middle of the screen, but upon zooming out, I could see one of my female 3-D anatomical models in the background layer, the decoration carefully rendered in the dip of her hip. "You think I do all my sketching the old school way? I know how to use illustration software, Haz."

"Well, you don't need to use mine to sketch tattoos for other women."

His grin almost turned feral as he reached forward, gripping my hip and pressing his thumb into the same place the tattoo had been on the model on the screen. "Who said it's for another woman, *kitten?*"

Shaking my head, I decided not to take the bait, stepping out of his hold and setting up the tripod next to the couch, aiming it toward where he was manspreading across my chair in a way that was way too alluring. I could probably count the number of times I'd seen Reid wearing something other than his typical bad boy uniform, and him in a suit was making things that shouldn't be fluttering inside me take flight.

"Can I do a quick warm up sketch before we…?" I trailed off, but Reid's eyebrow lifted in challenge, and I knew he was going to say something suggestive.

"Before I stroke my cock while you watch?"

"Do you have to make everything hard?"

His grin was almost sinister as he reached down, intentionally adjusting himself and drawing attention to the fact he was hiding something firm inside his snug dress pants. "I'm not the one making this hard."

"You knew what I meant."

"Hmm, not sure I do. Why don't you tell me, in detail, how I'm making things hard? Maybe I can give you a demonstration while you talk."

"Shut up," I hissed, pulling my phone out of the pocket of my leggings, and shoving one of my earbuds in after I pressed play. Reid watched my every move, his fingertips tapping on the armrests of the chair.

My stylus moved across the page quickly while I roughed in the general outline of the scene. The chair underneath his powerful form. The way his thick neck met the strong slope of his shoulders. To his credit, Reid sat still, letting my eyes flicker across his chest and along the strong jawline my fingers itched to caress.

Meanwhile, the audiobook in my ears detailed Serafina's reaction to the powerful mafia boss showing up on her doorstep to collect on a promise to watch her. They'd been dancing around each other until this point in the book, her pushing him away at every turn and him unable to resist the pull of her.

They weren't supposed to even know the other existed, but a chance meeting ignited a clandestine friendship between the two that violated the blood feud their families had been engaged in for decades. He shouldn't want her, and she shouldn't want him, but despite it all, they couldn't stay away from each other.

I hadn't sent Reid the audiobook on purpose, knowing it'd mirror our situation a little too close for comfort. And I hadn't wanted him to know about the scene leading up to her watching him pleasure himself in a chair across the room.

But I knew he'd read the scene as he watched me, his eyes focused on my every move while I tried to capture how he looked right now. Strong. Determined. Dangerous.

I didn't need to warm up, I'd spent the entire day working on another project, my wrist aching with all the abuse I'd put it through in the last few weeks as I flew through commission after commission—inspiration racing through my veins unlike it ever had before. But as my cheeks turned pink when Serafina pulled out a vibrator and settled in across from Gio to use it on herself while he watched, Reid's fingers dug into the chair in a way that told me everything I needed to know.

He didn't just want to recreate his part of the scene. He wanted to watch mine.

"Stop," he growled, his voice a rough command as he reached across the coffee table to pull the tablet from my grasp.

"Hey," I protested weakly, trying to pull it back, but he'd already switched gears, grabbing my phone from the table and turning it to play the audio from the speakers and not my earbuds.

His gaze was almost feral as he watched me squirm, unable to keep from reacting to the author's description of the scene. The flush on her skin, the way his eyes tracking her every move turned her on, the moans she couldn't keep in while her hands moved under his instruction since he couldn't touch her.

"Go get a toy," Reid commanded, his voice leaving no room for interpretation.

Shaking my head, I pulled my phone out of his hand, fast forwarding the audio to the part where Gio was stripping down across from her, roughly pulling on his cock as her cries increased in pitch.

"I wasn't asking you. I was telling you," Reid growled, grabbing my phone back and stabbing at the screen until the narrator's rough voice cut off.

"That's not what I was asked to draw," I protested, but as his jaw clenched, I knew he didn't give a fuck. Reid was a man who'd met his limit, and I had two options: beg him to leave to preserve my sanity or listen to him and fall into pretending with him for one more night.

"The fuck it's not. You want to see how desperate this character is for her; you do what I ask, so you get the picture you need to give this author the commission she paid for. She wanted a man on edge and desperate, and while that drawing on your tablet is close, we both know you can do better."

"Are you trying to neg my work to get me to touch myself in front of you?"

"No. I'm trying to give you what you need to show anyone who sees that piece that you are the best at what you fucking do."

"It's just a drawing," I whispered, suddenly feeling self-conscious.

"Now, or I will go rummage around in your nightstand until I find what I'm looking for."

Reid's imposing form didn't show any sign of backing down. And I realized maybe he'd been holding this part of himself at bay for the last week, letting me lead. But he wasn't letting me lead anymore, and when he stepped back, settling into the chair and watching me as he slowly unbuttoned his shirt, he knew I'd follow.

Tossing my phone on the couch, I hurried down the short hallway, my pulse pounding in my ears as I yanked open my closet and grabbed the small box from the top shelf. It only had three things inside it, not a terribly extensive collection, but they'd been used more than I would care to admit to anyone.

"You better not try to hide in there." Reid's deep voice carried down the hallway and I grabbed the contents, taking all three items with me as I returned to the living room.

Silently, I laid the trio of toys down in the center of the table between us, watching his reaction to each one. His eyes lingered on the thrusting toy in the center before flickering up to meet mine, a question in his gaze.

Deciding to give him back a little of the attitude he'd had since he strutted into my apartment, I let the thought I would've normally filtered before it came out of my mouth fly. "Just because I'm a virgin doesn't mean I don't like to get fucked."

"Fuck," he cursed before he reached forward to grab the little bullet vibrator from the table, tossing it in my direction.

I caught it, pressing the button to turn it on with my thumb while his eyes continued to watch my every move. "Can't take a little teasing, Reid?"

"Not right now, Haz. Especially since I now know exactly what you diddle yourself with after work."

Despite the tension between us building exponentially, a giggle escaped my lips at his choice of words. "Did you just say diddle?"

"What am I supposed to say? I feel like I'm corrupting your innocent little ears every time I say a curse word," he growled, his eyes still fixated on the bigger toy in the center of the table. I wondered if he was thinking the same thing I was. That it was only fractionally smaller than what I knew was in his pants right now.

Which meant despite my v-card not having been punched, I could take what he had to offer without question. "Just say I fuck myself with a vibrator when I get excited by my commissions."

"Is that what you were planning to do when I interrupted you the other night?"

Shrugging, I sat back into the cushions behind me, suddenly feeling powerful as I watched him squirm at my refusal to play this game by his rules. "Close your mouth, Reid. You're not the only one who gets excited by your job. Does inflicting pain turn you on?"

But he didn't let me keep control for long, sitting up and bracing his forearms on his knees, narrowing his eyes. "Does the thought of me stroking myself in my office after I touch a beautiful woman's body for hours turn you on?"

"Only if you're thinking about me when you do it."

His jaw clenched, and I watched as his fingers dug into his hair, tugging roughly as he tried to keep control of his emotions. "Haz, don't."

But I didn't want him to be in control. If he was here to push the envelope tonight, I was going to push right back. "Because I think of you when I touch myself."

"Fuck. Don't tell me that if you want me to keep my hands to myself."

Going in for the kill, I taunted him, hoping he wouldn't do what I thought I wanted before now. "Why? Afraid you won't live up to the fantasy?"

"No, because if you tell me any more details of what you think about while you're touching yourself, my resolve to respect your wishes is going to be nonexistent. Kind of like your virginity once I get my hands on you."

And that was the sentence that had me stripping off my leggings, spreading my legs and pressing a vibrator to my clit while Reid frantically unbuttoned his pants and tugged them down a few feet away.

Chapter
Twenty-Six

REENACTING THE SCENE OF a romance novel was not how I ever expected to see Hazel like this for the first time, but every inch of creamy skin she revealed drove my desperation for her up a notch. She was fucking stunning, and my fingers literally ached at the thought of touching her. I'd traced the curves she was uncovering through various stages of being undressed, but never with her bare like she was now.

Shaking my head, I tried to focus on her movements, and not fantasizing about things I couldn't have.

That wasn't what this was about.

Tonight was about one last night where we could be together like this, working on a common goal, only the goal of getting pictures she could use for her commissions had shifted into one of mutual satisfaction.

My eyes were still drawn to the vibrator on the table with the long handle. I'd seen enough faux equipment in my lifetime to know exactly what that one did, and my brain had short-circuited when Hazel told me she liked to get fucked. Because that was not something I ever expected to come from her lips outside of a filthy fantasy scenario that my brain had concocted inside my shower while I touched myself to thoughts of her.

And those scenarios had been in overdrive for weeks as she revealed more and more of the person she'd been hiding from me—and everyone else.

Hazel had a secret naughty side, and I was ready to see her let it loose.

"Oh fuck," she whimpered as she settled back against the couch cushions, spreading her legs wide without hesitation and holding the vibrator unabashedly against her clit. This wasn't some inexperienced fumbling as she tried to figure out what to do. Hazel had played with this toy before, and if I had to guess by the practiced motions of her fingers, she played with it often.

My mouth watered at the sight of her pussy, which had my fingers frantically wrenching down the zipper on these damn fucking suit pants and then my thumbs shoving them and my boxer briefs to my ankles.

Her eyes tracked my movements, her pink tongue darting out to wet her lips while she hungrily watched me grab my aching cock and squeeze. At this rate, it wouldn't take much effort to get me there, but I didn't want to miss the show in my desperation to get off.

There wasn't time to appreciate that this was the first moment we'd really had to look at each other in the flesh, not hidden beneath layers of clothes or a strategically placed bedsheet. She was just as perfect as I'd imagined, lightly freckled skin, a pink flush staining her chest and neck from her arousal, guileless brown eyes framed by long dark lashes blinking up at me through the haze of her desire.

The teenage girl I'd once sat across a table from had transformed into a gorgeous specimen of a woman with subtle curves that were going to be my complete and utter undoing. Hazel had always been an important part of my life, and I hadn't lied about her being family earlier, but she was also so much more. At this moment, blinking up at me and hungrily watching the movements of my hand, she wasn't just the woman I wanted anymore; she was the woman I needed to keep breathing.

"You're stunning." My words came out in a low growl, and I struggled to focus long enough to settle into the chair across from her. "I fantasized you'd be like this."

"Like what?" she gasped, dipping the tiny vibrator inside of herself and then pressing the glistening toy back to her clit with a whimper.

"Unashamed," I groaned, flexing my forearm as my fist squeezed the head of my weeping cock. "Wanton."

My thumb passed over the head of my dick, her eyes widening when it slowly brushed against the ring protruding through the tip, causing a rumble to build in my chest. "Seriously fucking sexy."

"You…" she whimpered, eyelashes fluttering as her fingers continued to move between her quivering thighs. "You're sexy too. So strong."

She'd seen me shirtless before, but not like this. Not fisting my bare cock to the sight of her pleasuring herself. But I was trying to hold off, to savor the sight and sounds of her pleasure. Because I knew this might be the only time she let me in like this. This might be the *last* time she let me this close to her as something other than a friend.

And while my motives for putting her in this situation were not exactly altruistic, I also knew that if I came too soon, she wouldn't have the picture she needed.

"That's it, kitten, keep going," I murmured, watching her squirm against the vibrator. Her hips danced across the cushion beneath her, and I could tell she was close by the way her eyes could barely stay open to focus on me. She was lost to the haze of pleasure, and I had a front-row seat. "Turn the speed up, make yourself come. I can see how much you want it."

Her fingers shook as she listened, the buzzing sound that had just been background noise becoming higher pitched, along with the moans she couldn't hold in anymore.

My fingers flexed as my cock throbbed in my fist, but I didn't dare move for fear that watching her would set me off. And whether or not I was actually touching her, Hazel's pleasure would always come first.

"I…" she gasped, her neck arching and her head falling back to the couch behind her. "I can't…"

"You can." My voice was low, filled with gravel as I encouraged her, knowing she was close but not quite there. "Concentrate on how every touch feels. Each movement of your fingers against your overheated skin. The slick sound it makes with every pass of that toy against your clit. How desperate you are. Just let go and feel the euphoria coursing through your veins."

"Reid," she moaned, her eyes locking with mine, her movements frantic as she chased the high she was so close to reaching. "Oh, God."

Adrenaline roared through my veins as I watched her hit the peak, tipping over the edge with a whimpery moan, her legs shaking. Her beautiful body arched against the couch cushions as she let go, pleasure coursing through her body while I watched with rapt attention.

My pulse hammered in the side of my neck, my restraint skirting a very fine edge, but I kept myself under control, just watching her as I waited to see where she wanted to go from here.

I easily could have chased her into oblivion, used the scene in front of me to seek my own pleasure and it'd be over in seconds, but I waited, my fist flexed against the head, trying to keep myself in enough control that I wouldn't risk going off too early.

Hazel slowly drifted back to her body; eyes closed as she stretched her arms above her head languidly with a satisfied hum. But I could tell the moment she remembered she wasn't alone. Her movements faltered, her eyes drifting open until we locked gazes.

"You didn't?" she asked, voice uncertain as she nodded at where my fist had a stranglehold on my dick.

"I didn't," I confirmed, waiting.

"Why didn't you..." her voice trailed off as she grabbed a blanket from the end of the couch, moving to wrap it around herself.

"Don't," I growled, barely restraining myself enough to stay seated instead of flipping the coffee table out of my way and covering her body with mine.

"But..."

"No. If you want this picture, don't cover yourself up. He's desperate, remember?"

She nodded, slowly reaching forward to pick up her tablet and stylus. Her eyes were wide as she continued watching me, likely cataloging how I looked right now.

I hoped this scene would remain imprinted in her memory, so every time she closed her eyes it would haunt her like it was going to haunt me.

"What do I..."

"Play the audiobook, grab the remote for that camera to take pictures if you need to, and draw. You know exactly what to do, kitten." And if she didn't do it soon, I wasn't sure I could hold back any longer.

She nodded, getting everything into place and settling back onto the couch with her tablet in her lap.

As the narrator's voice filled the space between us, my movements mimicked the character, following the description of Gio's frantic need for the woman sitting across the room from him. It didn't feel like I was imitating a fictional character. My desperation was real. I was head over heels for the woman whose expressive eyes were taking in every nuance of the scene in front of her and recording it on the tablet in her lap.

Watching her draw was almost as sexy as the fact she was naked while she was doing it, and I greedily took in her every movement.

"Fuck, Haz. I don't think I can hold on much longer," I panted, my pulse roaring in my ears as I twisted my wrist, thrusting up into my grip as I could feel my balls tighten, threatening to end this very, very soon.

"Just a little longer," she murmured, the stylus in her hand moving furiously as she tried to capture this moment.

"I'm so close. I don't know if I can." My pained groan had a smirk pulling at the corner of her lips, threatening to send me right over the edge. She was enjoying this. And that thought had me using every trick in my arsenal to keep me from coming.

My thoughts were hazy as my movements slowed; my grip intentionally firm to keep from getting there. I wouldn't come until she told me to. And she knew it as her motions faltered, her gaze on my body lingering while she drew things out.

She was torturing me, and she knew it. The little minx.

"Please." I wasn't above begging, my head falling backward as my cock throbbed in my hand, but I kept myself under control. For her. No one had ever made me feel this desperate, but I would do whatever Hazel asked me to.

"No," her voice was stronger, and I tilted my head sideways to watch her, but she wasn't even looking at me anymore. She was completely absorbed in the character on the tablet, bringing him to life in the way I knew only she could.

"Please, baby. I can't fucking hold off any longer. You're too beautiful."

My rough voice echoed the words of the character on the phone speaker, and her eyes drifted to mine, filled with more emotion than I would have expected, given how adamantly she'd been pushing me away before.

She reached forward, stopping the audiobook and setting the tablet in her lap, eyes squarely focused on my hand.

"Then don't hold back," she said, voice confident and sexy.

That was all the encouragement I needed, my fist flying along my length as she watched, her eyes widening as my entire body tensed. I tried to keep my eyes open, but my orgasm hit like a freight train, my cock pulsing in my hand and my release erupting in spurts that dripped down the back of my fingers.

The moment the pulses stopped, Hazel was grabbing the tablet and her stylus; concentration squarely on finishing the last details of the drawing while I tried to breathe, a complete wreck slumped in the chair across from her.

A smile crossed her face as she finished, bright eyes meeting my drowsy ones.

I was sure from the outside, this scene would look ridiculous, me half-dressed with my pants around my ankles and my hand covered in cum, fingers frozen on my waning erection. Her naked, sitting across from me with a tablet in her lap, vibrators spread out across the table in between us.

But I wouldn't change a fucking thing.

"Get what you need?" I asked, afraid to move and ruin the moment.

Her smile spread, her cheeks turning pink as she nodded.

"Now is when you decide to blush, kitten?" I chuckled, watching as the flush deepened, her eyes twinkling when the humor of the situation set in and she joined me, her laughter ringing out into the quiet room.

But as the gravity of the moment set in as the endorphins faded, her laughter slowly stopped, her eyes wary as she looked at me.

"What's wrong?" I asked, reaching to the side table and grabbing some tissues to wipe my hand.

"Did we just ruin this?"

I faltered, my gaze snapping to hers. "Ruin what?"

"Everything. I don't know how we come back from this."

"Maybe we don't come back from this," I whispered, reaching down to pull up my pants. "Maybe this is when things go forward."

"Reid."

Shaking my head, I resisted the urge to look at her, quickly buttoning my shirt and fastening the buckle on my belt.

"You can't just pretend this doesn't change things."

Sitting back with my fingers gripping the armrests, I finally lifted my eyes to find hers. "I'm not pretending anything, Haz. This changed everything. And if you weren't so scared of taking what you wanted, you'd see how good we could be together. It wouldn't matter that there is a reveal tomorrow, and it wouldn't matter that you have feelings you don't know what to do with for someone you've never seen. What would matter is how I feel about you, and what you want to do about that."

"It's not that easy."

"That's where you're wrong. It *is* that easy. Letting yourself feel what I *know* you feel for me is easy, it's overcoming this bullshit fear that I don't feel the same thing—that I'm not fucking desperate for you—that is keeping you from realizing that."

Chapter Twenty-Seven

T HE LOOK IN REID'S eyes last night as he let himself out of my apartment haunted me. But in typical avoidant fashion, I'd thrown myself into rendering the last parts of the commission instead of facing the truth of what he'd said. I'd finally finished attaching the files to an email at 3 am before I'd hidden under my covers and eventually fallen asleep.

I'd survived on only a few hours of sleep before, but I'd never felt quite as weary doing it as I did today. I should have been excited that I was going to meet Seven in a matter of hours, but I wasn't.

My nerves and anxiety had nothing to do with the anonymous man who I had thought I had a connection with. It had everything to do with the man who had walked away from me last night when I'd hidden behind my insecurities instead of telling him I felt the same as he did.

"What is going on with you today?" Charley asked, straddling the barstool next to where I was tying bows onto the heart-shaped ornaments she'd planned to string from the copper ceiling tiles overhead.

"Nothing."

"Yeah, that avoidance thing may get your brother to stop asking questions, but you know I'm not gonna fall for that shit," she laughed, carefully prying the thin pink ribbon from between my fingers and pushing what I'd been using to distract myself out of reach.

"It's...everything's fine. I'll be fine." And maybe if I repeated it enough, it'd come true.

"And now I *know* you're full of shit." Which was why she held the title of best friend. Charley had always been able to tell when something was bothering me, and until now, I hadn't minded her need to fix those things. But she couldn't fix this. The only person who could change the situation was me. And the more I thought of tracking down Reid and telling him how I felt, the more panicked my mind became.

"I think I love him."

Glancing to the side, my best friend was the poster child for the phrase gob smacked, her mouth dropped open and her eyes wide as she stared at me.

"What?" she finally asked, regaining her ability to speak. "What the hell happened in the last forty-eight hours? I thought you were going to see how things went tonight before you decided what to do. You mentioned *nothing* about being in love with one of them."

"Reid. Reid happened. I think I'm in love with him, but I didn't realize that's what I was feeling until it was too late. And now he hates me, and I'm going to die alone."

The more I let myself acknowledge the truth, the stronger the feelings I'd been denying felt. While I hadn't been sure they were real last night—and not caused by the endorphin rush of what'd transpired—in the stark, dreary light of day, my doubts had lifted. But the damage was done. And the fatalistic part of my brain had decided that it was now literally the end of the world.

I knew it was anxiety, and I should just talk to him, but I was also terrified of what would come out of my mouth if I did. And every single scenario my fucked-up subconscious conjured up was worse than the last. My vivid imagination had done more damage to me this morning than Reid ever had. And then my thoughts drifted to having to show him this side of me, and the panic started all over again.

"Wow, you're fucked. Aren't you?" Charley's amused laughter that normally made me feel better only reminded me how terrible I felt. "Although that might be funnier because you're fucked without having ever been fucked."

Waiting until her amusement had run its course, I picked at a loose thread on the side of my jeans.

"I'm not kidding," I whispered as I tried to fight off the urge to cry. "Things got a little heated last night, and I got scared…and then he left. And now I don't know how to fix it."

What if, after he left last night, he changed his mind?

What if, when I saw him next, he pretended nothing had changed between us in the last two weeks?

What if he decided that my hesitations because of another man were something he couldn't overlook?

What if…

"I'm gonna fucking kill him," she muttered, her hands balling into fists in her lap.

Shaking my head, I let the tears that'd been pooling in my eyes fall.

Charley's hands framed my face, urging me to look up as she rubbed her thumbs beneath my eyes. "Did he try to take things too far last night?"

"No, he's never done anything without making sure I was okay with it first."

She let out a relieved breath. "Then why are you so sad right now?"

My chin quivered as I shook my head, my throat too tight to answer with words.

"I thought you were staying away from him until after tonight." Charley patiently waited for me to calm the fuck down, and I hoped my friend would help me figure out how to do what Reid had asked of me. He'd been so sure I was brave, and I'd told him I wasn't with him. But I wanted to be.

"I was having trouble with a drawing, but I didn't want to ask him to help me with it because he'd have to…" I trailed off abruptly, trying to figure out how to tell her what happened without revealing details I didn't want her to know. I'd accidentally overheard way too many whispered conversations to know she was into unconventional playtime with my brother that had something to do with

UNO cards and probably wouldn't judge me. But I didn't blush on command for no reason.

"And Reid's pierced package is now a part of your peen pics?"

"That was a lot of alliteration." And I frowned as I ran what she said back through my head. "And how do *you* know about his...?"

"Accessorized dick?" she asked when I didn't finish my thought. "Pretty sure anyone with ears in this building knows about that. His lady friends talk."

Of course they did. As if that wasn't hard enough. Now, if he suddenly started dating someone for real instead of continuing his string of meaningless hook ups, how many whispered comments was I going to deal with about his past?

"Don't change the subject. You may try to hide behind that adorably innocent looking face and a thin veil of sarcasm, but I know exactly what you've been working on for the last few months. You forget I know what your Instagram handle is, and while you tried to be sneaky and leave it off your website, I found that secret subscription service you started as a little side gig."

It was my turn to be gob smacked as my best friend yet again laughed at my expense, but it'd done the job of stopping my panic spiral in its tracks.

"Huds doesn't know about that, does he?"

"Fuck no. And I'm sure as hell not going to tell him. He thinks you shoot sparkly rainbows out of your ass and will be a virgin forever. I am not going to be the one who tells him that his angelic baby sister draws penises like a pro and has been giving sneaky through the clothes blow jobs to his best friend in the middle of the night in the apartment above the bar he owns."

"Yeah, that's probably a good idea."

"Ya think? Your brother is laid back about a lot of things, but overprotective when it comes to you might be an understatement. There are some things he doesn't need to know." When my eyes widened, she placed a hand on my forearm. "I meant he didn't need to know that you draw dicks for money, not that he shouldn't know you're in love with his best friend. But that is all you."

"It's tasteful bookish dick *art*, not just gratuitous dick illustrations. You sure you don't want to tell him about Reid?" I asked, knowing she was going to laugh at my expense yet again.

"Nope. I'm good." The door behind me closed, and judging by the secret smile Charley aimed over my shoulder, it seemed like my brother might find out sooner rather than later.

My hands began to sweat as I waited for him to join us, and I averted my eyes when he placed a tender kiss on her cheek, running his hand down her arm. "Hey there, little devil. You're not encouraging my sister to do bad things tonight, are you?"

"Not exactly," Charley laughed, standing up and grabbing my much taller brother by the shoulders and forcing him to sit on the stool she'd just occupied. "She's being naughty all on her own."

He cringed, eyes darting between the two of us. "Not sure I need to know that."

"Haz." Charley stood behind my brother, not so subtly nodding my head in his direction. "Now might be a great time to talk to your brother about that project you were telling me about."

Eyes wide, I mouthed, *you're dead,* but she just laughed and escaped into the kitchen, likely to eavesdrop while she pretended to give us privacy.

"You finally going to tell me about that secret project you've been working on for the last few months?" Hudson looked amused, but I knew he wouldn't pry if I stuttered my way through an excuse to run away and hide upstairs until the embarrassment wore off, which would likely be never.

"Not exactly."

He nodded, propping his boot on the bottom rung of my barstool, and tapping his foot while he waited for me to speak. "You know both of us could get on with our days if you just tell me. Because you know Char won't let us leave until we talk."

"So, obviously you know that I've been working on some artwork on the side while I've been taking classes."

He nodded, smiling as his eyes filled with mirth.

"Well, I've been taking private commissions to illustrate some scenes from books." He never needed to know what types of books they were from, and my meddling best friend had better keep that information to herself.

"Sounds pretty cool. I've noticed you buried in your tablet a lot down here. So, what's up? Do you need to cut back on your hours or something?"

"No, not exactly... I kind of wanted to talk to you about something else."

"Okay. We going to do this the Hazel way, or are you just going to tell me?"

My entire family knew that I was completely incapable of talking to them without laying out all the extraneous details I thought they needed to know ahead of time before I just awkwardly spit out the point, but maybe now was the time to just get on with it and fill in the details later. Not that my brother ever needed to know all the details when it came to what had happened in the last few weeks.

Charley's head popped up over the counter in the expo window and she mimed me taking in a deep breath, followed by the two words Reid had used last night: *Be Brave.*

"I think I might, sort of, maybe...beinlovewithReid."

My best friend's hand covered her mouth as her shoulders shook with laughter, but my brother didn't seem to find the situation quite as comical.

"Say what now? You're in love with who?"

"Um...well, you see... I..."

Hudson's hands balled into fists, and his eyes suddenly flashed with something that I rarely saw from him, a bit of disappointment mixed with anger. "Did he touch you?"

"Huh?"

Hudson's jaw clenched, and he shook his head once before refocusing his gaze on me. "What exactly is going on here? Did Reid come on to you or something? Where is this coming from? You've barely talked to him in years and suddenly you're in love with him?"

"It's not suddenly. I've had feelings for Reid for a long time, it was just in the last few weeks that..."

"That he decided he needed to fuck my baby sister?" he yelled, and I flinched, hating that was his response. Hudson loved Reid, and if anything, while he had come on strong about insisting on helping me with my commissions, I was just as much of a willing participant in what had happened between us.

"First of all, *no one* has fucked your baby sister." Hudson flinched, but I didn't stop, suddenly angry that he was just assuming that Reid was the bad guy. "Second, he's your best fucking friend. Do you honestly think he would do anything if he wasn't serious about his feelings for me?"

"But he doesn't take anything seriously, and he's never had a serious relationship in his life. Do you really want to be the person he tries out monogamy on? You think it's gonna last?"

He wasn't saying anything I hadn't thought in the last week, but Reid had also shown me multiple times that he was patient enough to wait for me to be ready for him—even though I'd repeatedly pushed him away. My relationships hadn't exactly been serious until this point, either, so it wasn't like we were on an uneven footing.

"I don't know if it's going to last, just like you don't know if what you have with Charley is going to last."

"But at least I—"

"No, there isn't anything you can say right now to dismiss that you never know if any relationship is going to work out. Just because a relationship lasts a long time doesn't mean it's a good one. Can you honestly say that your relationship with Viv was more important than the one you have with my best friend—who fucking adores you—"

"Stop cursing, Haz," Hudson muttered, but I growled at him and a surprise laugh echoed from the kitchen.

"No. I won't quit *fucking* cursing. Because you're going to fucking listen to me. I may have been afraid to say something—hell, I was afraid to admit it to myself to begin with—but I love your best friend, and he has done nothing to show me he doesn't deserve it, so I'm going to get through this stupid reveal tonight, let down the guy who would probably be the safe option, and then I'm going to find your best friend and I'm going to tell him he is worth being brave for."

Hudson's expression had shifted from anger to something else, understanding maybe, I wasn't sure, but whatever it was had him nodding a moment later and reaching forward to hug me. "He's never going to deserve you, Haz. But I really want him to prove me wrong."

"Me too," I whispered, squeezing him tighter before I broke from his hold. "And you will not be an asshole about it."

"I make no promises," he laughed, leaning back into Charley as she snuck up behind him and wrapped her arms around his shoulders.

"Don't worry, Haz. I'll keep this one in line." He tried to look grumpy about it, but when she kissed him on the cheek, a smile broke loose. He was a total softie even when he pretended he wasn't. "You sure you want to wait until tonight to talk to Reid?"

"Yeah, I should probably tell Seven in person."

She bit her lip, then leaned forward to whisper something in Hudson's ear. He got up from the stool and she sat back down, reaching forward to grasp both of my hands once he was gone. "You know I love you, right?"

"What did you do?"

"It's not my place to tell you, and honestly I don't know the entire story, but maybe go into tonight with an open mind."

"Not your place to tell me what?"

She shook her head, but I couldn't prod her for more answers because a shouted curse from the kitchen drew our attention.

"Are you fucking kidding me?!?"

Then asking her was off the table when Hudson started swearing up a storm that the compressor in the freezer had seized and everything had thawed overnight.

The afternoon was spent in a flurry of activity as we tried to salvage what we could from the freezer, and I got to work hanging the decorations for the party while the two of them scoured every store in town for replacements since we couldn't exactly open the bar on a holiday without things to feed people. And if we tried to close the kitchen for the night, we wouldn't be able to serve alcohol because it violated the liquor license if we didn't serve food after 8 pm.

But as we tried to avert the logistical crisis threatening to close down the bar, a lingering sense of unease grew within me. Because I had a feeling everything was about to change.

And I was afraid it wouldn't be for the better.

Chapter
Twenty-Eight

"**D**O YOU THINK IT'D be okay if you stayed longer?" Colette asked, throwing the bar towel she'd been using over her shoulder and taking a deep breath as we finally got a slight break from the crowd filling the tasting room at the distillery.

In his hurry to leave town, Jay hadn't exactly told me he'd arranged with the event planner at the ski resort to host a special tour and tasting with the guests who were staying there over Valentine's Day. So, when I'd come over to cover for the morning tours, I'd expected to have the rest of the day to track down Hazel before tonight and beg her to forgive me for not saying something about Seven—about me—sooner.

I knew she'd be hurt, and while I'd asked her to be brave with me, maybe I should have followed my own damn advice and not waited until the last fucking minute to come clean.

Jay had called me in a panic, completely apologetic for not giving me the details, but the damage was done, and I couldn't exactly leave his best friend Colette alone to deal with a few dozen tourists by herself. Of course, I'd forgiven him because that's what family does, and after asking for an update on Tristan, who was still stable but being treated for third-degree burns and smoke inhalation, I'd agreed to stay until late afternoon to help.

"I've got something going on at five, so I have to be out of here at four-thirty or I'll never get back on time."

"Oh! Are you helping Hudson out with that dating event that Charley planned? I heard about it from the Wests. They're super excited that she's going to be working for them in time for wedding season." The fact she knew about it showed exactly how interconnected small-town life could be, even from the next town over.

Hudson and Hazel's cousin Colette was a ski instructor during the winter, but she was a trail guide for the outdoor adventure business that Charley's aunt and uncle ran during the summer and fall. We'd all grown up together, and I'd spent the afternoon doing a double take every time Colette walked by because Hazel was like her several years younger twin with nearly identical long wavy red hair.

"No, not exactly. I kind of, um...was part of the event? Sort of."

Colette laughed, clearly getting a kick out of the thought of me agreeing to do something like that. While we'd run in similar circles in high school, she was too busy focusing on her budding professional ski career to pay any attention to boys. Much less ones like Jay, Hudson and I had been.

Looking back, we'd been absolute dumbasses, thinking we were God's gift to the women of the mountain, and I was honestly surprised we'd all turned out as halfway decent, responsible adults who ran our own businesses.

"I'm assuming Charley had something to do with it. I can't exactly see you signing up for that without some outside influence."

"Yeah, no one says no to her." Despite her and Hazel being so much younger than the rest of us, we had all known for decades that once Charley had something in her mind, she wouldn't let up until everyone else had bent to her whim.

"My mom said she convinced Hazel to do it. Did you just have to skip talking to her or something? I can't see my cousin dealing well with you being a part of it. Even though I was out of the country at the time, I still heard about that night at the bar with you and a girl in the storage room."

"Or something," I muttered, hoping she'd change the subject, but I knew she wouldn't.

"Hazel knew you did it too, right? So, she knew not to give her number to you?"

Thankfully, a group of resort guests decided it was an opportune time to get refills, and we spent the next ten minutes mixing cocktails and talking about whiskey production.

I thought maybe she'd drop it, but as a bar towel cracked against my arm and she hissed my name from a few feet away once the crowd had cleared, I knew she hadn't.

"Reid! You didn't fucking tell her." Opening my mouth to respond, she snapped the towel against me again. "And let me guess, she gave you her number, and you spent the entire weekend secretly flirting with my baby cousin without her knowledge."

"I…" Another towel crack had me jumping away from her, but I didn't fight back when she pushed me through the door that led to the warehouse.

"What the actual fuck is wrong with you, Reid Harding?"

As Hazel's furious cousin—who was about an entire foot shorter but still scared the shit out of me—twisted the bar towel around her fingers, clearly wanting to continue beating me with it, I was asking myself the same question.

I *had* asked myself the same question about a million times over the last two weeks. It would've been awkward as fuck, and Hazel probably would have stopped talking to me *again*, but I'd had plenty of opportunities to come clean about my secret identity and hadn't.

Every bit of ire headed my way from the people in Hazel's life who I knew would jump to her side in a heartbeat was deserved, but it didn't really change anything. If given the opportunity to go back and change things, I wouldn't. Not if it meant giving up the time I'd spent with her—both by phone and in person.

"I love her."

Colette stopped in her tracks, blinking up at me, clearly not expecting that to be the excuse that came out of my mouth. Not that it was an excuse. It was the truth. And it had been for a while. It may have started off as a mutual fondness between a shy teenager and an arrogant young twenty-something who thought he had life figured out, but it'd shifted into something I'd always wanted, just never thought would happen. Especially not with her.

"She's gonna kill you. And I might help," she responded, crossing her arms in front of the apron emblazoned with the distillery's logo.

"I just hope she listens to me and doesn't shut me out again."

"Yeah, well, you deserved to be shut out after your dumbass behavior back then, and you still probably deserve it now." She was right. I knew what I was doing was wrong. Hazel probably wouldn't have taken me seriously if I'd have confessed how my feelings had been changing for a while, but now I wasn't sure what was worse… Her not believing my intentions toward her were real, or her deciding that building a foundation on lies and half-truths wasn't something she would forgive.

"I know, I fucked up."

"Yeah, you did. How much time before this reveal?" she asked, pulling her phone out of her pocket at the same time I looked up. The clock read 4:40 pm on the wall over her shoulder, and my eyes widened as I realized I was cutting it too damn close and should have left already.

"Fuck. I've gotta go."

Colette playfully snapped the towel at me as I yanked off my apron, throwing it on the desk by the door before I burst back through it into the tasting room and grabbed my stuff.

She followed me toward the side door, holding it open against the icy February wind as I covered my face, yanked on my helmet and pulled up the zipper on my jacket to protect me from the cold, fastening the snaps on the part that wrapped around my throat.

"Do *not* fuck this up," she growled, but the smile on her face gave her away.

"Pretty sure I already did that, but I'll try not to make it worse."

Shaking her head, Colette leaned forward and gave me a pat on the shoulder before she pulled me into a half hug. "I'm sure Hudson will be the first one in line to fuck you up if you do, but if you don't, please don't break her heart."

I nodded, unsure of what else to say. My decision to leave last night instead of staying to tell her the truth may have already sealed my fate, but the only thing I could do right now was to show up and hope she didn't hate me.

Flipping the visor closed on my helmet, I crossed the parking lot, straddling my bike and backing it out of the spot it'd been in all day. The snow had been sparse, so I hoped the roads would be mostly clear for the ride over the pass back to Sage Springs, but when I hit traffic coming back into town caused by a few cars sliding into a ditch because of ice on the main road, I knew I wouldn't make it on time.

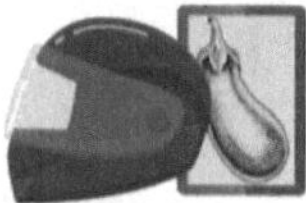

T HE BAR'S PARKING LOT was packed as I finally turned the last bend coming down the mountain pass, coasting slowly onto the gravel. County services had been able to get trucks out to clear the cars from the road and I followed a plow half the way, trying to stay far enough back so I wasn't getting sprayed with ice melt, but I was still really fucking late.

Charley had been blowing up my phone, the speaker in my helmet chiming each time my pocket buzzed, but because of the conditions, there was no way in hell I was pulling over to check a text message. I may have been a daredevil, but I didn't actually have a death wish.

She was waiting inside the door to ambush me when I finally showed up, pushing me out of sight with two hands and slapping a lanyard against my chest. "You're fucking late! As if you hadn't already made this hard enough."

"Yeah, I know," I sighed, inspecting the tag hanging from the lanyard with the number 7 printed on both sides in a blocky font. "You're lucky I got here at all. The temperature dropped, and the pass was like a fucking ice-skating rink. I had to walk my bike along the shoulder through part of it, so I didn't go slipping off the edge of a fucking mountain."

"Well, she's waiting in there to break up with you—"

"What?" Disappointment flowed through me, and I squeezed the paper in my fist, but stopped when Charley kicked me in the shin.

"Don't ruin that. And don't fucking interrupt me. Hazel confessed everything to me this morning and told me she needed to come tonight to let Seven down easy."

I didn't want to let hope set in prematurely, but I sighed, relieved that she'd chosen me. Not that Seven wasn't me too, but if she wanted to let him down easy, that meant that Hazel had been thinking about what I said to her last night about moving forward instead of letting the last two weeks ruin our friendship.

"Well, I wouldn't get my hopes up, because Ten has been in there flirting with her since the minute he walked in the door. And despite her watching the door like a hawk, clearly waiting for you, she's also had to deal with half the girls in the bar gossiping about the mysterious Seven, who they all gave their phone numbers to but never got a text from."

"Fuck."

"Yeah, dumbass, fuck. Why would you flirt with all of them if you wanted Hazel?"

"I didn't, I swear. I was bored as fuck half the time and didn't even hesitate to throw every number but Hazel's away the second you handed them to me."

"Well, don't tell them that because I am not protecting if you do. Thankfully, there seemed to be some people who matched up despite falling for your dismissive bullshit and deep voice, so I'd appreciate it if you could not cause a scene."

"I won't." But as I shifted to the side, pushing my visor down so no one could tell who I was, I saw Hazel throw her head back with laughter as that dipshit baseball player ran his hand down the outside of her arm. When her hand touched the back of his, her head tilting to the side as she looked up at him, I wasn't so sure I could keep my promise.

Chapter
Twenty-Nine

D ESPITE FEELING ABSOLUTELY NO spark with him, I had to give Christian—who'd, much to my surprise, ended up being number Ten—some credit; he kept me laughing instead of crying as the clock neared six and Mr. Seven still hadn't shown his face. Maybe he *had* been trying to tell me something when he said to follow my heart and just hadn't wanted to hurt my feelings.

Although, apparently, I was the only one of the women who Seven had texted. Several of the others had also given him their phone number, but never heard from him. Now there was a bet over whether he'd show up. And if he did, who he'd show up for. But I guessed that would make it easier to tell him I couldn't go on that date with him since he'd have his pick of women who'd be waiting to console him. Not that I expected him to be that devastated.

Not wanting to risk an uproar, I just quietly backed out of that discussion without a word. That was when Christian had cornered me.

Glancing at the clock again, I sighed, wishing I could just go home and curl up into a ball. Or muster the courage to sneak across the parking lot and try to talk to Reid. He had also been missing all evening. I would have expected him to be around to help with the freezer fiasco, but he had been at the distillery all day yesterday since Jayden was out of town, so maybe they needed him again.

Not that I'd know because he also wasn't talking to me. Or I was overthinking things again, and he was giving me space to figure out what I was going to do about tonight, but my text messages had been disappointingly empty today.

"I'm sorry again that I didn't just come out and say something before. I was afraid that maybe I'd saved your number wrong in my phone, and I was messaging some other random person."

"It's fine. I probably should have figured it out when you kept hinting you'd see me soon."

He leaned in close, glancing around before he whispered in my ear. "Did you give your number to anyone else? None of these guys have come to talk to you, so I was just curious if I had any competition."

"Um..." I fidgeted with the numbered lanyard Charley had roped around me as soon as I got back downstairs after changing into the red off the shoulder dress we'd picked out the other day.

A distorted deep voice saved me from having to answer, instead my eyes widened as a palm skimmed my side and a warm body stepped close behind me, his chest brushing against the bare skin between my shoulder blades. "Yes, she did."

"Hey, man." Christian chuckled, extending his hand toward my side. "Decided to keep them thirsty by making an extremely fashionably late entrance?"

"Not exactly," his muted voice answered. Seven's arm brushed mine as he reached around me to shake Christian's hand, my body reacting to his proximity. Fuck. That wasn't good. I'd come here to let him know about Reid, not become even more confused about which one to choose. "I only came here for one reason."

"You know you can take that off, right?" Christian nodded, and I turned, bracing myself and expecting to come face to face with the man who'd charmed me through a wall, but I didn't expect him to be wearing his motorcycle helmet into the bar. I guess that explained why his voice sounded strange.

"Yeah, I'm aware. Actually, can I steal this one from you for a few minutes?"

"Not mine to steal, apparently, but if you screw this up, I'd be more than happy to," Christian commented, aiming a flirty smile at me before he took a few steps backward.

I frowned, studying the details on the helmet out of the corner of my eye as Seven towered over me. The glossy black finish had a decal on the side I couldn't make out, but it looked familiar.

As Christian turned to approach a group of women who'd been standing off to the side, talking amongst themselves, I tried to calm my thoughts so I didn't start word vomiting all over the poor guy once he got me alone.

"Can we talk?" he asked, holding out one of his hands, still covered by a leather glove. I was pretty sure under any other circumstances, a tall, dark and mysterious man in a motorcycle helmet asking me to go with him would have been fantasy inspiring. My fingers itched with the need to draw how he looked right now, but I needed to concentrate.

"Yeah, um, I know somewhere quiet we can go." Taking his hand, I pulled him behind me as I moved toward the back hallway. Hudson was too busy behind the bar to mind me using his office.

Charley watched with a strangely neutral expression as I towed Seven behind me, but the whispers that followed us as people noticed the giant 7 hanging from his neck had my nerves building.

Thankfully, Hudson's door was unlocked as I twisted the knob, gesturing for him to follow me inside the quiet office.

A sense of déjà vu hit me as I took a seat in my brother's chair behind the desk and gestured for him to sit in the one across from it. Maybe it'd make it easier for me to say what I needed to say if he was separated from me by a cluttered piece of furniture.

"Okay, so I know you wanted to talk, but I feel like I need to go first so you aren't wasting your time," I started, and he leaned back in the chair, nodding once in concession.

Even without being able to see his face, I was kind of kicking myself that I needed to end this. He was tall, with strong looking broad shoulders, wearing a blue dress shirt covered by a leather jacket. Dark denim clung to his legs and disappeared into a pair of worn, brown leather riding boots. It was weird to know that I had fond feelings for him without ever seeing his face, but I also knew those feelings weren't enough to stop what needed to come next.

"When we talked at the event, I honestly didn't think you were being serious. I'd never had an instant connection with someone like that. And I didn't expect to flirt with you like we did, because normally I am an absolute hot mess around people, much less around men whose voices made me feel the things that yours did."

To his credit, he just sat there waiting, not trying to interrupt me, and weirdly, also not removing his helmet. But maybe that would just make this easier. Being distracted by his face might make my resolve waver or send me into a tangent that would just make all this more confusing.

"And don't get me wrong, I looked forward to every one of your messages. I felt like you were someone who understood me and would let me express myself without judgment, which is rare in my life." I could count on the fingers of one hand the number of people who treated me like that outside of my immediate family.

"I sense a but coming," he said, leaning forward to brace his forearms on his thighs.

"Yeah. There's a but," I whispered before I took a deep breath. "*But* it wouldn't be fair of me to give you a false sense of hope. Because while the timing was epically shitty, I kind of have really strong feelings for someone else. And I don't know if he's going to break my heart, or if it's a terrible idea to pursue something more with him, but..."

It was harder than I thought it'd be to admit this, especially to a stranger that might have feelings for me. "But he is someone I've liked for a long time, and while my feelings used to be a girlish crush, they've turned into something I don't think I can deny any longer. And to be completely honest, I don't want to."

Seven sat there silently, one of his legs bouncing nervously.

"Can you maybe say something now? I know we barely know each other, and this is probably not as big of a deal to you as it is to me..."

He sat upright, his hands framing the side of the helmet. He hesitated, and I could hear him exhale a loud sigh before he started pulling upward. His face was covered by a black balaclava, but as his eyes came into view—even closed—a surprised gasp escaped my lips.

"But…"

"I'm sorry, kitten," Reid's deep voice was muffled by the fabric covering it, but it was like a punch directly to the gut.

"How? I mean, what… Oh my God."

My pulse pounded as he reached up to drag the fabric covering off his head. His hair was sweaty and sticking up, his cheeks pink from being inside the helmet for so long, but I'd never seen him look so handsome…yet devastated at the same time.

He opened his mouth, but I held up a hand between us, trying to blink away the tears that had pooled as I sat there and stared at him. I wanted to shout at him, to scream and throw things from my brother's desk at his face, to shock and injure him as much as I was feeling right now.

But only one sentence managed to escape my mouth.

"How…how could you?"

And then I was on my feet, running toward the bathroom across the hallway to escape from him, and this time he really could fucking keep the penis—and the jackass attached to it—because I'd apparently fallen for the biggest fucking dick on the planet.

Chapter
Thirty

A s Hazel disappeared from view, the sounds of the bathroom door slamming shut, and the lock being flipped, were like shots directly to my heart. I *knew* I had fucked this up, but the sight of unshed tears and so much disdain in her eyes was almost more than I could handle.

Everyone had begged me not to fuck this up, but I still had. Because instead of talking to her, I'd greedily sucked up as much of her time—both as Seven and Reid—as I could get. I'd pursued her. I'd messaged and charmed her. I'd pushed my way into her business and forced myself into this harebrained idea to help her get reference photos for her commissions.

She had every right to be upset. She had every right to be mad at me for how I'd handled this. Or not handled this, because I'd had more than one opening to confess to her what I'd done.

But I didn't. Because deep down, I was afraid that she wouldn't love me. And now I'd pretty much guaranteed she never would.

Maybe it was better that she'd only confessed to having strong feelings for me. Maybe that would make it easier to convince myself I hadn't meant as much to her as she'd meant to me. Because I knew I would be in a ball crying on the floor if she'd shared the fact that she loved me with another man before she told me.

But it didn't fucking matter now, because she never would. And the longer I waited, staring at that damn bathroom door, the more it set in that she wanted absolutely nothing to fucking do with me.

So, while I wanted to break the lock and pull her into my arms and apologize for how I hurt her, I did what I knew I should. For her.

Gathering my helmet from the floor, I tucked it under my arm and took a deep breath, shaking my head as I walked out the door of Hudson's office, quietly closing it behind me. Two steps and I laid my palm against the worn wood of the bathroom door, leaning in to brace my forehead on it as I tried to come to terms with the fact that I had probably pushed away the one woman who could love me because I was a selfish fucking asshole.

"I'm sorry, Haz," I whispered to the door, but I couldn't hear anything from the other side. She was probably in there crying and cursing my name and I couldn't even comfort her, because I didn't deserve to be around her right now. Or maybe ever.

When the other side of the door remained silent, I stepped away. The walk to the back door was eerily quiet, everyone out front having a good time while I snuck out, knowing in my gut that this was infinitely worse than when I'd left after her accident. Because she wasn't just going to avoid me because of embarrassment for a few years. No, she was going to avoid me for the rest of my life. And to make matters worse, there was a man on the other side of the building more than willing to go after her and maybe deserve the feelings I'd hoped she had for me.

Keeping my head down, I briskly moved down the hall, but as I passed the storeroom, a figure emerged, blocking my path.

"Where are you going?" Hudson asked. "Does Charley know you're leaving?"

He hadn't said anything outright over the last few weeks, but I had a feeling his girlfriend had told him how she convinced me to do the event. Not that it'd taken much convincing for me to agree.

"Yeah. It's all good. Heading home. Just didn't vibe with anyone." Even to my ears, it sounded like a lie. I may not have vibed with anyone *else* during the event. But I'd shared much more than vibes with the woman hiding from me in the bathroom.

"I think we both know that's a lie." Hudson's arms crossed his chest. We were probably built about the same—although I was a few inches taller—but he had a menacing expression suddenly taking over his face. It was then I knew he had more information about what had been going on in the last two weeks than he'd let on.

"What?"

"You think I'm that stupid? I'm only gonna ask you this once, and I deserve an honest answer."

I nodded, suddenly afraid that fucking this up had lost me more than just the woman I was in love with. "You know I've never lied to you before."

"Yeah, you just sneak into my bar after hours to come after my little sister. Lies by omission are still fucking lies."

Taking a step back, I blinked, wondering exactly what he knew and where he'd gotten the information from.

"She told you?"

"Gonna need to define who she is, asshole," he growled, continuing to block my path. "Charley finally confessed to me a few days after the first event that she'd asked you to take part. And while I didn't want you to make Hazel uncomfortable, she assured me that everything was fine."

"But I wasn't sure how true that was this morning, because I come in here to get set up and Char is consoling Hazel about something, and I thought it was because of some Seven dumbass. I'm not ashamed to admit I eavesdropped a little, and concluded that my sister was about to let this guy down easy tonight."

I wasn't sure if he was done talking, so I just stayed quiet.

"But then my sister shocks the shit out of me when she confesses that she's in love with you. I'd always kind of known she was attracted to you. Even when she ran away from you, she watched you. I hadn't realized that I needed to be worried about my best friend fucking around with my baby sister until now."

"I wasn't..."

"And after she talked to me, before I spent all day having to run around because my fucking freezer died an awful death, I realized that I'd been getting weird alerts from my security cameras for the last two weeks. The cameras that send an alert to my phone after hours. I hadn't checked the footage until today, because the alarm never went off, so the person coming into the bar late at night had the code to disarm it. But when I did, I was a little shocked that it wasn't just recordings of Hazel coming and going after midnight."

My eyes widened as he stepped in closer, staring directly into them.

"Kind of curious that you've been here almost every night for weeks and never said a damn thing. So, right now, you're going to tell me what the fuck is going on."

I wasn't sure what to tell him. He could see from the lanyard hanging around my neck that I was Seven, the guy Hazel had been talking to. And now he knew I'd been sneaking over here at night as myself. I hated fucking lying to him, but my loyalty was to the privacy of the woman in the bathroom right now, so I told him as much of a truth as I could manage without giving away secrets I didn't have permission to give. "I've been helping her with her illustrations."

"So that's why you left with sex hair last night," Hudson scoffed. "Did you fuck my little sister?"

Shaking my head, I took a step back, but he raised an eyebrow. Backing away from him only made me look guilty as fuck. "No, but..."

"What the fuck, Reid. You couldn't have just gone after someone else? She's a fucking virgin, dude. And you're my best friend—at least I thought you were. You can't just fuck my sister and then expect me to be okay with it." His anger had transformed into disappointment, and I realized maybe I deserved to lose them all over this. "When you get bored, Char and I are going to be the ones left picking up the pieces. She'll leave. And then every time she refuses to come somewhere she thinks you might be, I'll want to beat the shit out of the man who I thought was going to be my best friend until we were old fucks sitting out on our front porches scaring away the neighbor kids."

"So that's it, you don't trust that my feelings for her are genuine? That it didn't kill me to see her face drop when I took off my helmet and she realized what I'd been hiding. That she is locked in the bathroom right now, hiding *from me*. And that I won't ever be able to do anything about the fact that there is some fucker out there who doesn't deserve her. Someone she'll decide to give her heart to instead."

"And you think you deserve it? You're bailing before things have even started." He shook his head, looking at me like he didn't know me. I didn't know myself anymore either after the last few weeks. At least the person I thought I was.

"I fucking *love* her, Hudson. Like my heart pounds every time I walk into the same room. I can't go for five minutes without thinking about her. When I'm not around her, all I think about is the next time I'll get to talk to her. She's all I see..." I confessed, my voice cracking. "And the worst part of it is, she doesn't want me."

"Did you even ask her that?"

"She made her choice clear," I said, defeated, as I gestured down the hallway to the closed bathroom door. If she had any desire to talk to me, she wouldn't be hiding. And she wouldn't have looked at me like I broke her heart. The way she'd looked at me was going to fucking haunt me.

"Fine, be a chickenshit," he scoffed. "Go ahead and leave. Maybe you're right. Maybe you aren't good enough for her because you're just rolling over like a coward without even trying."

"Fuck off," I muttered, my eyes stinging. "You don't know how hard it is to know I'm not the right guy for her."

Hudson stepped to the side, gesturing toward the back door with a look of disgust on his face. "Guess we'll never know now."

Chapter
Thirty-One

I WASN'T SURE HOW long I'd been sitting on the closed toilet seat lid, staring at the latch on the bathroom stall I'd locked myself inside, but judging from the tingling sensation running up the back of my legs, it'd been a while.

When I'd escaped in here, swiping tears from my eyes, I'd been crushed. Because yet again, I'd been gullible enough to believe that I was a good judge of character.

It seemed my fatal flaw was seeing the best in people. Blindly assuming unless they did something truly, overtly malicious, that they had my best interests at heart.

And now it was clear that not only had Reid kept things from me, but so had my best friend. Who was in love with my brother, who'd I'd just told this morning that I was in love with his best friend. Joke was on me, because apparently, they all fucking sucked.

If Reid had told me who he was pretending to be even a few days ago, before I confessed what was going on to Charley, then I might have been able to salvage my dignity. But now I was going to have to spend the rest of my life in this toilet stall.

Because there was no way in hell I was leaving it to face what happened.

I didn't want anyone's pity, and I really didn't want to have to explain how epically unobservant I clearly was. Although, considering he'd been purposely texting me from a number I'd never seen before, Reid had known exactly what he was doing.

The only question that still bothered me was why.

If he knew when he volunteered to help me with my commissions that he had already earned my number as Seven, then why did he even bother with the ruse? What exactly was in this elaborate plan of his to get close to me?

I wasn't sure what to think of him right now. He'd never gone to lengths like this before—at least not that I'd heard of—to get the attention of a woman. So why me? What was so special about me he felt the need to not only deceive me under the guise of anonymity but invade my life in such a personal manner and share all the intimate moments we had the last two weeks?

Was this all a game to him? A way to fool an inexperienced girl into believing that he had genuine feelings for her.

If I read this in one of the countless romance novels I'd devoured over the last several months, I would want to kick the heroine's ass for being so clueless.

I'd also probably want to kick her ass for not immediately calling the hero out on his bullshit and demanding answers from him. But hindsight and firsthand mortification were 20/20.

"Haz? You in here?"

"Fuck," I hissed under my breath, carefully pulling my legs up so she couldn't see them from underneath the stall door. Maybe if I just pretended I wasn't in here, then she would go away and let me wallow in peace. But, of course, she knew I was in here, because she'd had to unlock the door to get in.

"Come on, sweetheart. Come out and talk to me. Hudson told me Reid left right after he told you. What happened?"

"Oh, you mean you don't already know? I thought maybe since you'd been in on the whole thing that you'd already gotten a full update on how fucking shocked I was from your lying little bestie."

"I know you're mad, honey, but..."

"*Mad*," I scoffed, shaking my head. "I'm not fucking mad. I'm heartbroken. And I feel really fucking stupid that I fell for whatever in the hell was going on. And not only did you know about it; you encouraged it. This is what you were talking about this morning, right? When you said I needed to keep an open mind because it wasn't your story to tell?"

"Yeah, but…"

"There is no, *yeah, but* Charley. You should have told me. I guess at least he revealed himself in Hudson's office and not in a room full of people. Because then I might be able to forget what happened, or at least fake it long enough to show my face in the bar again. Hopefully, no one else finds out, because if this hits the small-town rumor mill, I'll need to change my name and move across the country. I guess I can at least draw fucking dicks from anywhere." My voice continued to rise as the panic mixed with anger flowed through my veins. "What if someone was walking down the hallway long enough to put together what happened? What if one of those women out there who also apparently fell for his charming bullshit found out that the only person Seven messaged was really his best friend's naïve little sister?"

"Hazel, none of that happened, but it might if you keep yelling about it in here."

"I'm not fucking yelling," I hissed, standing up and pulling the stall door open, but of course I couldn't even do that right and the pocket of my dress caught on the latch. I heard the material rip before I looked down to see the several inches long gaping hole in the side seam where the stitches had now come undone. "Great, just fucking great. Now I'm gonna flash my underwear at anyone who is loitering in the hallway when I finally decide to make a break for it and go hide in my apartment where I'm going to have to buy a legion of cat plushies to fulfill my life's mission of becoming a fucking cat lady before I'm twenty-five."

"Haz, breathe." Charley mimicked breathing in slowly through her nose and out through her mouth, eyes widening as I stomped to where she was standing against the closed door.

"I. Don't. Want. To. Fucking. Breathe."

"You're kind of scaring me right now," she whispered, eyes wide as she flattened herself against the wood at her back.

"Good. I hope I am. Because I am fucking done with all of you keeping things from me to manipulate my life." Shaking my head, I bit my lip to stave off the tears. I wasn't sure if they were from anger or sadness, but either way, I was about to fucking blow. And Charley was right in the path of Hurricane Hazel.

"We weren't trying to..." she trailed off when I stomped my foot, pain radiating up my calf because it was still half asleep, but I was running on adrenaline and anxiety, and I couldn't stop if I wanted to right now. "I mean, I wasn't trying to—"

"Well, maybe you should have fucking tried harder."

"I'm sorry. I shouldn't have asked him to do it, but I kind of guessed how he felt about you, and you two were going to continue dancing around each other for another two years if I didn't do anything and now..."

"And now I'm miserable, and he's back home being whatever the fuck he was, and now I don't know if I can trust any of the people in my life. But yeah, that's so much better than just letting things happen naturally."

"Oh, you think things would have happened naturally?" she scoffed, crossing her arms and cocking one eyebrow. She'd been spending too much time with my brother. His mannerisms were rubbing off on her, as well as other things I would never acknowledge, because ew.

"I mean, maybe."

"Yeah, right," she laughed, shaking her head. "He would have tried to flirt with you, and you would have retreated into your shell so hard no one could coax you out."

"I seemed to do just fine while he was flirting with me for the last two weeks. He didn't need your help to pretend to be someone he isn't to get me to confess personal things to him under the veil of having anonymous text conversations."

"I don't think he was pretending, Haz. He seemed genuinely crushed when Hudson talked to him."

"Yeah, I'm sure he did. And I'm sure you were right there eavesdropping on that conversation because you just can't fucking help yourself. You're so fucking nosy that you had to meddle in my life, and now I really am going to end up alone. And someone I thought I had actual feelings for was a fucking sham, and my brother is going to hold this against him. So not only did you ruin my life, but you also ruined my brother's too."

Her head shifted back as if I had slapped her. "I didn't tell Reid to do this, Hazel. He never told me he was going to go after you in real life. I didn't even know if you were going to give him your number to begin with."

"Well, since you both lied to me, now I wish I fucking hadn't."

"So, you wish the last two weeks never happened? Is that what I'm hearing?"

Nodding, I crossed my arms, trying to hold myself together now that the adrenaline was wearing off. "Yeah. I kind of do. I wish you'd never talked me into this stupid experiment."

"Then maybe your feelings for him aren't as strong as you thought they were. Because the Hazel I know wouldn't be standing in a bathroom fighting with me if she were really in love with her brother's best friend. She'd be yelling at him instead."

"It doesn't matter how I feel."

"Why not?" she asked, approaching me slowly and then carefully pulling me into her chest, cupping the back of my head and urging me to lay it against her shoulder as my anger waned.

I sniffed, trying to keep my voice from cracking when I spoke, but I failed. "Because he clearly doesn't feel the same way. I don't know what the whole point of this was."

"Then why don't you go ask him?"

Chapter
Thirty-Two

A ND THAT WAS HOW I ended up standing in front of his apartment door, nervously bouncing on my toes while I waited for him to answer.

The adrenaline from yelling at Charley in the bathroom was wearing off, but I could tell my brain was still riding the wave of anger infused dopamine.

She had made it sound like Reid had come back home after he left the bar, but as the silence stretched on, I wondered if he'd gone somewhere else. Not that he went to many other places than across the parking lot.

Which had me wondering if he was now going to avoid spending time there. Hudson had been too busy at the bar to notice I'd left, but I was sure he had all kinds of opinions on how epically fucked tonight had gotten.

Closing my eyes, I reached up and pounded on the door again, telling myself that I would wait for another thirty seconds before I went back home and started ordering my furry stuffed companions. By the time I got to twenty-five counting in my head, a noise from the other side of the door had my heart rate picking up.

I could do this. I could be brave. Even if I currently felt like throwing up.

"Hud, you know I love you, man, but I'm not in the fucking mood. Just go fuck Charley and leave me alone. You can kick my ass tomorrow."

Reid's tired voice carried through the door, and he sounded about as defeated as I felt.

"Well, I'm not gonna say I've never thought about fucking Charley, but she's kind of disgustingly in love with my brother. So, I'm going to pass," I responded—trying not to immediately turn and run in the other direction screaming—as the door crept open. "But I might take you up on the ass kicking part."

A shirtless Reid was standing in the doorway wearing a pair of low-slung plaid pajama pants. His hair was wet, so he'd clearly been in the shower, but I was here to get answers, not ogle him. Even if he was disgustingly attractive while I was out here fidgeting in the hallway with a hole in the side of my dress, tear tracks on my cheeks, and my once sleek ponytail chaotically styled from the wind outside as I'd run across the parking lot.

"Why are you here?" he asked. Not exactly the romantic declaration that had flashed through my mind in the five minutes I'd been standing in the hallway. Clearly, we were going with option two, him not wanting to see me. "*How* are you here?"

"You think you're the only one with keys and alarm codes?" Charley had left me to wash my face while she'd gone in search of Hudson's spare keys to Reid's shop. She pressed them into my hand with a sticky note that had the code for his alarm system and practically pushed me out the back door. "The real question is, why aren't you over there?"

"Because I realized no one wanted me over there. It was easier to come back home and keep myself from making it worse. Not that I could imagine much worse than knowing you want nothing to do with me."

"Sucks, doesn't it?" I laughed humorlessly, and he tilted his head to the side as he stared at me.

Finally, he sighed, looking away while he scrubbed a palm over his beard. It was a nervous tell I'd noticed he had months ago. At least it was confirmation he wasn't totally unfazed by my presence. "Just go, Haz. We both know you don't want to be here. As soon as you found out it was me, you couldn't get far enough away."

"Well, it's a little upsetting to find out that the guy you've been falling for was lying to your face. And your phone. For weeks. And that he apparently thought it was a joke. Because not only did he have your number, but he had the numbers of every single girl in the room."

He shook his head, still not looking at me.

Fight for me, God dammit. I wanted to yell, but it was like he couldn't follow his own advice. He wasn't even trying to be brave. He was throwing in the towel. And the sadness I'd felt before just seemed to multiply.

"No. He didn't. Because he threw away every number but yours."

As his cautious gaze lifted to mine, I tried to fight the urge to look away. "You expect me to believe that? You saw some of them. I'm not even in the same league as them."

He nodded, standing straighter and crossing his arms. "You're right. You're not."

What the actual fuck? "Fuck you—"

But he shook his head, raising his voice over mine. "They've all got nothing on you, trust me. I had to suffer through dates with them when all I could think about was you."

"But you shouldn't have even known it *was* me. The whole point was to text with someone you'd never seen. Because then you'd get to know each other without the distraction of physical attraction clouding your judgement." Shaking my head, I tried to fight off the hurt that was still underlying all the other conflicting emotions I felt. "But you knew who you were texting. I was just the idiot who was out of the loop. The sucker who fell for your, *follow your heart,* bullshit."

He opened his mouth to speak, but I held my hand up, deciding to just ask him what I'd come here to ask. "I know I'm not as experienced as you, *clearly.* But I meant every word I said and texted you over the last two weeks. And now I just feel like the punchline of a joke. Did it actually mean anything to you?"

My voice cracked, but I managed to keep the tears at bay. He didn't deserve to see me cry.

"Haz, what the fuck? Of course, it meant something. It meant *everything.* I felt like the last two weeks had made everything in my life fall into clarity. That I'd been so listless for the past few years, and all I needed to anchor me was you."

His words made my heart skip a beat. But anchors didn't just hold people in place to keep them from drifting away, they could weigh people down.

"You could've told me sooner. Based upon the way you were going back and forth bantering about Seven and Ten like it was an inside joke, my best friend also knew what you were doing for over a week. And you two purposely kept it from me. You could have told me that day and I would have been embarrassed as hell, but at least I wouldn't feel like I do right now."

He sighed, leaning against the door frame with his shoulder. Part of me didn't want to have this conversation standing in a doorway, but I'd never been inside his apartment before, and call me crazy, but the first time I was, I wanted to be invited, not because I forced myself on him.

"Why couldn't you have just opened your fucking mouth and told me? Said 'Hey, Haz. By the way, your sneaky best friend conned me into participating in her blind dating event. And she fed me information, so I'd know exactly how to charm you into believing I have genuine feelings for you. And then you'll fall for a lie.'"

As soon as the words tumbled out of my mouth, his body tensed, and he shook his head with his jaw clenched. "My feelings for you are not a lie!"

I was a little startled at his raised voice, but if he wanted to shout, I could shout back. "Then why didn't you just open your mouth and say something?"

"Because I wanted you to want *me*, not him."

"Do you realize how fucking stupid that sounds? You *are* him," I hissed. I understood his words, but they made absolutely no sense.

"And being in love with you has made me epically fucking stupid," he said, his voice lowering. "I was also terrified that you didn't feel the same way. That I had gotten myself in so deep with you that when you inevitably found out what I'd done, you wouldn't want anything to do with me."

"Yet here I am, fucking chasing you because no matter how hurt I am, and how stupid I feel, the thought of never finding out why you thought you needed to do this was unbearable." I hid from a lot of things in my life, but if I hid from this, the unanswered questions would eat me alive.

"I thought the reason was obvious, kitten. All of it—every text and every time I pushed my way into helping with your commissions—was because I haven't been able to get you out of my head for months."

The tone of his voice made it seem like he was annoyed by the whole situation, but his gaze was doing funny things to my stomach that should have had me running in the opposite direction.

"I did it because I love you, Haz, and I was prepared to do just about anything to make you mine."

Chapter
Thirty-Three

A S SOON AS THE words were out of my mouth, I suddenly wanted to do what Hazel had done and go hide in the bathroom. Because I was not prepared for the response I got the first time I told a woman I was in love with her.

"*Was*? You're not prepared to do that anymore?" Hazel asked, and that damn sass bleeding into her tone made me want to throw her over my shoulder and cart her off to my bed to shower her in apology kisses.

I hadn't expected my brave girl to embrace her fire and chase me down. I honestly thought that earlier in Hudson's office might be the closest that I ever got to her again. That she'd double down on avoiding me and I'd be forced to greedily catch glimpses of her that never quite satisfied the craving that ran through my veins.

When I didn't respond right away, she narrowed her eyes and propped her hands on her hips, stepping in until her chest was almost brushing mine. It was the worst kind of torture, being this close and knowing I shouldn't touch.

"So, you not only lied to me...you manipulated me...you toyed with my feelings and made it nearly impossible to focus on anything else the last few weeks, and now you're just going to walk away?"

Her hand flattened against my chest, my heart thudding against her cold palm. It physically ached not to touch her, but as the pink blush I craved stained her cheekbones, I knew I was about to face the wrath of a very pissed off Hazel Rivera.

"I guess I never realized that for someone who's gotten so much of it you were such a fucking pussy," she seethed, pushing her hand against my chest until she was forcing me backward into my apartment. She punctuated each word with another push until the back of my legs hit the edge of my leather couch. "That as soon as things got complicated, the man who spent hours talking to me and encouraging me to embrace who I was over the last few weeks would retreat like a goddamned coward."

"Haz, I..."

"Don't fucking interrupt me," she snapped, bringing both hands up and shoving my chest hard enough that I was forced to sit down. "Because I'm not even close to being done."

I'd seen her mad before, but it'd never been aimed at me. And I knew it shouldn't turn me on, but I couldn't look away as she towered over me, living up to my nickname for her. My kitten had brought out the claws, and even if I got scratched, I'd let her take every ounce of frustration out on me because I deserved it.

"I get your MO is to hit it and quit it. And that you've never spent more time focusing on a woman than it took to get in her pants and then run in the other direction because clearly feelings are a hard concept for you to grasp." The flush that crept across her chest and shoulders when she was aroused apparently also appeared when Hazel was pissed, and my eyes were transfixed as she yelled at me. "But if you think you're going to get away with running away from me with a half-assed apology and spouting off some bullshit line about loving me, then you don't really know me at all."

"I..."

"Nope," she said, holding her hand out to stop me from talking. I closed my mouth and nodded for her to continue. "So, you have two options right now, Reid Harding. Are you listening?"

I nodded, balling my hands into fists so I didn't succumb to the urge to haul her into my lap.

"You can choose to hide from what you did, and we'll go back to how things were after the accident—with me pretending you don't exist. And this time I really will hate you."

Her voice faltered on the last two words and her lip quivered, but my fiery girl took a deep breath and kept going.

"Or you can take your own advice and be brave. And you can mean it when you apologize. Promise me you will never lie to me ever again—especially not under the bullshit excuse of it being for my own good. *Prove* that you love me, and that you're willing to be the man you showed me you can be and fight for me. Because I—"

But I didn't give her the opportunity to finish what she was going to say, because I couldn't hold back any longer. I surged up from the couch and grasped the sides of her face.

My lips covered hers, my heart hammering in my chest when she didn't initially respond. But then her hands wrapped around my neck, her fingers digging into the hair on the back of my head and pulling me closer while her tongue plunged into my mouth.

Kissing Hazel was everything I thought it'd be…but also so much more. Her lips were soft and tasted like the amaretto I knew she liked to drink when she was nervous. I expected her to be timid, but she didn't hold back one bit. She was the strong girl—*woman*—who'd been hiding under my nose for years that I never expected needing like I did right now. I'd never felt this kind of desperation before, the need to pull someone close and melt into them.

"Fuck, kitten. I missed you," I whispered into her mouth when our lips broke apart. "I'm so sorry."

"Good, you should be," she growled, her raspy voice doing things that made it hard to hide how much I wanted her beneath the flimsy plaid pants I was wearing. When she pushed up on her toes and pressed her body close to mine, there was no disguising her effect on me. But I didn't want to do anything to scare her. Although I should have known better when she noticed my hesitation to push things too far and took things into her own tiny hands, reaching down to cup the front of my pants and squeezing. "What are you going to do to make it up to me?"

"Fuck," I grunted as her thumb rubbed against my piercing suggestively.

"That sounds like a good start," she teased, pressing against my chest until I fell back onto the couch. Then she shocked the shit out of me by hiking up her dress and climbing into my lap, her hands framing my face before she slanted her mouth over mine and stole not only my breath, but my heart, too.

Instinct took over, and she ground into me as she devoured my mouth, whimpering as my desperate cock pressed against her through a few thin layers of fabric. She kissed me until I was drunk on her, panting when she pulled away a few moments later and gathered the hem of her dress to yank it over her head.

"God, you're gorgeous," I murmured, leaning in to drag my lips across her soft, flushed skin, apologizing to her with kisses and nips that had her gasping and grinding against me in a way that threatened to make me embarrass myself.

My fingers traced the exposed skin that my lips couldn't reach, eventually digging into her ass and pulling her tightly against me until she couldn't get any closer. Our hips rocked against each other while I sucked on her neck, eventually pulling her down so I could capture her lips again.

Her thumbs rubbed against the bars piercing my nipples, the sensation making me throb beneath her. If this is what it felt like to touch her while we still had clothing between us, I knew it'd be explosive when I was finally inside her. But we weren't ready for that. I knew she wasn't, and I didn't think I was either, to be honest. She was right; I had a lot of making up to do. And this wasn't something I could apologize for with my dick.

"Fuck me," she whimpered, reaching down between us and tugging at the waistband of my pants, but I captured her wrist, bringing her hand up between us and placing a lingering kiss in the middle of her palm.

"Not like this," I groaned, trying to keep myself in control. While I ached to be inside of her, I didn't want her to decide like this in the heat of the moment. Hazel may not have made a big deal about her inexperience, but I wouldn't fuck her on my couch after such an emotional day. I didn't want to wake up in the morning with her gone because she'd changed her mind and regretted what happened between us.

"Please," she whimpered, slipping her hand under the flannel pants that barely covered me, gripping my dick in her palm.

"Fuck, kitten." But there wasn't anything I could do to stop her as her touches became more desperate, her grip firmer and more self-assured as she drove me to desperation. "This shouldn't be about me. I'm the one who needs to be making things up to you. Let me take care of you."

"No," she breathed, leaning in to nip at my ear, but her free hand grasped mine, leading it between her legs. "We don't need to choose. We can both get what we need."

Nudging away the flimsy lace covering her, my fingers caressed her slick skin. Each touch elicited a different noise from the wanton woman in my lap. A whimpered moan when my fingertips dipped inside her, my cock throbbing in her palm. A gasp when they pressed further, caressing against a place that had her rocking and grinding down against them how I imagined her riding me. A growl when I slowly drew them out, followed by a groan as I thrust them back inside, enjoying the way she clenched around them.

"Make me come," she whispered against my cheek as she rocked with me, both of us chasing the high that the other brought through desperate touches.

"Fuck, Haz," I groaned, throbbing in her palm much closer to the edge than I wanted to be, but utterly incapable of resisting how she made me feel.

My thumb found her clit, and I tried to concentrate on getting her there before I embarrassed myself.

"Oh God, Reid...fuck..." she moaned, throwing her head back and whimpering as she rode my fingers, squeezing them rhythmically as she let go. I was seconds behind her, pulsing in her hand and spilling inside my pants as she wrung every drop out of me, my heart hammering in my chest.

Leaning my head against the back of the couch, I watched her face. Her eyes were closed, a smile pulling at the corner of her lips, and her chest heaving with each labored breath she took. She was stunning as she came back to me, lashes fluttering before her bright eyes locked with mine. When her smile grew as she looked at me, her teeth coming out to nibble on the corner of her lip, I couldn't keep it in anymore.

"I love you," I whispered, my voice low and rough, but her smile grew, until a laugh escaped her.

She leaned in, laying her head against my shoulder and tucking her face into my neck while her fingers dug into my hair, scratching my scalp as she snuggled against me. I wanted to make a joke about her rubbing up against me like a cat, but when she whispered the words I wasn't sure I'd ever hear into my skin, I wrapped my arms around her and never wanted to let go.

"Love you, too."

Chapter Thirty-Four

"**M**MMM." REID'S CHEST VIBRATED against my back, his fingers twitching and his hips flexing forward as he drifted out of the relaxed and exhausted sleep we'd fallen into last night. After our impromptu couch humping, he'd carried me to bed and wrapped himself around me, stroking my hair until I fell asleep. "Want to wake up like this every day."

I wholeheartedly agreed that waking up in his arms was nice. Okay, it was more than nice. When my eyes had fluttered open, I noticed dawn breaking through the gap in his curtains, and I'd freaked out that last night had actually happened.

Not only was my virginity problem not resolved despite the intense orgasm last night, but Reid had been the guy I'd been falling for in real life *and* in the texts we'd been exchanging. Residual anger still lingered at the edges of my mind, but I'd stood up for myself last night in a way I never had before, and he'd seemed genuinely contrite about his part in the deception.

Hating and avoiding him for the *next* two years wouldn't help either of us, especially if I'd had to watch him decide to try out a relationship with someone else. The thought of losing what had been building between us was more painful than what had happened.

In a twisted sort of way, I was flattered that Reid had stacked the deck to charm me into falling for him. And I trusted he didn't really have nefarious plans to love me and leave me, because he easily could've seduced me into his bed long before now.

Hell, he could've just let Seven drift off into a mystery, never revealing what he did. Then I would never have confessed how my feelings for him had changed. *That* would've been much more deceptive than coming clean, even if it hurt.

But the question that had been plaguing me was, how long had these feelings for me been building? Until a few months ago, my existence had seemed like something that lingered in the periphery of his life. I was just his best friend's little sister who once had considered him a friend—despite the clandestine nature of our late-night drawing sessions.

Back then, the nearly six-year age gap *had* been a big deal. I was a lovesick teen, and he was an adult, but he'd never said or done anything that could've been misconstrued as inappropriate. And despite the way I'd avoided him for the last few years, he'd done nothing to push me or make me intentionally uncomfortable.

"Did you sleep okay?" he asked, squeezing me tighter as his hand slowly crept down my belly and played with the waistband of my lace panties.

"Yeah."

"Are you hungry? Do you want me to make you some breakfast? I'm not sure what food I have in my refrigerator, but I'm resourceful."

"Maybe later," I whispered, and his hand froze. He scooted away slightly and rolled me to my back, leaning over me to look into my eyes.

"What's wrong?"

"Nothing." But I could tell by the flash of disappointment in his eyes that he realized I wasn't being truthful with him.

"Haz. I know when you're overthinking something and freaking yourself out. I can tell by the tone of your voice. Just tell me. You'll feel better after you get it off your chest."

Instead of asking what was really bothering me, I asked another question I was curious about. "How long before you knew fourteen was me?"

His expressive brown eyes traced my face, lingering on mine for a moment before he sighed and rolled onto his back beside me. He grasped my hand, interlocking our fingers. I didn't know if it was to ground himself or keep me from running away, but it worried me he was hesitating.

"I wasn't completely sure until before the motorcycle commission. Charley offered to tell me, but I didn't ask."

He seemed a bit too timid to share the details with me, but he wasn't lying any longer, so that was a start. And when he turned his face to stare at me, all the passion and intensity I'd been convinced might not exist sparked brightly between us. But tucked underneath his warm covers, his large hand anchoring me to him, it was time to come clean with each other. I was serious when I'd told him I wouldn't tolerate any more lies.

"But you suspected something before that." Looking back, all the teasing comments with Charley about Seven were a red flag. If I hadn't been so worried about his overwhelming presence, I should have noticed that something wasn't right.

"The rambling during the date was when I started wondering, but after our first conversation, I didn't want to stop. The better I got to know you, the easier it was to ignore that I wasn't telling you the truth. Although, I was jealous of myself there for a few days, when you seemed to be more interested in talking to him than me."

He'd said that last night, too. That he wanted me to choose him and not Seven. But looking back on it, even though I didn't know it at the time, the parts of Reid's personality that drew me to him in real life were what gained my attention with Seven.

"Which I still think is stupid, but I get it now. You wanted me to like you for you, not because of a man who charmed me through a wall when I let my guard down."

"I know I should have come clean right away, but I knew you'd be embarrassed about the things you said to me and would probably pull away. I'm not ashamed to admit I saw an opening to make you see me and I took it."

"Did the two of you plan the whole thing? Was it all a lie? Am I that gullible?"

Charley's part in orchestrating and concealing the whole thing still hurt, too. She'd been my best friend since we were children, and to have her go behind my back and help with manipulating my emotions was hard to reconcile.

"No, she didn't ask me to do it until you were locked in that bathroom you love so much after telling me I could keep the penis."

My cheeks heated at my unintentional slip, but I could honestly say I no longer wanted Reid to keep the penis. It was mine now. Or it would be once he gave up the goods.

"Are you sure she didn't tell you what my number was? Feed you flirty things to say to me?"

"No Haz," he whispered, leaning in and pressing his lips to my forehead. "Our conversation was genuine, and it also kind of cemented what I'd suspected for months. That maybe my feelings for you weren't so one sided."

"But I didn't know it was you."

"And that's why you let your guard down and actually talked to me. Because we both know if I randomly started flirting with you in real life, you would've gone back to pushing me away."

"But then you *did* start flirting with me in real life."

He chuckled, drawing me in close and tucking my head beneath his chin. His warm hands cupped my shoulders, and my body relaxed as his fingertips traced my shoulder blades. "I think that conversation through a wall unlocked something inside me. I told you I was willing to do just about anything to make you mine."

"There's that *was* word again. Makes me think that you're planning to phone it in now that you've gotten me into your bed."

"Then maybe I need to do something about that. Since I didn't exactly get the Valentine's date that I'd been hoping for."

"You mean having your bestie's little sister yelling at you for being a dumbass and then shoving her hand down your pants isn't your idea of a romantic date?" I giggled, tracing my fingers through the dark hair covering his chest. One of his piercings was almost at eye level, and since it was right there, I moved my head forward, grasping the little ball on the end with my teeth and tugging. Reid's answering groan and the flex of his hips into mine was like a shot of adrenaline, and I did it again, enjoying this newfound power over him.

"*Kitten*," he growled, pulling me closer and digging his fingertips into my skin. "What are you doing to me?"

"I would've thought with your extensive experience you could figure it out," I whispered into his chest, my fingertips skating down his firm stomach toward the trail of hair my hand had followed last night.

But Mr. Suddenly Responsible intercepted it, interlacing our fingers and pulling them between our chests instead of letting me greet his morning wood in a mutually enjoyable manner.

"While I would love to rip that lace off of you—"

"Yes, please," I giggled, placing a lingering kiss on his collarbone.

"You asked me to prove that you could trust me, and while I know we would both enjoy it, fucking you this morning isn't the way to do that."

Pouting, I tried not to be disappointed at his rejection, but the romantic inside me was swooning a little at his restraint. Even if he was being a giant cockblock. Which I had not known he was capable of. But I had to admit, his protective and respectful side was sexy.

"You don't want to play a little, *just the tip*?" I teased, thinking that the hardware on his tip would probably do some very enjoyable things to my lady parts.

"Haz, you're killing me," he groaned, rolling onto his back and pulling me on top of him. I rested my chin on his chest, and his fingers combed through my chaotic hair as he gazed up at me.

The way he looked at me now was still a bit shocking. It was laced with a tenderness that made me want to throw my panties at him, but it was also helping with his case to convince me that his feelings were genuine and not just driven by secondhand, horny illustration hormones.

Part of me wished his camera was set up right now, because I wanted to capture this moment, to draw the two of us in his bed, our bodies pressed together with only some scraps of lace and a pair of inconvenient plaid pajama pants separating us. Maybe I'd have to start drawing some illicit illustrations from memory soon, because I knew my mental source material library was going to get a catalog update—and soon.

At least, it would when Reid finally stopped being so honorable about it.

"Let me take you out before I—"

"Slip it in?" I supplied, enjoying the way his eyes rolled and the rumble that ran through his chest at my suggestive interruptions.

"What am I going to do with you?" he whispered into my lips, craning his neck forward to kiss me.

"I told you I had a list."

I should have been worried about morning breath when his palm cradled the back of my head and his tongue slipped into my mouth, slowly coaxing mine in a way that had my toes curling, but it only made me want him that much more.

Chapter Thirty-Five

Reid

S INCE HE NOW OWED me one, I didn't feel bad about commandeering my cousin's distillery for the morning to carry out my plans. Because while I wanted to show Hazel how much I wanted to spend time with her on an actual date, it was also mid-February in the mountains of Colorado, so it was cold as fuck outside. And it provided the privacy I wanted with her from prying eyes.

There were too many people in Sage Springs and Butterfly Ridge that would start spreading things through the rumor mill if they saw me suddenly becoming affectionate in public with my best friend's little sister.

I wasn't trying to hide her. I just didn't want to share her. I wanted to greedily soak up all her lingering looks and savor all her suggestive touches without the prying eyes of others diluting the way she made me feel.

"I'm going to run to the store. I'll be back in an hour, and I expect you to be ready and waiting for me."

"Aren't you suddenly bossy?" she teased, pushing up to her tiptoes and ghosting her lips along the edge of my jaw.

The wind whipping behind the building of the bar had her shivering and burrowing further into my chest as I held her next to the back door, reluctant to let her out of my sight or my arms.

She'd blushed through the story of how she'd torn her dress last night, but it was too cold to send her home wearing it anyway. I'd pulled out a pair of flannel pants that were huge on her and rolled them at the waist before I covered her up with one of my hoodies that hung down to her knees. Long socks and a pair of much too large slides had been used to cover her delicate feet instead of the high heels I was carrying. Every part of me resisted saying goodbye to her so soon. Even if it was only for a short time.

"You haven't seen bossy yet," I growled, turning to nip at her cheek before I bent my knees and placed a lingering kiss on her cold lips. Now that I had unlimited access to her lips, I hadn't been able to resist kissing her all morning as I fed her breakfast and tucked her into my bed to sketch on my tablet while I rushed through a quick shower.

"I'm gonna call the cops for trespassing," Hudson's voice boomed through the small speaker on the camera mounted in the eaves above the door. *"Quit trying to seduce my sister underneath my fucking camera."*

Hazel and I both thrust our middle fingers in its direction as we deepened the kiss, finally separating with a laugh and agreeing to part for long enough to get ready.

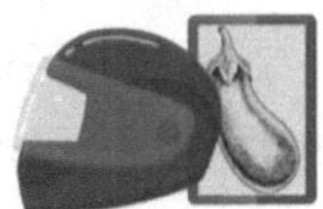

CLIMBING OFF THE BIKE behind the warehouse on the edge of the ridge, I quickly unbuckled the strap on Hazel's helmet and then pulled mine off, gently setting them on the ground next to my bike before I pulled her into my arms and kissed her breathless.

The entire ride to the distillery had been an exercise in restraint as her fingertips traced maddening patterns on my stomach underneath my jacket. I still didn't know where she'd stashed her gloves, but I was enjoying her touch too much to stop her while I navigated my bike over the roads that'd thankfully had been deiced since yesterday.

"You're a naughty girl, Hazel," I groaned against her lips.

"You don't call me kitten for nothing," she whispered while nipping at my lip. Then she reached down to grab what was now *her* helmet. She did indeed make a warm little backpack companion, and I couldn't imagine riding with anyone else.

"Killing me," I groaned under my breath, pulling the food I'd brought with me from the storage on the side of my bike and following her down the packed snow-covered path to the back door.

She bounced in place while I unlocked the door, rushing into the warm building and stripping off her coat as I followed behind, finding a place underneath the windows overlooking the woods at the back of the building to set up our picnic.

"Brought me back to the scene of the crime?" she teased, wrapping her arms around me from behind and laying her cheek against my back. For a woman who'd been resistant to get within a few feet of me only weeks ago, she hadn't had any trouble transitioning into being able to touch me now. And her continued affection had me falling even harder for her, because last night I had thought my questionable decision making would drive her away for good.

But she'd chosen to give me another chance, and I wouldn't squander it, because she deserved a man who wasn't afraid to show her how much of a treasure she was.

"If I remember correctly, you seemed to enjoy your time here quite a lot."

"For someone who refused to play *just the tip* with me this morning, you don't seem to be doing a very good job of keeping my mind off it. Because you just set up a romantic picnic in the same spot where we played just the finger*tip*."

"Shut up and sit down so I can hand-feed you grapes like the goddess you are," I growled. Spinning around, I pulled her giggling form into my arms. I dipped her back, pressing my lips to the hollow of her throat, and my chest warmed at the way she clung to me just as tightly as I held her.

"And you told me no one threw their panties at you in this building."

Laying her against the blanket and propping myself onto my side next to her, I whispered words in her ear that would have had her scurrying away from me even a few days ago. "Let me romance you like you deserve right now. You can take off your panties and throw them at me all you want once I get you in my bed later."

"Promises, promises," she sighed, leaning over to dot a kiss on my nose before she sat up, reaching for the bowl of grapes and holding them in front of my face. "Now, feed me, since you won't fuck me."

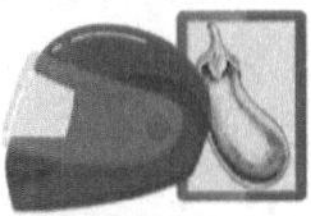

IF I THOUGHT HAZEL was shy before, I clearly hadn't been paying attention very well.

We spent the morning and well into the afternoon flirting and talking and kissing in the darkened warehouse until I knew we needed to go because Colette was coming to lead a few last tours and tastings while Jay was still in Wyoming.

While I knew her cousin wouldn't judge us for sneaking off somewhere secluded and quiet for some alone time, I also didn't want to share my time with Hazel.

She was finally showing me a whole new side of her personality that I was becoming hopelessly addicted to. The introverted, blushing, sometimes rambling adorable person she'd always shown me before was still very much there in her personality, but there was this new confidence in the way she interacted with me that was undeniably sexy.

And while I'd managed to resist her last night, and then again, this morning; I was now fighting the urge to rip off her panties before she could throw them at me.

But getting caught frantically deflowering her on a blanket on a concrete floor wasn't how I'd imagined being with her the first time. I wanted to unwrap her like a present and kiss every inch of her skin before I slipped inside her.

"You ready to go home?" I whispered into her neck, enjoying the way she pressed herself back into my chest while she rested between my thighs with my hands idly tracing the skin on her stomach.

"You ready to fuck me?" she asked, turning her head to the side to look back at me. "Now that you've shown me how much of a secret romantic you are, I'm having trouble resisting you."

"The feeling is entirely mutual." My lips traced the soft skin on the side of her neck suggestively as my fingertips dipped below the waistband of her pants. I wanted to take things further, but the beep of the alarm system chiming at the front of the building had me pulling her up and quickly shoving the remnants of our picnic back into my bag.

"Fuck, Colette is here to do the afternoon tours."

"Trying to hide me?" she asked, but I could tell she was just teasing me.

"No, just really don't want to fucking share you."

Hazel laughed, helping me clean up and scurrying toward the back door as her cousin's voice echoed back to our hidden corner.

"You don't have to run off on my account!"

"Sorry, Coley. Talk later. Gotta go violate my boyfriend now!" Hazel giggled, yanking the front of my jacket toward her to steal a kiss before she darted out the back door toward my awaiting bike.

Colette peeked her head around the partial wall that concealed our hiding spot as I pulled the door back open.

"So, you must not have fucked up too badly," she laughed, swinging a bar towel at her side, clearly a hidden threat to start snapping me with it like she had yesterday.

"Oh, I did," I chuckled, still a little unbelieving that Hazel had actually come after me last night. "But I'm working on fixing it."

"Good. She deserves someone who won't give up on her. And I guess if you're serious about finally growing up, you do too."

Smiling, I grabbed the rest of our gear. "Aw, that was almost sincere, Col."

"But don't fuck it up. Because I know every trail on this mountain where no one would think to look for a body."

She laughed as I nodded and escaped out the back door, eager to get back home with her cousin. Because now that I'd given Hazel what she deserved in a date, I wanted to end the night inside her, showing her exactly how she should be worshiped by a man.

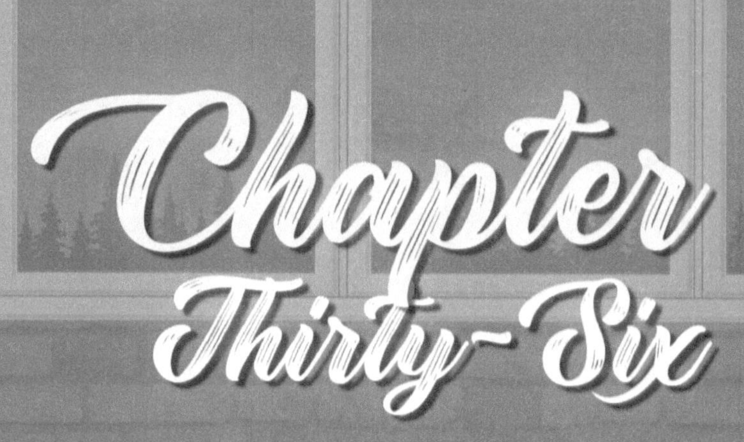

Chapter
Thirty-Six

Reid

THE RIDE BACK DOWN the mountain was just as torturous as the ride up it, and I was fucking aching by the time we pulled into the parking lot behind the shop. I wanted to take her to *my* bed, but there were cars parked out front, and I really didn't want my employees to know what it sounded like when I made Hazel come.

Nodding toward the bar's parking lot after I helped her off the back of the bike, I was thankful for small miracles because Hudson's car and his bike were absent, despite him typically coming in by now to start on prep work. "Your place?"

But I couldn't hold out any longer, and he would just have to fucking deal with it if I was fucking his little sister when he showed up for work.

"I don't care as long as you have that hard cock inside me in the next ten minutes," Hazel whispered in my ear, her hand gripping me through my jeans and sending a shot of adrenaline licking up my spine.

"Deal," I grunted, pulling her hand away and kissing her cold lips before I snuck in the back of the shop to stash our helmets inside the door before I was grasping her hand and towing her across the parking lot behind me.

Hazel's laughter surrounded us as I crowded against her back, watching her shaky fingers punch in the code on the lock. The sound warmed me from the inside out, and I wanted to keep her this happy always, but I was also in a hurry to get her naked.

Grasping her around the waist with one arm, I carried her toward the stairs with my hand sealed over her mouth, just in case someone was here that we didn't know about. I wasn't risking any more interruptions.

We crashed through the door to her apartment moments later, ripping at each other's clothes as we stumbled down the hallway toward her bedroom. Her shirt was long forgotten, tossed over my shoulder as we passed the couch. She toed off her shoes and ripped down her pants as I tried to unzip my coat and unbuckle my belt. By the time we made it to her bed, my pants were around my ankles and her hands were tugging at my boxer briefs.

"Fuck," I grunted as her chilly hand wrapped around my dick, but it turned to a loud groan as she pushed me to sit on the edge of the mattress and dropped to her knees. Her tongue darted out, tracing up the underside slowly. When she reached the tip, her teeth tugged at the little ring on the end before I could fully appreciate that she had her mouth on my bare skin.

The last time Hazel had my dick near her mouth, I'd come embarrassingly fast in my own boxers and this time wasn't any better as she sucked the tip—her tongue playing with my piercing—and then opened her mouth, my hard cock disappearing between her kiss-swollen lips.

"Oh fuck, slow down," I moaned, lacing my fingers into her hair and flexing my hips into the movements of her sinful mouth. My kitten was a natural and had me riding the edge within minutes, desperately trying to hold off, because this shouldn't be all about me.

Using my leverage on her hair to pull her head back, I rubbed the thumb on my other hand against her bottom lip while she panted, enjoying the way she hummed against it.

"Get on this bed, because the next time I come, it's going to be inside you," I growled, pulling her up and spinning her around to sit on the bed. She lifted her hips, scrambling backward across her covers. She laid back against her pillows, spreading her legs and caressing her tits as she watched me yank off my boots and my pants, leaving them in a heap next to her bed.

"You're so fucking gorgeous," I groaned, crawling up the mattress to shove my shoulders between her legs, hooking my arms around the backs of her thighs and yanking her hips toward my lips. She could suck my dick another day, because I had some apologizing to do. First on my list was her pussy.

Hazel's back arched as I sucked her clit between my lips, her fingers diving into my hair and pulling me closer as she rocked against my tongue. If I would have known she'd be like this, I would have seduced her years ago. Because I was mentally kicking myself for watching her from afar for far too long.

"Oh, fuck, I'm gonna come," she gasped, yanking my hair as I lapped at her, concentrating the tip of my tongue on the spot I knew would send her over the edge. She moaned my name as her pussy pulsed against my tongue and I growled into her flesh as her fingernails scraped my shoulders in her frenzy to get me closer.

Kissing my way up her stomach, I nuzzled her neck, but she wasn't having any of it, grasping my cheeks and shoving her tongue into my mouth despite the evidence of her orgasm all over my lips and beard.

My hips ground against hers as she kissed me, not so shy any longer. And I fucking loved that she was as desperate for me as I was for her.

"Nightstand," she panted, blindly reaching to her side as I sucked on her pulse point. I was bound to leave a mark on her delicate skin, but I really didn't care, so long as everyone knew she was mine. "Now, Reid, please."

Leaning over, I pulled open her drawer, resisting a laugh when I saw she'd apparently put the thrusting vibrator inside of it after we were done the other night. I wanted to watch her with it, but that would have to be another time, because there was no way she was coming on a silicone toy when I was moments away from being inside her.

Pushing it out of the way, I grasped a condom, tearing the edge of the wrapper open with my teeth before I pushed myself up on one arm, our hands disappearing between our overheated bodies to secure it into place.

Hazel's chest heaved as I settled over her, her eyes desperately seeking mine as I teased her entrance with the head of my dick, watching as the covered ring pressed against her clit. She ground her hips up into my teasing motions, riding the tip and covering the condom with the evidence of her desire for me.

She panted and gasped as I teased her, winding her up to where she was desperately squirming underneath me. A needy moan escaped her lips, cutting off with a gasp as I inched my way inside, grinding my teeth at how tight she was.

She'd been snug around my fingers last night, but she was about to strangle an embarrassingly early orgasm out of me at this rate.

"Breathe, kitten, breathe. I've got you."

"I know," she gasped again, tilting her hips and I groaned as I slipped inside further. "But it's so big. I mean, I knew it was big, but now it's big and inside me and it feels so... and..."

I smothered her rambling with a deep kiss, coaxing my tongue against hers until I felt her body melting into the mattress beneath her. It was understandable that she was nervous, and I knew she rambled when she was overwhelmed, but I needed her to relax. Because I only wanted to make her feel good. I had to make this something she'd look back on fondly.

She deserved to have a memorable first time, even if it was with a piece of shit like me who didn't deserve this. Who didn't deserve *her*. But I wanted to, desperately.

"Oh God," she moaned against my lips, arching her back and pressing her chest against mine, the pitch of her voice almost as desperate as her hard little nipples dragging across my chest. "You're everywhere. I didn't know it'd be this overwhelming."

"Being inside you is fucking addictive," I murmured, tilting my hips and pressing forward until I didn't know where she ended, and I began. "This feels so right. It's never..."

"Felt like this before," she finished my thought, chasing my movements with her hips as I pulled back and then seated myself fully inside her tight, wet pussy—that was now mine. She was mine. And I was a selfish fucker who never wanted her to belong to another man. Ever. I was the only one who would ever touch her like this. The only one who would ever be inside her.

"And you were worried you wouldn't know what to do."

Her eyes danced along my face as I gazed down at her flushed cheeks, cataloging every nuance of her features. She was so beautiful, and part of me still didn't believe that her feelings were as strong as mine.

"I...oh, fuck, right there...right fucking there...love this...you feel so...I didn't know...I wanted it to be you...I...I...love you," she babbled, her nails digging into my back as my hips faltered, the intensity of it all driving me way too close to the edge.

"I love you too. I told you whoever was lucky enough to be inside you like this would be hopelessly in love with you."

Her eyes shined as I traced her temples with my fingertips, watching her every expression as I rolled my hips. My eyelids fluttered as her pussy squeezed my cock tightly every time I pulled away, clearly as desperate to keep me inside of her as I was to be there.

But the friction had me slowly losing my mind, driving into her harder. Craving every whimper and moan as I fought the urge to fuck her into the mattress until she screamed.

"I never wanted it to be anyone but you. Always you," she gasped, turning her head and moaning into her pillow. Needing to get closer, I wrapped my arm around her back, holding her tightly to my chest as I drove into her. My mouth rested on her neck, her pulse thrumming against my lips.

"I knew being inside you like this would drive me insane."

"Harder," she whispered, her hips bucking into mine. "I need it harder. Want to feel you for days."

"I'm gonna come if I go harder. You're too tight. It's too much."
She murmured agreements as I kept up the steady pace of deep

thrusts, feeling her body light up as my cock dragged against a place inside her that made her clench each time my piercing grazed it.

Despite only watching her come a few times in person over the last several days, instinctively I knew she was close.

Pushing away from her, almost laughing when she tried to drag me back down, I pressed my knee forward and angled my hips, my chest rumbling at the surprised moan that escaped her at the change in angle.

"Again. That felt so good. More. Please. Fuck... Reid. I want to come so bad. I can feel it building but..."

My hips rolled in firm but fluid movements, her stream of words punctuated by her desperate moans as I felt her riding the edge. Desperate to fall over but not getting quite close enough.

"Breathe," I exhaled, bringing my hand to where we were joined and slowly rolling my thumb across her clit the way I'd seen her do to herself.

The way I'd been desperate to at the time but so lost in a haze of arousal that I'd been simultaneously chasing my release as I watched her fall apart on the couch across the room.

But I couldn't think about the times I'd watched her come in the last week. The way she sounded when she pulsed around her own fingers instead of mine.

Because I needed her to get there.

I needed her to come.

Now.

"Fuck. I can feel how close you are. You're so fucking wet. And tight and I want you to breathe and let go. I need you to come on my cock, kitten."

"I...I..." she gasped, her eyes rolling back and her neck arching as she bucked into my movements.

"That's it. Feel it. Feel how fucking spectacular we are together. How right this feels."

"Harder," she whimpered, and I gritted my teeth, doing as she asked and barely holding on as I tried not to let how amazing she felt drag me under before her.

"Whatever you want. Just want to make you feel good."

"So good," she sobbed, a tear rolling from the corner of her eye as she stared up at me through glassy eyes.

I knew if I kept things up at this angle, I could get her there, but I needed her closer.

Cradling her to my chest, I rolled my hips, driving her up the mattress with each thrust. She clung to me, her chest heaving as she let the pleasure drag her under, crying out into my neck as she came.

"Fuck, Haz. *Yes*. I didn't know it could feel like this. I don't want to stop."

"I want you to come inside me," she whimpered, her short nails digging into the center of my back, urging me to join her.

I tried *desperately* to drag it out, to feel her for just a moment longer, but I couldn't hold on, my release spurting into the condom moments later while I crushed her to my chest, clinging to the woman who I couldn't imagine my life without.

Epilogue

Reid

"OH, MY GOD! OH! MY! GOD!" Hazel's excited voice had me rushing up the stairs to the apartment, wishing I'd been the one to make her scream like that, but I hadn't hesitated to haul ass across the parking lot when she'd texted me she'd gotten a package this morning.

Using my key to let myself inside, I found her bouncing on the couch, a hardback book clasped tightly to her chest.

"Did it come?" I chuckled, knowing how much this moment meant to her. This was a big deal, and I was so fucking proud of her.

"Oh my God, I love it so much," she cooed, cradling the book in her arms and rocking from side to side with elated tears escaping the corners of her eyes.

Crossing the room, I sat down on the coffee table in front of her, holding out a hand as I watched my girlfriend lose her damn mind over a book. "Well, let me see it."

She tilted her head, her eyes flashing to mine as she clutched it a little tighter.

"Oh, come on, kitten. I helped, you could at least let me see it for a second before you run off with it. If I didn't know better, I'd think you loved a book cover more than me."

"Never," she cooed, reluctantly offering me the hardback, one of her illustrations wrapping around the entire book jacket.

In the last five months, her growing business had flourished, and when a publisher out of Boston had contacted her to commission a special edition cover for two of their authors, we'd celebrated by fucking on my bike hidden behind her parent's cabin in the mountains before we got to work taking dozens of source photos for her to work off.

"This is fucking amazing, Haz. I'm so proud of you, baby."

She swiped away happy tears, grinning at me in a way that made my heart pound. "I still can't believe my work is in bookstores now and that I've actually talked to Chastity Rose and Stone Evans. Pinch me!"

Chuckling, I carefully set the book down on the table beside me, cupping her cheeks and rubbing away the wetness, my lips covering hers until she was sighing into my mouth and trying to crawl into my lap.

As much as I wanted to enjoy more celebratory sex, I had plans for her this morning, and I hoped she'd be just as excited as I was about them.

"I've got a better idea," I murmured against her lips, halting her wandering hands before she could pull down the zipper on my pants.

Hazel was insatiable, and I fucking loved it, but right now I wanted to get her pants off for another reason.

"Better than me riding your cock on the living room floor?" she asked, tugging at my ear with her teeth.

"You can ride me later if you aren't too sore," I groaned into her cheek, wanting to kick my own ass for not letting her have her way with me, but I'd been booked solid all month and had finally cleared an afternoon in my schedule to surprise her.

"Sore?" she asked, trying to pull back to look at me.

But I ignored my slip, tugging on her hand and hoping I could distract her before she asked too many questions. "Come on, come to the shop with me."

She huffed, but didn't hesitate to follow. I'd given my staff a paid afternoon off, so the back hallway was quiet as I ushered her inside.

Hazel knew the way to my private workspace well, spending lots of time curled up in the corner drawing while I worked on sketches for clients. She'd been delighted to finally see me in action, not realizing that I had a very similar software to the one she used for her commissions.

But today she was going to be the client in the chair, not just an observer or my sketching companion.

"Take a seat," I said, passing her and moving to the sink to wash my hands before I pulled on a set of black gloves, her eyes widening when I playfully snapped the band against my wrist.

"You planning to play naughty doctor and patient?" she asked, draping herself across the crinkly paper covering my reclining chair.

"Not exactly," I chuckled. "But I need you to take off your pants."

She glanced toward the open door, but listened, slowly inching her leggings down. I watched, my fingers twitching with the need to touch her, but I just waited with my hips leaned against the countertop behind me as her smooth, flawless skin came into view.

"Panties too."

Her head tilted to the side as she shot me a cheeky look, wiggling her eyebrows as she did what I asked, tossing them toward me once she was uncovered from the waist down.

"Want me to take off my shirt now, too?" she cooed, playfully tugging on the hem and flashing me the bra that matched the panties clutched tightly in my fist.

"Later." My voice was gruff, my body betraying me as my cock tried to negotiate a detour to my afternoon plans. "Lay back on the chair."

"Want me to spread my legs?" she sassed, flashing me an enticing view of her bare pussy, but I had to be strong, because I wanted to see my ink on her skin more than I wanted to fuck her right now. As wrong as it felt to be turning her down, I had my reasons.

"Nope, I need you to lie on your back, hands on your stomach."

She pouted, pretending to walk her fingers lower to touch herself, but eventually listened, heaving a deep sigh with her hands folded across the tank top covering her stomach. I sat down on my stool and rolled in close. Swiping an alcohol pad over the dip on the side of her hip, I expected her to ask a million questions, but she just watched quietly while I shaved the downy hairs from her skin. Her eyes widened when I followed up by laying the stencil in place and carefully rubbing with firm strokes of my thumb to transfer the image onto her skin.

Curious eyes lit up as I peeled away the paper, revealing the abstract outline of the kitten I'd sketched on her tablet months ago while I plotted the first thing I wanted to ink on her skin.

"What about the calf wrap?" she asked, knowing I'd spent the last few months perfecting the illustration of the vined peonies for her next tattoo.

"I thought it might be a good idea to start small for the first one," I murmured, getting my tools unwrapped and set out across my rolling cart. "This one won't take very long, and if you decide you want to wait on the calf piece, you won't have a partially finished tattoo on your leg in the meantime."

She inhaled a shuddering breath as I loaded the ink onto the needle, hovering above her hip, while I gave her a moment to calm down.

"You ready?" I asked, wanting to lean in to kiss the tiny temporary mark on her skin, but also knowing I'd just have to delay things to sanitize again before I could get to work.

"Yup, go for it," she squeaked, nodding.

"Deep breath, kitten. Then let it out slowly."

She listened, taking a deep breath in before she released it through her nose, her eyes watching my hands as the needle brushed her skin for the first time.

There was something satisfying about knowing that she'd given me another one of her firsts, a grin tugging at my lips while I worked. Hazel had let out a surprised gasp at the first few strokes of the needle, but then she'd melted into the chair, watching me mark her with hooded eyes.

Which made resisting her that much harder, and by the time I smoothed the clear bandage over the quarter sized tattoo, I was glad I'd cleared the building for the afternoon.

"You want me here or my bed?" I asked, knowing exactly how turned on she'd gotten while I inked her. Timid Hazel would have been mortified to see the wet mark on the paper beneath her hips, but horny Hazel just grinned when I growled at the sight of it.

"Bed," she gasped before I leaned in, kissing her lips while I blindly reached over to leave my gun on the cart and ripped the gloves covering my hands off so I could touch her. I should be responsible and clean up my equipment, but that could wait until later.

Right now, I needed to fuck her while I stared at the permanent mark I'd left on her skin. When she ripped my belt from the loops and her hand dove into my pants, gripping my hard cock, I knew she needed the same thing.

Carefully gathering her into my arms, I cradled her body against my chest and headed for the stairs, pausing every few steps to kiss her while she clawed at my hair.

My motions were intentionally gentle as I sat her on the bed, watching her pull her top over her head and discard her bra as I yanked off my clothes. While I shoved down my briefs, I calculated the positions we could use to keep from rubbing her ink, but I wanted to watch her face when she fell apart. Although she had come to appreciate the use of walls during sex.

Sitting down in the center of the bed, I carefully pulled her toward me, maneuvering her to straddle my legs with hers outstretched behind me. Pulling one leg up and over my shoulder, I grinned as she gasped and reached back to brace her palm against the mattress between my legs. "You're lucky I'm so flexible," she giggled.

Her inked hip was straight as it extended past me, but I stopped briefly to check that she was comfortable before I poised myself at her entrance and urged her to lift her hips. "And while I'd love to fold you up like a pretzel and fuck you into the mattress right now, I want to watch you use my cock to make yourself come knowing you've got a permanent reminder of me on your skin."

"Such a romantic," she sighed, reaching down to rub the head of my cock to her clit. She teased herself with my piercing before she fit my cock to her entrance easing it inside her glistening pussy. It throbbed as it disappeared inside her, my deep groan joining her gasping moan as her hips rocked against me.

"That feel good, kitten?" I asked, thrusting my hips to match her movements, holding her calf and dragging my lips across her scar as she rode me with her head thrown back.

"Ohh, fuck yes," she moaned, chasing the high she knew I could give her, leaning back until I could feel my dick hitting the spot inside that would tip her over the edge the quickest. "You know I love your cock."

Hazel had been shy about riding me when we first started having sex, but she'd quickly gotten over her nerves, often preferring to watch me fall apart beneath her now that she knew exactly how to control the angle to use my piercing to her advantage.

She knew I was hopelessly addicted to watching her come. Especially when I was inside her. Although she enjoyed making me jealous by forcing me to watch her with a toy until I couldn't take it anymore and flung it across the room before I replaced it with my cock and showed her who really owned her pussy.

"I love you," I groaned into her skin as I felt the telltale flutters of her orgasm building, her fingernails digging into my shoulder as she ground down against me.

My eyes drifted to the tiny, inked kitten, my hand holding her waist steady to keep her from disturbing it too much with her frantic movements.

"Love you, too," she moaned, her head tipped back, and a look of ecstasy painted across her delicate features as I pulled her onto my hips. "Oh, fuck, I'm close."

Groaning, I thrust harder, yanking her hips to mine, watching as a flush raced across her bouncing breasts and up her neck before I felt her finally come with a loud moan. I followed her moments later, pulsing inside her as she gasped out my name.

Her eyes found mine with a satisfied smile before she rolled her shoulder, collapsing back to the mattress between my legs with a giggle.

"So, you like your new kitten, *kitten*?" I chuckled, rubbing my thumb along the edge of the clear film, careful not to disturb it.

"You're not allowed to tattoo women anymore," she giggled, rolling her head to the side, her hair a chaotic mess against the rumpled sheets. "Because it was unreal how horny that made me."

"Not interested in fucking anyone but you after a session," I laughed, reluctantly lifting her hips and slipping out from beneath them. She curled into my chest after I stretched out onto the mattress next to her, fingers tracing the dark ink over my pec.

I'd had Gray tat a tiny matching kitten in white ink over my heart that almost blended into my skin tone almost a month ago, giving me shit the entire time. Luckily, it'd coincided with Hazel making a trip to Boston to meet with the publisher in person to finalize the cover design. It'd healed enough by the time she returned, and she hadn't noticed yet.

Capturing her fingers, I moved them to the center of my chest, holding her finger as I used it to trace the shape, watching with a soft smile as she noticed the faint mark, her eyes meeting mine as her chin quivered.

"For me?" she asked, eyes filled with emotion.

"Nope," I teased. "It's for that other feral cat lady who lives across the alley."

"Fuck you," she giggled, pushing against my chest, but when my lips flattened against her forehead, she let me pull her closer to breathe her in. "She doesn't live there anymore."

"Hmm," I hummed, smiling against her skin. "Glad she finally came to her senses and took over my apartment."

"Me too." Her voice was quiet as her fingertip returned to tracing the mark on my chest.

Hazel still worked in the space above the bar, and sometimes we crashed there after her sporadic shifts if we were too tired to come back home. But over the last month, most of her clothing had migrated to my closet, and her chaos had spread out over most of the flat spaces in the apartment. I didn't care, though, because it meant I got to come home to her every night.

"We should get dressed before the kids get here," she whispered, leaning in to kiss the skin over my heart.

"Yeah, since we're supposed to be modeling responsible behavior. Probably not a good idea to corrupt their young minds by letting them catch you ravishing your live-in girlfriend above the shop."

Hazel had jumped in with both feet to help me plan and advertise the summer workshops I'd mentioned as Seven. She'd even gotten a few of the art supply companies who now sponsored her on social media to donate the materials we needed.

We'd advertised the program at the two local high schools, the art teachers nominating students to take part. There was even a set of workshops being planned for over winter break next year because we'd ended up with a waiting list of students wanting to attend.

They'd almost been more excited than I was when they found out that one of their mentors was going to have their work featured on an internationally distributed book cover.

"You need to go get the book to show them." Pushing up, I crossed to where I'd discarded my clothes, quickly yanking them back on before I disappeared into my closet and grabbed a long summer dress for Hazel to put on. While I didn't like the idea of her not wearing panties around a group of horny teen boys for a few hours, it was flowy and long, so they wouldn't know.

Hazel groaned, finally sitting up so I could put her bra back on, dropping a kiss on her shoulder as I fastened the clasp in the back. She lifted her arms and watched with amused eyes as I pulled the dress over her head, carefully smoothing it into place once I'd pulled her to stand in front of me.

"You're a catch, Mr. Harding," she murmured, laying her cheek against my chest. "Such a *good boy*."

"I'm just glad you let me catch *you*." Wrapping my arms around her, I held her tightly, thankful that despite my unconventionally risky antics jeopardizing things between us, she'd given me a chance to earn her heart.

"You're kind of hard to resist."

THE END

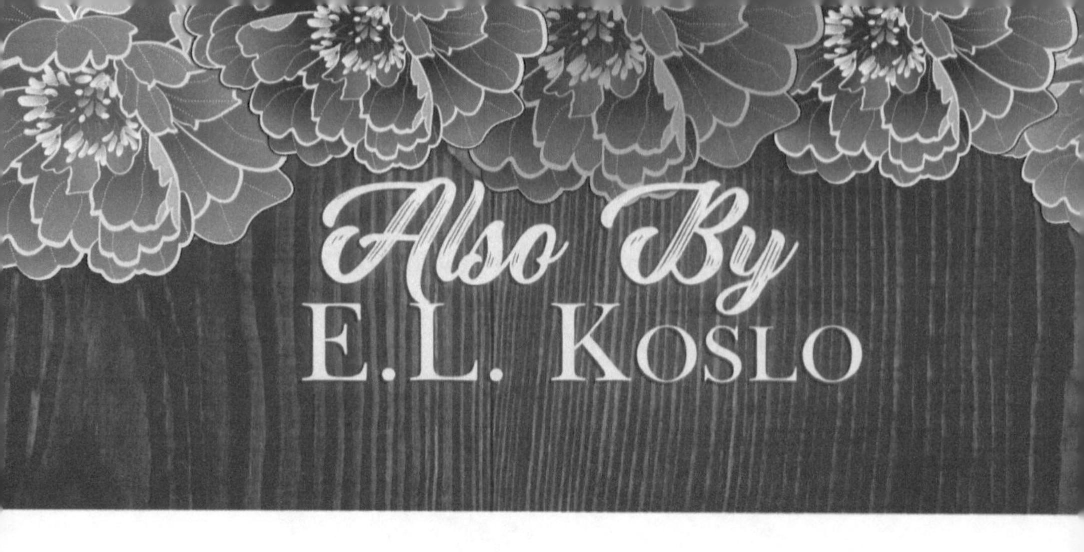

THE DIRTY WORDS SERIES

Foreplay on Words (Amazon)

Book One of The Dirty Words Series
Evan and Chase
Preview of Foreplay on Words: https://BookHip.com/WCJHJGA

Mark my Words (Amazon)

Book Two of The Dirty Words Series
Sam and Kristine
Preview of Mark my Words: https://BookHip.com/QHWGXTZ

Bound by Words (Amazon)

Book Three of The Dirty Words Series
Nathan and Kelly
Preview of Bound by Words: https://BookHip.com/NRRHRBN

More Than Words (Amazon)

Book Four of The Dirty Words Series
Adrian and Isobel
Preview of More Than Words: https://BookHip.com/TARMSTL

.

.

MASKED MEN OF SAGE SPRINGS

Accidental Abduction (Amazon)

Book One in the Masked Men of Sage Springs Series
Hudson and Charley
Preview of Accidental Abduction: https://bookhip.com/CDPWX
AB
Coming to audio soon!

Illicit Illustration (Amazon)

Book Two in the Masked Men of Sage Springs Series
Reid and Hazel
Preview of Illicit Illustration: https://bookhip.com/CDPWXAB

Smokin' Situation (Amazon)

Book Three in the Masked Men of Sage Springs Series
Annie and Tristan
Preview of Smokin' Situation: https://bookhip.com/FCDAKTZ

.

.

STANDALONES

The Midnight Voyeur (Amazon)

Now available in Duet audio featuring Branden Davis-Butler, Cole Eubanks and Troy Duran: https://books2read.com/themidnightv oyeur
(Wide at all audio retailers)
Spicy, taboo, reverse age-gap, stand-alone – Ginny
Preview The Midnight Voyeur: https://BookHip.com/SZXGKKQ

The Mystery Correspondent (Amazon)

Steamy Christmas novella, stand-alone – Ryder and Stella
Preview of The Mystery Correspondent: https://BookHip.com/X PBVAMB

Meet Him at the Altar

New Adult coming of age, written like a romcom/mystery
Kendall & The Groom
Preview of Meet Him at the Altar available on ELKoslo.com

Acknowledgments

To my readers, thank you so much for all of your support, I truly appreciate each one of you more than you know.

To my ARC team of amazing, kind, hilarious souls—thank you for always being so excited when I send you a new set of characters to fall in love with.

To my dear team of Alpha readers—Katie, you are my rock. I don't think my books, or my life would be where they are right now without you. Having you as a friend and plotting partner keeps me going more than you know. Kelly, you have been there since the beginning of my writing journey, and I still look forward to your reactions each time I send you a new book—and a new book boyfriend to lick. Veronica, your enthusiasm and love for Hazel's character mean the world to me. And I always know I must be doing something right as an author when you leave a "Dammit Koslo!" in one of my alpha docs. Jody, having you as a part of the team this time was amazing, and having another neurospicy queen validate my portrayal of Hazel's character meant so much to me. Nikki, thank you for always making time for my books and being willing to jump right into the chaos of my unpredictable writing schedule. Cheyenne, thank you for appreciating Hazel's obsession with potatoes, emotional support tater tots are absolutely a thing, and I love that you're on this journey with me.

Thank you to Brittni who always makes my words look pretty. I'm always excited to see your insight into my writing.

To my dear husband, who has now loved me and my crazy ADHD antics for two decades, and I will cherish the next two decades with you. You encourage me when I'm feeling low and make me laugh when I am sad. None of my MMCs would exist if I didn't have a green flag, golden retriever book boyfriend doing this thing called life with me.

.

.

.

Make sure to follow me on Instagram - @ELKoslo_writes, Tiktok - @elkoslowrites and sign up for my newsletter at ELKoslo.com

.

I hope you enjoyed Reid & Hazel's story, if you would leave a review with your thoughts, it'd mean the world to me—Until next time,

.

E. L. Koslo

Website: ELKoslo.com

Instagram: @elkoslo_writes
Threads: @elkoslo_writes
TikTok: @elkoslowrites & @elkosloauthor

Facebook: E.L. Koslo
Page: EL Koslo Romance Writer
Private Reader Group: E.L. Koslo's Dirty Words Brigade

Pinterest: @elkoslo

X: @ELKoslo
BlueSky: https://bsky.app/profile/elkoslowrites.bsky.social

Amazon: amazon.com/author/e.l.koslo

Linktree: linktr.ee.Elkoslo

Newsletter: https://elkoslo.beehiiv.com/

About E.L. Koslo

FIND THE FUNNY IN YOUR LIFE.

E.L. writes spicy romantic comedies with a variety of cinnamon roll heroes and strong heroines. She grew up in the midwest US, married her college sweetheart, now lives in one of those flyover states with her four spirited children and emotional support/writing companion Bernedoodle, Quinn. Banter and second-hand embarrassment are her jam, so be prepared to laugh with or at her characters.

Her novels combine her love of steamy romance, awkward but loveable leading males, and headstrong heroines with a dash of humor and a little bit of kink.

www.ingramcontent.com/pod-product-compliance
Lightning Source LLC
Chambersburg PA
CBHW021155010826
48971CB00014B/1561